KU-481-148

SPEC OPS SQUAD

SQUAD

SUCKER PUNCH

RICK SHELLEY

2003
50TH
ANNIVERSARY

ACE BOOKS, NEW YORK

SPEC OPS SQUAD: SUCKER PUNCH

An Ace Book / published by arrangement with
the author

PRINTING HISTORY
Ace mass-market edition / January 2003

Copyright © 2003 by Rick Shelley.
Cover art by Michael Herring.
Cover design by Judy Murello.

Visit our website at
www.penguinputnam.com
Check out the ACE Science Fiction & Fantasy newsletter!

ISBN: 0-441-01007-5

ACE®
Ace Books are published by The Berkley Publishing Group,
a division of Penguin Putnam Inc.,
375 Hudson Street, New York, New York 10014.
ACE and the "A" design
are trademarks belonging to Penguin Putnam Inc.

PRINTED IN THE UNITED STATES OF AMERICA

10 9 8 7 6 5 4 3 2 1

If you want to know about the war between the Alliance of Light and the Ilion Federation, I'll tell you—straight and true, to the best of my ability. You won't get all the pious posturing and the highfalutin philosophy and moralizing you've been hearing from the politicians and generals. I've got a different perspective, and I see the war up close and personal—which none of the politicians and damned few of the generals can honestly say. My name is Bart Drak. Friends call me Dragon to my face. Others sometimes use that nickname behind my back. That's okay with me. I'm a buck sergeant leading a Special Operations Squad in Ranger Battalion of the 1st Combined Regiment. *Spec Ops*—we get the dirtiest, most dangerous jobs. If the mission is something no sane individual would attempt, the big shots dump it on us, Spec Ops—the SOS.

CHAPTER 1

THE 1ST COMBINED REGIMENT RETURNED TO Earth after the bloody mess on Olviat, the living and the dead—at least, all the dead who left remains that could be retrieved—human, divotect, abarand, biraunta, porracci, ghuroh. According to the logic of the military, Earth was our home base, though not even all the humans in the regiment came from Earth, so that was the first stop for the dead. The dead humans and aliens who came from other worlds were either shipped home from Earth or buried there, with full military honors. Maybe that does mean something, to their survivors, if not to them. Right now, I can't see what.

Those of us who had survived Olviat needed time to mend. Okay, not all of us had physical injuries, but that fight had wounded all of us, one way or another. The slight wound I had taken in the foot was nothing. By the time we got home, it was just a bad memory, when I thought of it at all. Even the scar was fading fast and would be gone within weeks.

For a few days after we returned to base—getting back to the routine of life in the barracks and preparing for some much-needed furlough time—I was okay, physically and mentally. We had been back at Fort Campbell for eight or nine days before the reaction set in. I have no idea what triggered it, but I got to a point where I couldn't eat anything without either gagging or throwing it back up before it got all the way down.

For a couple of days, I tried to fight it on my own—first by forcing myself to eat and trying in vain to restrain the need to vomit, then by not eating at all, so I wouldn't have anything to puke back up. But it didn't take long before I couldn't even keep water down, and you get in trouble in a hurry if you can't hydrate your system. All the fancy medical nanobots floating through my system couldn't make water out of nothing. They had to take it from what stores my body already had, and there was nothing to replace what they took. I had no choice but to report for sick call, and the doctor put me in the hospital. I spent three days taking in everything through tubes while a team of . . . specialists got me to talk my way through the problem. Yes, it was all in my head. If it had been physical—say, an imbalance in brain chemicals—the medical nanoagents in my system would have kept it from getting so far out of hand.

Those doctors kept busy. I wasn't the only one who needed a little tightening of the brain bolts after Olviat. I later learned that the percentage of men requiring post-trauma counseling was nearly 30 percent higher than normal after that campaign. It was Captain Fusik, our company commander, who told me that. You see, he spent three days getting his head straight again, too. Olviat had been that bad.

Every unit in 1st Combined Regiment had suffered heavy casualties. Ranger Battalion had lost the most men. That *is* considered normal. It's the special operations units that always draw the most dangerous assignments in combat. That's why we're considered to be elite units. Sometimes I think that "elite" is a synonym for "stupid"—as in too stupid to know this job is going to kill you if you stay at it long enough.

THE FIRST MONTH WE WERE BACK ON EARTH WAS fairly well wasted—from the military point of view. It was a time to let men get their heads back together and let off steam. We took furloughs and passes. Those men who were present and not in the hospital pulled the usual variety of fatigue details, just to keep them busy, whether the jobs they were stuck with were needed or not. The army can always find jobs for idle hands. And when we were off duty, evenings and weekends, we all let off steam however we could. That meant a lot of men got roaring drunk as often as they could, until they ran out of cash and friends to borrow from. Our officers and the military police cut everyone more than a little slack. A drunk was more likely to get helped back to his unit and given a medical patch to counteract the alcohol and detox his system than a ride to the stockade.

Replacements started arriving and were parceled out. The integration of species in the regiment complicated that somewhat, especially in Ranger Battalion, and there were transfers within the unit to help fill holes and meet the numbers and mix of species. Promotions were handed out, and medals, both part of the army scoring system. In B Company, Ranger Battalion, we all more or less expected Tonio Xeres, first platoon's sergeant, to be promoted to company lead sergeant to fill the vacancy left after Lead Sergeant Halsey's death on Olviat. Tonio had been filling the job on an interim basis and was the most senior platoon sergeant in the company by the time that campaign ended. That would have put me in line to succeed Tonio as platoon sergeant. Again, I was the senior squad leader in the platoon, the only human squad leader in the platoon, and I had a few more medals than any of the other possible contenders. Those came the hard way because I had been in the human Ranger Battalion that had been training on Dintsen when the Ilion Federation started the war with an invasion there.

It didn't work that way. Tonio and I stayed right where we were. They brought in Herb Deelock from 1st Battalion and gave him the company lead sergeant job.

Captain Fusik told Tonio and me that we had been screwed,

only that wasn't the precise word he used. He had asked a few questions at regimental headquarters and found out why. I should have guessed. Major Josiah Wellman, the man who had volunteered me for the regiment in the first place, had managed to blackball the promotions because he wasn't going to let me get promoted no matter what—so long as he had any say in the matter.

Then, as if to add insult to injury, Wellman was promoted to lieutenant colonel days later. The only redeeming piece of the whole pile of crap was that the promotion brought a transfer for Wellman. He went from assistant operations officer on the regimental staff to commander of 1st Battalion. That took him out of the direct chain of command above me. The next time promotions were handed out, he wouldn't be in line to veto it.

Tonio and I shared a few beers in the noncom club, to drown our disappointment, after Captain Fusik let us know why we had been gypped. "Heaven help that man"—Wellman—"if he's ever too close when the bullets are flying," I mumbled, not sure if Tonio could hear me—and drunk enough not to give a damn. I laughed. "Even if he gets shot in the back, nobody'll ever be sure who shot him. He hasn't got the balls to stand and fight."

"He's not worth the bother, Dragon," Tonio said, his voice a dead, don't-give-a-damn monotone. "He's gotta live with himself, an' that's a worse punishment than anything *you* could do to him."

"Hell, I'm not so much pissed at him screwing me. I expected that. But *you* deserve to be lead sergeant. He's screwing you just to make sure he gets me."

"Don't make me no never mind. I told you right off I wouldn't get the job. Too many other guys around deserve it."

Well, Tonio always was too modest for his own damned good. I owed him my life, and so did everyone else who made it off Dintsen alive after that first fight of the war. We were caught with our pants down and bent over, and the tonatin of the Ilion Federation did us up royally.

People on Earth have never given the tonatin half the credit they deserve. Just because they look so much like the Neanderthals of our prehistory, folks write them off as perhaps only marginally sentient, certainly no match for humans. But the tonatin aren't Neanderthals; we've just been slow learning that. They have larger brains than we do, and the sad truth is they might just be smarter than us, as well as bigger and stronger. They've managed to dominate the Ilion Federation, even though it contains worlds populated by nearly all of the other spacefaring species. There are even a few human worlds in that federation.

"Just forget about Wellman," Tonio advised as he drained the beer in front of him and got to his feet, pushing himself up with both hands on the bar. Even supporting himself like that, he swayed. "He's not worth the grief."

"Maybe not, but it doesn't hurt to dream about it." If ever there was an officer destined to get blasted by one of his own men, it was Josiah Wellman, but I wouldn't be the one to do it. But I also knew that I wouldn't "see" anything if it happened while I was around.

THE REGIMENT HAD BEEN ON EARTH MORE THAN five weeks before we got back into a serious training regimen. Ranger Battalion had all its replacements, and everyone who was being transferred had already moved. There were only two men in the battalion still in the hospital having limbs regenerated. Well, that's really begging the question. There were several others still in the hospital, but they had been transferred out of the unit, to be reassigned elsewhere once they were fit for duty.

Since the military prides itself on logical actions, we started training on a Monday, the start of a new work week. It goes almost without saying that after three beautiful weeks the weather was miserable once we had to be out in it. We started our morning calisthenics in a light snow, with the temperature a couple of degrees below freezing. It was near the end of February, and winter wanted to get in one last lick before it gave way to spring. Maybe exercise does warm you up, but you can't go constantly, and every time we took a few seconds' rest, there was a sharp north wind hitting sweat and trying to make us feel like icicles.

Of course, not everyone suffered equally from the cold. Toniyi Ooyayni, the divotect in my squad, didn't feel it at all. Divotect have a reptilian sort of ancestry. They're cold-blooded—exothermic. They function at whatever the temperature is, though they get sluggish when it's cold; or they use heated clothing to keep them from shutting down altogether.

Neither Corporal Souvana nor Lance Corporal Kiervauna showed any discomfort either. As usual for porracci, they did their exercise in the nude, trusting their thick fur and heavy layers of fat under the skin to keep them warm. Weighing more than three hundred pounds apiece, they've got plenty of insulation.

Fur alone doesn't always do the job though. Our two bi-raunta—Oyo, who had been with the squad from the beginning, and Ala Vel Nuff, who was one of the replacements—had thick fur but only weighed about seventy-five pounds each. They shivered as much as the humans.

The ghuroh—Claw, one of the originals in the squad, and Razor, another replacement—were somewhere in between in their reaction to the cold. They're almost hairless but don't show the effects of cold as much as humans or biraunta do.

The other two humans in my squad, Lance Corporal Robbie McGraw and Private Neville St. John, shivered as much as I did. Maybe more: I've had more years to get used to it.

My squad. Except for the most recent replacements, we had been through hell together. Only five of us had been together from the beginning. I was surprised that there were still three humans in the squad. I would have offered odds that either McGraw or St. John would have been transferred, replaced by an abarand to get the mix within the squad back to what it had been at the start. But . . .

well, that's the army. Three humans, two porracci, two biraunta, two ghuroh, and one divotect.

I'm starting to get a little self-conscious at repeating the traditional descriptive analogies about the other species—porracci look something like orangutans, biraunta like five-foot-tall spider monkeys, ghuroh like mastiffs, divotect like iguana, tonatin like Neanderthals. It feels somehow wrong, even racist, to repeat the stereotypes, but if you're not familiar with how they look, that's the closest I can come to giving you the *flavor* of their appearance. If you see a holograph of one of them, the descriptions are good enough that you'll know which species the individual belongs to.

THE FIRST WEEK OF TRAINING WAS DESIGNED TO get us back in top physical condition. That meant a lot of calisthenics, long marches, and plenty of running. When you've been sloughing off for a month or more, it's like starting all over in boot camp. You've got to build up the muscles and endurance again, shed the extra fat that has settled in.

I pushed my men hard, and I pushed myself even harder. Those of us who had been around and seen combat didn't need much prompting. When you know what combat is like, you want to be in the best possible condition the next time you face it. Every noncom in the battalion was pushing the replacements extra hard, and every officer was urging us not to let up. Even though some of the new men had just come from basic training or Ranger School, and most thought they were in pretty good shape, they had farther to go. Men die in war, but I'd be damned if any of *my* men were going to die because I didn't push them hard enough in training.

Maybe you're thinking, *Why not just pump everybody full of specialized nanobots to go in and build all the muscle mass and nerve connections they could possibly need?*

Turn everyone into a frigging superhero. You could short-cut the training and make an invincible army.

There was a time when I wondered about that myself. A medtech in my first company told me that it was possible. "We could turn everyone in the army into Titans," he told me. "Eight feet tall, three hundred pounds, able to lift half a ton and run a mile in three minutes, ten seconds." But we're still pretty much the same as we were. The short answer is that physical strength and stamina aren't enough. You've got to train the mind and reflexes, and there are no shortcuts for that. A lot of the moves have to become automatic, and the only way to ensure that is through endless repetitions, drills, exercises. Besides, nobody wants to build an army of freaks—different from the rest of our kind. There was one other argument against it—probably the defining argument as far as the army was concerned. Those extralarge superhumans would eat more, and their uniforms would have to be larger. Food and fabric cost money that could be "better" used for weapons, ammunition, and training.

I'm sure there are high-level staff types somewhere who dream of an army of "superior" beings who can stomp through any opposition. And—*maybe*—somewhere along the line there have been experiments, tests. I can't say for a fact that there have been, but I've heard rumors. It wouldn't surprise me. But, then, eggheads and moldy staff types have never been high on my list of personal favorites.

"HEY, SARGE! CAPTAIN'S ON HIS WAY." ROBBIE McGraw stuck his head through the open doorway of my room just long enough to pass the word. Then he headed back out to his place in the squad bay.

It was half past ten, Saturday morning, the end of our first week of training. We were on a five-and-a-half-day work week, and the end of that week was an inspection. Like most soldiers, I usually consider barracks inspections to be a pain in the rump, but in this case it gave us our first break in the heavy physical demands that had been dumped on us. Once the inspection was over, assuming we passed, we would be free until Reveille on Monday morning.

I scanned my room one last time to make sure that nothing was out of place, that the bed was neatly made, and that there was nothing that would prompt the captain to give the room anything more than the most cursory of glances. Squad leaders are supposed to set a good example for their men, and if my area was screwed up, the rest of the squad would get a more thorough examination. Then I went out to the space between my room and the door to the latrine. The captain would pass between them coming into the squad bay.

For my money, George Fusik was an okay officer. The war had given him a chance for military redemption, only it hadn't been his fault that he needed it. Years back, he had been part of the force that had put down the Bunyan Rebellion in the Pacific Northwest. One of his superiors had screwed up an operation and gotten men killed, but Captain Fusik—then a senior lieutenant—had been made the scapegoat. If the war hadn't come along and given him a chance to show the brass what a good soldier he was, he would have remained an SL until he was forced to resign after being passed over for promotion too many times.

As the captain came in, trailed by Junior Lieutenant Torl'vi Trivauna, Lead Sergeant Deelock, and Platoon Sergeant Xeres, I shouted, "Attention!" and braced into the position myself. Trivauna was our new porracci platoon leader. Eso Vel Hohi, the biraunta JL who had moved into that position, and company executive officer, when his predecessor was killed on Olviat, had made senior lieutenant and was now the commander of D Company.

"First squad ready for inspection, sir," I reported.

Captain Fusik smiled and nodded. He glanced over my shoulder into my room but didn't bother to go in. He looked the other way for an equally cursory glance into the latrine. Then he started down the middle of the squad bay. The men were all standing at attention at the ends of their bunks, all in fresh fatigue uniforms. The captain went through the motions, taking a little time looking over the gear that the men had laid out and glancing in their lockers, but I could tell that he had no intention of nit-picking. He was taking the time to go through the motions because he knew that the men had put effort into getting ready. It's a way of saying, "Hey, you didn't waste all that effort. I appreciate what you've done."

The captain worked his way down one side and back up the other, with his entourage—which now included me— trailing along behind, ready to receive any complaints the captain might have. He didn't have any. When we got back to the corridor end of the room, he simply said, "Good work, Sergeant. You may dismiss your men for the weekend," and left. At the door, Tonio hesitated just long enough to give me a thumbs-up gesture.

I gave the group about ten seconds to get farther down the corridor—toward the nest squad bay—before I went back to the middle of the squad bay. "You heard the man," I said. "Good job. You're now officially off duty until the bugle blows Monday morning. Anybody going off base, don't forget to pick up your pass at the orderly room . . . and try to stay out of trouble."

No one made a run for the door. Most of the men would hang around for lunch in the mess hall. When you eat at government expense it saves money for drinking. Anyone going to leave base would also change into civilian clothes or a dress uniform. We're not supposed to go off base in fatigues except on duty.

"You got plans for this weekend?" Robbie McGraw asked, ambling toward me in that peculiar gait he has; it looks a lot slower than it is. Robbie was a lance corporal, assistant second fire team leader behind Souvana.

I grinned and grunted. "Nothing special. First off, I'm going to soak under a steaming hot shower until my muscles quit aching. Then I'm going to the mess hall for chow. After that, I'll probably pour a little beer down my gullet. One of the clubs. I'm too beat to go to town."

"I heard that," Robbie said. "I know how beat I feel, so it must really be tough on an old-timer like you."

"Watch it. I'm not so old I can't whup the daylights out of half a dozen kids like you." Far as that goes, Robbie wasn't more than five or six years younger than me. He was a good soldier, knew the business, and kept his head when it counted. You didn't have to watch your back if he was behind you. "You figure to paint the town?"

"Maybe later. I think I'm gonna sack out this afternoon. Catch up on my beauty sleep."

"There aren't enough afternoons in a year for that," I said, walking away.

Okay, it wasn't an important exchange, not on the surface, but in another sense it was a very important gauge. The mental pain was gone, and we didn't have the same level of tension within the squad we'd had for so long. After a lot of months in training together, and two bloody campaigns, the whole business of integrating the species was finally working. Robbie and I were both human, of course, but I might have the same sort of exchange with any of the men under my command.

Well, Souvana hadn't opened up all that much yet, but our relationship was no longer nearly as hostile as it had been in the beginning. The only really fragile relationship in the squad was between our two porracci, Corporal Souvana and Lance Corporal Kiervauna. A long time back, they had come to blows, and the strain was still visible between them. But there had been no repetition of the fight. They could work together.

I ATE A BIG MEAL, THEN DRANK SLOWLY ONCE I got to the enlisted men's club that afternoon. I *forced* myself to sip when I wanted to gulp. I still had memories of all the gab sessions the head doctors had put me through. I knew it would be easy to start using booze as a crutch. I'd been there. But there was soft music playing in the bar, and there were bowls of munchies within reach. The place wasn't particularly crowded. I guess a lot of guys were either sacking out like Robbie or had gone into town to have more freedom than they would on base.

Now and then I found myself humming along with one of the songs, doing a good job of not thinking about anything but my restful afternoon. It's good to be able to turn everything off for a while. I was on my fourth or fifth beer when Tonio came in and took the stool at my left. He ordered a beer for himself and a refill for me.

"Captain find anything to spoil his weekend?" I asked, after Tonio had a chance to take the foam off his beer. Tonio and I go way back. He's the best friend I've ever had, more like a brother than the real brother I was *blessed* with.

"No, he went home happy," Tonio said. He gave me a sharp glance. "How're *you* feeling?"

I shrugged. There was a lot in Tonio's question. He wasn't just asking if I was on my way to drunk. He was asking how my head was working as well. "Comfortable, somewhere between here and there. I'm getting by. How about you?"

"Keeping one step ahead of the brain bugs."

We didn't need to talk all the time. We sat and drank, with Tonio sipping as slowly as I had been. It was just a comfortable afternoon, and drinking with a buddy is almost always better than drinking alone. I bought the next round. We were near the bottom of those bottles before I said anything.

"Any news I haven't heard yet?"

"Not about the regiment," he said. "Nobody's started guessing how much time we'll have before they send us out again." Deal with the important stuff first. "The war news"—he shrugged—"I guess you've heard as much of that as I have."

"Doesn't seem to be any end in sight," I said. Mumbled. There was fighting in at least half a dozen places, worlds many light-years apart. The Alliance of Light hit the Ilion

Federation; they hit us. Men died. Bits of real estate changed hands. The war went on. And on.

"It can't go on forever," Tonio said.

"It can go on until there's nobody left to hold a gun but the honchos running the mess," I said, draining the last of my beer. It didn't taste so good now. It had a sour flavor. "Once we're all dead and buried but the politicians."

CHAPTER 2

TWELVE DAYS LATER WE HEARD THE NEWS THAT 2nd Combined Regiment had landed on Argent—a biraunta colony world that had only recently been captured by the Ilion Federation—with several allied units, and the invasion force was facing heavy resistance from the Ilion occupation army. Unlike the enemy armies we had faced, 2nd was up against a force that included two human battalions and a porracci regiment as well as two tonatin regiments. Four days after that, before we had heard any more recent news from Argent, Ranger Battalion, 1st Combined Regiment, was dropped into the Transylvanian Alps for our first extended field exercise since Olviat.

We were to be the "aggressor" force, sent in to see how well a mostly European regiment—only eight weeks "old"— was doing in its unit training. The exercise should have been a snap for us, since our battalion had been around for nearly a year, and we still had enough veterans to keep the newer men from screwing up too often or badly. The exercise didn't work out the way the brass planned it. We started out badly. Two shuttles carrying men from D Company collided during the landing. Only three men were killed, all from the shuttle crews, but most of the men in two platoons were injured. Thankfully, most of the injuries were minor, and after four hours all but one of the injured soldiers were fit for duty.

After that, one thing after another went wrong. There was a technical foul-up in communications channels that made it impossible for us to use our electronic maps to track movement of forces. One squad in C Company got lost and wasn't located for hours because of the breakdown in the system. A new man in A Company managed to set off a land mine by accident and lost both arms above the elbows. If the rest of the squad hadn't acted quickly to get tourniquets on the stumps, he would have bled to death. Two other men in his fire team received minor injuries from the explosion. A platoon from the European unit surrounded fourth platoon from B Company, forcing the platoon sergeant to surrender. Oyo, the biraunta in Souvana's fire team, managed to break a leg when a tree limb he swung to broke and he couldn't grab another. That put him in a medtank for three hours.

That was all in the first six hours of the operation. Things went downhill from there.

The exercise had been scheduled to last until after dawn Friday. It was canceled before sunset Tuesday, and we were lifted back to Kentucky. The mission critique for sergeants and officers was not a pleasant session.

THE NEXT FEW WEEKS WEREN'T PLEASANT EITHER, for anyone in the regiment. The army general staff leaned on General Ransom, commander of 1st Combined Regiment, who leaned on Colonel Hansen, commander of Ranger Battalion. Hansen leaned on his staff and the battalion commanders, who leaned on their company commanders, who leaned . . . Well, you get the picture. Pressure flows one way in the military, and it's those at the bottom who don't have anyone to scream at. Our days became longer, and we were given less time to rest between sessions. There were more frequent night exercises. On, and on. General Ransom and Colonel Hansen seemed determined to get us back to peak performance if it killed every last one of us.

With all the heat pouring down the chain of command, men made more mistakes. Even scores on the rifle range declined by 3 percent. There were accidents. Men were hurt in hand-to-hand combat training. More than a dozen men in the battalion suffered recurrences of post-traumatic stress disorders and had to be treated in the hospital. One biraunta in C Company was affected so badly he was sent home. The doctors despaired of being able to return him to military effectiveness.

Our next extended field exercise was more modest in its goals, and closer to home. It involved Ranger Battalion and one of the line battalions, and we only went as far as central Tennessee for that, up on the Cumberland Plateau. It lasted two days. While it wasn't wildly successful, at least there were no major foul-ups; no one was killed or seriously injured.

A little of the heat was lifted from us, but we knew the brass was still watching us closely.

EVEN THOUGH FEWER THAN A QUARTER OF THE soldiers in the regiment were human—and those divided among all of our major religions—we stood down from training for ten days for Christmas, from noon on the twenty-third of December to Reveille on January 2. There was furlough for anyone who had time coming and wanted to use it. Naturally, it was mostly the humans who took advantage of the holiday break. I was a little surprised at the long stand-down, and at the fact that we weren't required to keep a hefty portion of the regiment on duty through the holidays. In a war like the one we were in, nothing said that the Ilion Federation couldn't attempt something as hazardous as an invasion of Earth. From what I've seen of the tonatin—and they absolutely *rule* the Ilion Federation—I wouldn't have put it past them to attempt something as ballsy as that. I didn't think they could succeed, but they might cause enough damage to make a lot of Earth people lose any support for the war.

I didn't bother taking leave time, but Tonio pulled me a three-day pass for the end of the holiday. I went to Nashville for New Year's Eve, getting there a day early. I made the rounds of country music bars, drinking quietly amidst the bedlam of holiday revelers. Half the time, I don't think I even heard the music. I wanted noise, and I wanted alcohol. I got both. And I paid a holiday premium for the attention of a professional lady after all the fireworks and noisemakers went silent.

The fireworks gave me a few bad minutes. I *knew* they were coming. It's a New Year's staple. But when they started popping, I felt a tightness in my chest, an instinct to duck for cover. Maybe I came close to a combat flashback. Afterward, I needed something extra to settle me down, and the lady in question did do that.

I almost slept through the hotel's normal checkout time the next morning, but since I was a soldier and the hotel manager on duty was a veteran, they gave me an extra hour. It was past sunset on the first when I got back to camp, feeling a little more mellow than I had since the start of the war. I guess I had needed those days off more badly than I had realized.

EVEN BEFORE I CHECKED IN AT B COMPANY'S orderly room, I heard the news. A biraunta junior lieutenant in A Company had been found dead in his room in the BOQ—bachelor officer quarters—an apparent suicide. I didn't really know the dead JL, only who he was and where he belonged. He had just transferred in a month or so before.

Suicide is not exactly unknown in the army, even in peacetime. But what made this one notable was that it was an officer who swallowed his gun—as the idiom goes. He had stuck the muzzle of his needle pistol in his mouth and used a small wedge to make sure the pistol kept firing until the magazine was empty. That turned his brain into paté and sprayed it all over the walls of his room. Behind a locked door in a third-floor room. No one heard the pistol; needle guns make very little noise, and there weren't many people in the building at the time. When no one could get a response from him late in the morning of New Year's Day, they broke the door open. The autopsy determined that he had been dead for twelve hours before he was found.

The JL was a combat veteran. He had seen combat on two campaigns with a biraunta unit and earned himself a medal for heroism. He did not leave a suicide note. Neither the sergeants who served under him nor the other officers in his company had noticed any unusual behavior. There was no doubt it was a suicide. The circumstances precluded murder or accident. In any case, none of the men under his command had had time to get to hate him enough to waste him.

The suicide was the talk of the camp. That's about all I heard in the mess hall, then in the NCO club afterward. To get away from it all, I finally went to the library—not one of my usual haunts. I sat there watching old comedy videos for an hour or so, then headed back to my room in the barracks.

The squad bay was empty, which suited me. And I had the latrine to myself, so I took a shower, then retreated to my private room before any of my men checked in. I put a sleep patch on and slept straight through until just before Reveille the next morning.

There were three men in Ranger Battalion unaccounted for at Reveille the morning of January 2. It wasn't until the next day that we learned what had happened to the missing men. One had simply been AWOL. He hadn't returned to base on time; it was near noon on the second when he checked in. The second man had been jailed on a drunk and disorderly charge in Clarksville; the authorities there turned him over to the MPs, military police. The third man, an abarand private from D Company, had killed himself in a hotel room in Gavin City—the business area right across the road from Fort Campbell.

Captain Fusik spent fifteen minutes talking to the company—mentioning both suicides. It was part pep talk and part making sure that everyone knew that there were alternatives, a pretty sophisticated support system for anyone who had problems. There were plenty of people to talk to, and mechanisms for getting help. After the formation, the captain held a meeting for the officers and sergeants in the company and gave us more of the same, reminding us to watch our people carefully for any sign of potential problems.

"You've all had classes on how to handle this," Captain Fusik reminded us. "Sometime in the next few days, I'll bring someone in from base HQ to give us all a refresher. But we can't wait for that. The danger time begins *now*. Things like this can be contagious. Talk with your men. Watch them for anything unusual. *All* of them. You can't assume that some people are safe. It won't hurt to be a little paranoid about this. If we're going to make mistakes, let's make sure they're on the side of caution."

IT WAS A WEEK BEFORE WE STARTED TO GET PAST the tension of those first days of the new year. Our concerns about suicide pushed aside some of the concentration on training. We were tiptoeing around each other, looking over shoulders, wondering about hidden meanings in comments. It *can* make you almost paranoid, and I found myself wondering if too much of that kind of observation might make the problem worse. When we went to the rifle range, there were more safety officers behind the firing line, extra people at the ammunition supply point, and we were all a lot more careful than usual making certain no one took any rounds off the range with him.

There was war news, more good than bad for a change, but no one was ready to start planning a victory celebration. The Ilion Federation had given no sign that they were losing their will to fight. There had been some costly battles.

Both sides had lost a lot of soldiers. Maybe we were all getting more cautious about choosing new battlegrounds.

Closer to home, we learned that two more combined regiments were being created. A few officers and noncoms from the first two would be transferred to leaven the new units. We didn't know yet who might be leaving from our regiment. I kept my fingers crossed for Lieutenant Colonel Wellman to be one of them, but I doubted that my luck would be that good. I had used up all the luck I had coming on Olviat. I wasn't going to hope for another miracle.

Nothing had been said yet about how long it might be before 1st Combined Regiment went into battle again. When the regiment was formed, we were promised four months of training and didn't get that much. After Dintsen, we were again promised four months of training before we were committed to battle . . . and that's about what we got. This time, there had been no promise of four months or anything else. All we were told was that training would continue until we were told differently.

That January was also the coldest Fort Campbell had experienced in a century. We had more than twenty inches of snow that month, most of it coming in one storm on the twelfth and thirteenth. That month's snowfall was greater than the area's total snowfall for the previous ten winters combined. It only got us out of one day's field training though, while the blizzard was in progress.

February was also colder than usual, and wet—but at least the precipitation was rain. That didn't stop any training, but it gave us enough reasons to feel miserable.

Then we went from cold to hot. During the first two weeks of March, we were on a field exercise in the Philippines, and we went from that to a second exercise in the Australian outback; that one lasted eight days. In both cases, 1st Combined Regiment served as the aggressor force, pitted against two AustralAsian units, each of which had been augmented by battalions from offworld—porracci in the Philippines, ghuroh in Australia.

We made mistakes, but they were learning mistakes, not

the major gaffes that had put us in so much trouble a few months earlier. We critiqued each mission, then added extra training in the areas we had shown deficiencies in once we got back to Fort Campbell, near the end of the month.

ON THE THIRTEENTH OF APRIL, WE RECEIVED movement orders. As usual, we weren't given any information about where we were going, just orders to pack up and be ready to ship out within thirty-six hours. Until then, everyone in the regiment was restricted to base.

"Where do you think they're sending us, Sarge?" Neville St. John—he pronounced his last name Sinjin, after the British fashion—asked. Neville was the third man in the squad to ask me that question in half an hour, and I gave him the same answer I had given the others.

"I don't have any idea. Don't burn out your brain trying to guess. We'll know once we're aboard ship and burning toward our first hyperspace jump." I tried not to be short in tone, but the inevitable question had left me feeling a little more testy than usual. At that point, I doubt that anyone in the regiment except General Ransom and his top staff officers and battalion commanders had any idea where we were headed. They take security seriously. Espionage might seem quaintly outdated, but it exists, and it was theoretically possible for word to get to an enemy before we showed up. With all the species in the Alliance of Light except divotect also represented in the Ilion Federation, there was a chance that spies might be anywhere.

Yes, I was curious about where we might be going. How could I avoid it? Wherever we were going, it was almost certainly into combat, with all its routine dangers . . . like getting killed. But just then, idle speculation was driving me crazier than ignorance.

We fell out with our gear at four in the afternoon—1600 hours by military time—climbed aboard trucks that took us to the spaceport on base, transferred to shuttles, and headed up to the fleet in orbit. It takes time to move a regiment with its heavy weapons, supplies, and men. B Company, Ranger Battalion happened to be one of the first groups moved to the ships. It was past midnight before the last shuttles rendezvoused with their ships and the fleet started moving out-system.

IT TAKES GETTING USED TO, BUT YOU CAN TRAVEL between worlds faster than you can get between some places on Earth. It takes only a matter of a few hours to span hundreds of light-years, less time than it takes a company of soldiers to hike twenty miles. Once the fleet started moving out, accelerating, the ships made the first of two or three jumps through hyperspace, spending only enough time in normal space between jumps for the navigators to verify that the ships were where they were supposed to be.

That means they don't have to equip the ships with beds for all of their passengers. You sit in seats that aren't half as comfortable as the seats you might occupy flying from New York to Tokyo. There were enough beds for about a fourth of the men. If for some reason we had to remain aboard ship for any length of time, we would take shifts in those beds, six hours out of twenty-four, with no time for a bunk to cool off from one body before the next crawled in.

As soon as we were outbound, the officers received their mission briefing. Then they came back and passed the news to their sergeants. We gave our men the news.

"The world we're going to is Durestal," I said once I had my squad gathered around me. "That's the divotect colony the Alliance tried to take back from the IFers last year, the one where we lost four-fifths of the invasion force—killed or captured. We've gone back in, with more men this time. There are already four regiments of Alliance troops on the ground, heavily engaged with the enemy, with enough ships overhead to make certain the enemy can't reinforce their occupation force. We're going in as reinforcements because the force we have on Durestal hasn't been able to do the job on its own. According to the lastest intelligence, we'll be going in at a safe area and deploying once we're on the ground." I shrugged, to show that I wasn't giving that promise full credence either. "We should know more once we emerge from hyperspace over Durestal," I said.

I hesitated, then added, "Maybe we'll get lucky for a change and find that our troops there have finished the job without us."

Well, it *was* possible.

"There's one other thing that makes this campaign different from the two we've been on before," I said before anyone could comment on my wishful thinking. "On both Dintsen and Olviat we faced enemy forces that were virtually one hundred percent tonatin. That's not the case on Durestal. The reports we have indicate that there is one IFer mixed regimental-sized unit that includes a battalion of humans and a battalion of porracci along with a tonatin battalion. The other enemy units on the world are, apparently, exclusively tonatin."

CHAPTER 3

I DIDN'T THINK THAT THE PRESENCE OF PORRACCI on the other side would affect our porracci noticeably. If anything, I figured that it might put a little extra zest into them. They make more of a habit of fighting each other than humans ever have—and *that* is saying one hell of a lot. The macho dominance thing isn't just on the personal level among porracci, but extends through every layer of their society from what I've read. Some of it has become ritualized over the centuries, but even the most polite political or diplomatic debate at the highest levels can turn into a fight to the death. One estimate I saw suggested that the destructive nature of relationships among porracci may have held up their expansion into space by as much as a thousand years. Cooperation does not come easily for them.

We humans like to think we've outgrown that kind of warfare with our own kind . . . not that Earth has been totally peaceful, even in the last century. Our internecine wars are generally smaller, shorter, and less destructive than they used to be. The Paul Bunyan Rebellion in the Pacific Northwest had been the only serious conflict on Earth in several decades. And this was our first war involving other species. Call it progress.

We didn't have time for philosophical musings just then.

Charts of Durestal were downloaded to our maps, and we started going over the terrain and the latest known troop deployments, hostile and friendly, even though we had not received orders concerning our deployment once we were on the ground. When those orders finally came, we might not have time for study.

Durestal was the last divotect colony world still under the control of the Ilion Federation. Once it was liberated, the Alliance of Light would have accomplished the last of the specific official "war aims" enunciated when the Alliance decided to respond to the IFer invasions of the divotect colonies. That would leave all the vague stuff about making certain the Ilion Federation "paid for its outrages" and guaranteeing a peaceful future for the galaxy—the verbal diarrhea politicians and diplomats can't help spewing.

Preinvasion, the divotect population of Durestal had been under a million. It was the newest of their colony worlds and minimally developed, like most divotect worlds. Durestal had virtually no defenses. The IFer invaders had killed perhaps 8 percent of the divotect prior to the Alliance's attempt to kick the IFers off. More locals had died during our first try at that, some killed intentionally by the IFers, others simply unfortunate enough to get caught in the middle. By the time we mounted a second invasion, the divotect population of Durestal was estimated to be 750,000. That doesn't take into account the Alliance troops who died there, or the IFers.

Now 1st Combined Regiment was to reinforce the second force we had sent to liberate Durestal. We were supposed to be strong enough to finally bring the battle to a successful conclusion.

"I JUST CAN'T HELP FEELING THAT SOMEBODY near the top of the chain of command still isn't certain we're up to snuff," I told Tonio when we got a couple of minutes alone—off to the side of the compartment that housed the entire company—before the fleet's second hyperspace jump. "We're assault troops, special operations, not the mop-and-bucket brigade."

Tonio shrugged. "Maybe we were the only combat-ready unit available on short notice. Or maybe the situation on Durestal is more iffy than we've been told. Don't stick that chip on your shoulder until you know it belongs."

"Bullcrap! After that messed-up exercise, they don't think we can cut it anymore." Yes, Tonio was my superior, but he was also the best friend I've ever had. I knew I could say anything to him, in private, without getting marked as insubordinate or worse. And I knew he would give me any news, good or bad, as honestly as he could. "It's like the way Wellman has it in for me. Somebody farther up the line has it in for the whole regiment—maybe somebody who was against the idea of the combined regiment at the beginning and wants us to look like failures, no matter what it might cost the Alliance."

"Or maybe we've got a guardian angel who thinks we deserve a break after Dintsen and Olviat," Tonio said. "There's not a whole lot we can do about it one way or the other. We go where they send us and do what they tell us to do."

THEY DIDN'T SEND US TO THE SHUTTLES UNTIL after we came out of our last hyperspace jump—three hours out from Durestal. At least we would be riding the shuttles all the way in, not airsleds, and it still looked as if we could look forward to a peaceful ride and not have to worry about getting out of the box—the shuttle—fast on the other end to jump right into the battle. The last word we had before they sealed us in our shuttles was that we would be landing in an area forty miles from the nearest hostile ground troops, and that the Ilion Federation didn't have any aerospace fighters on station that could cause us grief on the way in.

I hoped they were right, mentally crossed my fingers,

and remained my usual nervous self through the ride in. I was relieved, not to mention surprised, that the ride in was everything promised—smooth, easy, and safe. More than that, once we were on the ground and away from the landing zone, there was a hot meal and coffee waiting.

"Maybe things aren't as bad here as we were told, Sarge," Robbie McGraw said during our meal. "If they can put a feed like this on for us, they can't be *too* worried about IFers."

"Don't start planning your vacation yet," I said. "The officers have already been pulled off for a briefing, so it looks like they're going to find something for us to do. And the nicer they are to us now, the worse the job is likely to be."

"Spoilsport," Robbie said with a laugh. "You're no fun at all anymore."

I didn't bother to reply. I was sitting where I could look off in the direction Captain Fusik and our lieutenants had gone, wondering how long it would be before they laid the news on us—and despite Robbie's buoyancy and my own surprise at how easily things had gone so far, I had the gloomy feeling that we were going to catch our share of hell before we got home.

The only joy to being a pessimist in the army is that you're right more often than you're wrong.

THE BRIEFING THE SERGEANTS GOT WHEN THE captain got back confirmed my notion. We weren't forty miles from the nearest enemy force, we were—maybe— fifteen. Probably less. That was where the heaviest current fighting was concentrated. The three line battalions and heavy-weapons battalion of 1st Combined Regiment were going to move in the direction of that enemy concentration. The line battalions were going on foot.

Don't say it, Captain, I thought, after Fusik laid that much of the situation out, but he said it anyway.

"We'll be going in by airsled, behind the enemy, to raise

what ruckus we can from that side." The shuttles had already gone back up to the ships to have the passenger seats folded out of the way and to have airsleds installed. Each shuttle can carry eight sleds, just enough for a ranger platoon. "All of Ranger Battalion is going in—various places," the captain continued. "B Company will operate in four platoon-sized teams. Some of the other companies will be broken down to squads. If the situation warrants, we might split up as well." He shrugged. "It depends on what we find and what we're able to do. Get back to your men. It'll be an hour before the shuttles get back in."

I went back to where my men were sitting and gave it to them the way the captain said it. "Get your rest while you can," I added. "No telling how long we'll be on the go once we start." I sat at the edge of the group and shrugged off my pack, then used it as a pillow. I knew I wasn't going to get any sleep, but I would conserve as much energy as I could . . . and try to keep the butterflies from multiplying in my stomach.

DIVOTECT HAD BEEN ON DURESTAL A CENTURY, and they're not as rough on the environment as some of the other sentients are. They build small communities and leave a lot of greenery between buildings, blending in with their surroundings. Probably more than 95 percent of the planet was virgin wilderness. The primary continent—the one we were on—was about the size of the Americas on Earth, but shaped something like Australia, tilted about forty degrees counterclockwise, with ocean all around it. From my study of the map, it looked as if about 70 percent of the continent was forest, broken only by the occasional region of savanna or prairie and the rivers—a couple of them as broad and grand as the Mississippi or Amazon on Earth. To the west there were thousands upon thousands of square miles of obvious prairie, with desert to the south-west.

We didn't have long-term meteorological records of the

world, but it looked as if perhaps only the northernmost section of the continent might see really heavy winter weather. Where we were, two thousand miles south of the northern edge, it was late spring, almost summer, with the early evening temperature not far below seventy degrees. Beautiful . . . if you could get past the possibility of a kill-or-be-killed situation.

To my surprise, I did doze—for a few minutes. We had adjusted our day-and-night routine before leaving Earth so that we would be set for the different cycle on Durestal, which meant that I couldn't have been really tired, but somehow I dropped off anyway. The noise of incoming shuttles shocked me out of sleep quickly enough.

"Up and on 'em!" Tonio shouted over the platoon radio frequency. I was awake by his second word and halfway to a sitting position before he finished. I used my rifle to help lever me to my feet. By that time I was also saying pretty much the same thing Tonio had, on my squad frequency, while I started moving around the circle, ready to use a boot to encourage anyone who was moving too slowly. But they were all getting to their feet, most of them more spryly than I had.

The order to "fall in" came three minutes after Tonio's first shout. Shuttles were still coming in, three or four at a time, and a few platoons from the battalion were already boarding the lead shuttles. We stood in formation for ninety seconds before Captain Fusik started us moving at the double. We were told which shuttles were ours and got aboard with a minimum of fuss . . . then squeezed into airsleds by fire teams.

As far as I'm concerned, an airsled is the ultimate torture chamber. Basically, it's a length of sewer pipe, barely large enough for the five soldiers of a fire team to squeeze into. We fit together like the members of a bobsled team, but with less elbow room. The sleds protrude in through the bottom of a shuttle. The shuttle takes us partway, then drops the sleds, which have a little more lifting surface than a rock and just enough rocket power to do minimal steering and brake us before we can plow into something at two hundred miles an hour. A sled hits the ground and skids. Then we get out as best we're able and get away from the box.

It's *always* a miserable ride.

We didn't get much information on our mission before we were sealed into the sleds. Detailed instructions don't always mean a lot. Once you're on the ground and out of the box any mission profile can be blown sky-high. You can't expect the enemy to cooperate and do exactly what you want them to. Captain Fusik linked to all the sergeants in the company—he had a specific radio channel for that— to remind us that we were going behind enemy lines. "Not very far behind," he added. "When we land, get your men out and move to the rendezvous point as quickly as possible." That rendezvous would be one hundred yards to the right of the tracks our sleds left going in, and fifty yards in front of the lead sled—the one that landed farthest north, not necessarily the first one in. No one would stay at the rendezvous long. The general idea is to get as far from the sleds as possible, quickly. Those airsleds generate a lot of heat landing, and the trails they left on the ground would be brilliant beacons in infrared to anyone looking for us . . . like several regiments of IFer soldiers.

WE LOST ONE FIRE TEAM FROM FOURTH PLATOON going in. Their airsled missed its landing point by thirty yards and smashed into a rock outcropping headfirst at two hundred miles per hour. The five guys inside didn't have a prayer. Airsleds don't leave any room for error. Even if you do everything right, there's a chance a sled will bite your head off.

A squad from C Company landed almost in the laps of half a battalion of IFer porracci. Our people didn't make it out of their sleds. The IFers used two rockets at short range. The second fire team of fourth squad in my platoon was luckier. They had a rough landing that cost two men broken legs and effectively put the team out of action for the next several hours.

This is starting to look like that exercise we blew on Earth, I thought, when the reports started coming in. Sometimes it's hard not to be superstitious. Having so many things go wrong at the beginning of an operation had the words *bad omen* running through my head. I needed a few minutes to shake them loose. I don't believe in omens. Most of the time.

WE COULDN'T HANG AROUND THE RENDEZVOUS. The men with broken legs were hauled by comrades, though that slowed us considerably. We go into battle loaded down with about as much weight as we can carry and still function. But we were not going to abandon injured comrades, except in the final extreme. The other three men in that fire team had minor injuries, but were ambulatory. Junior Lieutenant Trivauna and Platoon Sergeant Xeres got us gathered and moving. The lieutenant was with our platoon. That was okay by me. That gave us one more rifle and pistol. And you know a porracci is going to give any fight everything he's got.

All of fourth squad was left as soon as we got far enough from the landing zone and rendezvous for safety. That would give the injured men a little protection until they could be evacuated, or until medtechs could get to them with the gear to treat their broken legs. The rest of us changed direction and kept moving. We received our briefing in two doses—thirty seconds at the rendezvous, maybe twice that when we left fourth squad. We were observing electronic silence, not using radios, so the briefings had to come while we were stopped and the lieutenant could talk to us without using the radio.

The battle plan still wasn't elaborate or elegant, so the

lieutenant didn't need a lot of time to lay it out. We were to move toward the rear elements of one of the IFer battalions, take them under fire, then pull back and move to one side or the other and hit them again. Our job was strictly harrassment. With most of Ranger Battalion involved, we would be like a massive swarm of killer bees, attacking at will, swarming in to get in a lot of stings, then regrouping to do it all over again.

I once saw a bull that had been killed by bees like that.

NIGHT IN THE FOREST. THERE'S NOT MUCH MORE that a spec ops squad can ask for on a combat mission. Trees and darkness both contribute to survival. We moved at a steady—and fairly rapid—pace toward the nearest known enemy positions. But we moved carefully, with biraunta out as advance scouts, most of them up in the trees. On the ground, the three squads of the platoon moved along separate tracks. My squad had the point. The others flanked us and held back about fifty yards—about the same distance each was off to its respective side.

Ala and Oyo, our biraunta, were twenty feet or so up in the trees, thirty yards ahead of the first man on the ground. That was Toniyi, our divotect. Kiervauna, my assistant fire team leader, came next, then Claw, then me. Except for Oyo, the rest of my squad's second fire team was behind me, with Souvana at the tail. Souvana was that fire team's leader and assistant squad leader. According to the "book" he shouldn't have been the rear guard, but he liked that position, and I couldn't have asked for a better man watching our backs.

Looking through a night-vision system, the night is a strange combination of greens and grays. Depth perception suffers, and you can't see quite as far or as well. That's the drawback. The advantage is that any enemy will have the same degradation of vision. You swivel your head frequently, trying to watch the darkness around you, looking for movement that doesn't belong. Ears strain for any noise—anything that might give you a fraction of a second's warning of trouble. The longer you go without contacting the enemy, the more the tension builds. Each step can seem to take an eternity. You worry about giving yourself away by the proverbial snap of a twig or by a motion that's too abrupt to be natural.

It was fifty minutes after we left fourth squad when Ala dropped out of a tree ten yards in front of Toniyi and gave a hand sign that we were approaching the enemy. I stopped my squad and relayed the information—by hand signals—to Tonio and Lieutenant Trivauna, who stopped the rest of the platoon and called the squad leaders to him. I brought Ala along so he could tell what he had seen.

"I believe it's an enemy command post," Ala whispered. The six of us were gathered close, all with helmet visors tilted up out of the way so we could talk—whisper—without using our radios. "A camouflaged position with at least three humans inside. About a platoon spread in a loose perimeter around it, and about forty yards out."

I did the quick math. That would mean about five yards of perimeter per man. I also noted that Ala had specified humans. We knew there were human IFers on Durestal. It didn't help that I wished we hadn't been the ones to come up against them. They were still the enemy.

"A complete perimeter?" JL Trivauna asked.

"Yes, sir." Ala also nodded. "Oyo and I went far enough around on either side to be certain. The spacing between men is regular, not weighted to one side or the other. This is not part of a larger line. If there are other units, they are far enough off that the line is not continuous."

"Lieutenant?" Tonio used the one word, asking for permission to speak. Trivauna nodded. "If our job is to mess with their minds as well as inflict casualties, we might really stir the pot if we hit them from the far side. Even if this group has a complete perimeter around a CP, they must know that all the landings were on this side. If we make them think that we're between them and the bulk of their forces . . ."

Trivauna hesitated for half a second before he nodded again, then bared his teeth in a grin. "It would help if there were one or two survivors to spread that news," he said. "We'll do that, circle around, first and second squads to the left, third to the right. On my order we'll hit from three points—ten, twelve, and two by the clock, considering our current position six." He looked around to make sure everyone got the message. "We will engage only briefly. When I give the order to cease firing, first and second squads will withdraw due west. Third squad will go north far enough to break contact with the enemy before also heading west." He unfolded his electronic map, found our current location, the position of the enemy command post, and pointed to a spot three-quarters of a mile west of the enemy position. "This is where we'll rendezvous afterward."

IF EVER THERE WAS A "TEXTBOOK" SPEC OPS action, this should have been it—a quick night raid against a lightly fortified position. It's something a single squad should have been able to handle without much trouble, inflicting enough enemy casualties in the first volley that there would be no difficulty getting away. We had three squads, and the majority of us were combat veterans. Our only serious concern *should* have been making sure that we left those one or two survivors JL Trivauna mentioned—someone to make sure the enemy higher-ups knew we were around.

I don't know what went wrong. Maybe we didn't spot an electronic snoop planted out away from their perimeter. Maybe someone on that perimeter spotted movement and gave the alarm. Whatever the reason, the IFers opened up on us before Trivauna gave the order to fire. We were more than a hundred yards from the IFer perimeter. We came under both rifle and RPG—rocket-propelled grenade—fire, coordinated and disciplined. Second and third squads were hit simultaneously. My squad was a little luckier. We had time to go to ground and seek what cover from tree trunks we could find before any of the heat came our way. I don't *think* that the IFers spotted us until we opened fire on them—trying to take pressure off the rest of our people—but I couldn't swear to it.

JL Trivauna was with third squad. He didn't survive the first volley. Neither did the squad's sergeant. Tonio was with second squad, which also lost its squad leader—and two other men. There were several wounded men in both squads as well.

The rest of us put down all the firepower we could, but it was no longer a question of hit-and-run. We had too many wounded to pack along and withdraw under fire. We had to finish off that command post and its defending platoon before we could see to our wounded. It was them or us.

CHAPTER 4

MY SQUAD WAS IN THE BEST SHAPE, SO IT WAS
up to us to carry the burden of the fight. We put out every
round we could. Both of my men with grenade launchers
popped RPGs into the enemy positions as quickly as they
could, Kiervauna working clockwise, Razor working
counterclockwise. The rest of us kept our fingers on rifle
triggers, spreading long bursts at the enemy positions. For
maybe twenty seconds, my squad was the only one firing
against the IFers. Then we picked up a little help from the
survivors in the other squads.

It was only then that Kiervauna took time to launch a
pair of grenades toward the camouflaged site at the center
of the enemy positions. Kiervauna was an artist with a
grenade launcher. Both his RPGs hit the tent directly, ripping through the camouflage netting and the fabric be-
neath. I hadn't seen anyone move away from that tent, but
I might not have noticed if they had.

Once we were fully engaged, it didn't take long before
the volume of enemy fire diminished drastically. After
three minutes, Tonio radioed for me to work my squad
closer to the perimeter while the people left in second and
third squads provided covering fire.

We moved slowly, using fire-and-maneuver tactics, with
two or three men advancing while the rest of the squad

provided covering fire. As close to the enemy perimeter as we were, that was a very slow procedure, allowing us to advance only two or three yards at a time, spread along a squad front thirty yards wide. The biggest break we got was that we put down the enemy grenadiers quickly. All we had to worry about was rifle fire—not that automatic rifle fire isn't enough to worry about.

Eighty yards out, I held up our advance. There was no way to get closer without losing half my men. I told Tonio that we were stopping, and he okayed my decision. From eighty yards, Kiervauna and Slash could put their RPGs down with the precision of sharpshooters with rifles. Four minutes later, the ranking survivor of the IFer unit raised a white flag. There were only four IFers left alive and unwounded of the fifty who had been there at the start of the fight.

THE WAY THINGS WORKED OUT, THAT WAS THE only fighting our platoon did on Durestal. Not long after dawn, the commander of the IFer army of occupation surrendered.

Our regiment did not exactly cover itself with glory on Durestal. A company from 1st Battalion had mistakenly put a company from 2nd Battalion under fire during the final battle. By the time they got the mistake sorted out, we had twenty men killed by friendly fire and another thirty wounded. The rest of Ranger Battalion hadn't fared any better than B Company. A lot of things went wrong, like on that exercise on Earth.

"There's gonna be a lot of finger-pointing when we get home," Tonio told me that afternoon. Our wounded had been treated and returned to duty—except for one porracci who had lost both legs to a grenade. The dead had been retrieved and ferried up to the ships for the voyage home. Ranger Battalion had assembled near where we landed originally. The rest of 1st Combined Regiment was being assembled ten miles away.

The units that had been on Durestal all along took care of the surrendered IFer units—and liberated the Alliance soldiers who had been taken prisoner during the first attempt to take the world back. Not many POWs had survived, but we didn't know that yet. There was some hope that they had simply been moved to another IF world. It wasn't until the interrogations of the occupation force had gone on for quite a few hours before we learned that most of the POWs had been killed.

"You think the finger-pointing will wait till we get home?" I asked. "One'll get you five that it's started already."

Tonio shrugged. "You're probably right," he conceded, "but it'll really hit the fan when we get home." He hesitated, frowning. "It wouldn't surprise me if there's a big shake-up in command. General Ransom might get the sack, maybe even some of the battalion commanders. The brass have to have a scapegoat."

Like what they did to Captain Fusik after the Bunyan Rebellion, I thought, knowing that Tonio was thinking the same thing. "It was one of Wellman's companies that screwed up, firing on our own people," I said, as much to myself as to Tonio. I shook my head. "Much as I hate him, I hate to see something like that happen to anyone even more."

JUST BECAUSE THE FIGHTING WAS OVER ON Durestal didn't mean we could count on heading back to Earth the next day. It *might* have happened that way, but it didn't. Since 1st Combined Regiment had come in only for the last scene, we got stuck with a lot of the cleanup afterward. We took part in the search for casualties, trying to make sure that all friendly bodies were retrieved. We looked for IFer ammunition dumps. We confiscated weapons and electronics from the IFer dead and prisoners. We also searched for Alliance equipment, to make sure nothing was left behind that could be put to any use. Even gear that was too badly damaged to use could be recycled, and that was important—not for protecting the ecology of Durestal but for the practical reason that it's cheaper to recycle metals and composites than it is to find and process raw materials.

A secondary mission was to help the divotect residents start to rebuild their infrastructure. They had lost 15 percent of their population to the IFers and to the fighting during the two Alliance invasions. Power plants had been destroyed, buildings had been destroyed or damaged, and many food replicators had been damaged or confiscated by the IFer occupation force. Until they could get more help from Divo—the homeworld of their species—they needed all the assistance we could give them.

The fight to liberate Durestal had been over for twelve days before 1st Combined Regiment left. General Ransom was relieved of command five minutes after he stepped ashore at Fort Campbell. Somehow, Lieutenant Colonel Josiah Wellman escaped the axe.

THREE DAYS LATER, WE FELL OUT IN DRESS UNI-forms for a full regimental formation to meet our new commanding officer. Brigadier General Montgomery Jones had never commanded any troops but human, but he had spent the past three months on the staff of the Combined General Staff of the Grand Alliance. He had gone along on one combat campaign as an observer attached to a ghuroh regiment. He had also been on one other campaign and acquitted himself well. The rumor mill had given us some information about Jones. He was supposed to be a strict disciplinarian, but he had shown a cool head in combat. A few men I talked to who had served under him in peacetime said they respected him.

Jones was six feet, eight inches tall and looked as if he had just stepped out of a recruiting poster. He looked as starched as his dress uniform. He didn't say a lot—and nothing that I couldn't have guessed he would say. It was a standard new commander speech. We were going to train hard and when the time came we would fight hard and acquit ourselves as honorably as we had in our first two combat assignments. He would be hard but fair. *Blah, blah, blah.* He made a ten-minute speech feel as if it took an hour to deliver.

"Well, what did you think of our fearless leader?" Robbie McGraw asked, after we had been dismissed.

"I'll reserve judgment," I said. "And so should you. He's got a good reputation. No matter what, he's the boss now. Maybe a new hand at the top will get us past all the foul-ups."

Robbie snorted. "He's a cardboard cutout, Sarge. Give him a uniform without starch, and he'd melt into his boots."

"I don't know that, and neither do you," I said, making my voice firmer. Even if I agreed with Robbie, I would have had to stick up for Jones. It's up to the sergeants and junior officers to make sure a new CO has a chance to prove himself. We've got to make sure the grunts don't screw it all up—because that would screw us all, not just the man on top. "Give the man a chance. Don't go undermining everything at the start."

Robbie stared at me for about twenty seconds. Then he walked away. Obviously, he wasn't going to surrender his opinions because of what I said. Well, I understood his attitude. I've been the same way most of my life.

THE NEXT MORNING GENERAL JONES SCORED points—in my book, at least. He relieved Wellman of command of 1st Battalion and put him back on the regimental staff, this time as the operations officer. Technically, it was a lateral transfer, not a demotion, but I enjoyed the thought that Wellman had to take it as a reprimand. It was one of his companies that had caused those friendly-fire casualties on Durestal.

That same day the regiment went straight into an intensive training regimen. There was going to be no grace period after a combat mission, no weeks put aside for furloughs and passes, no waiting for our dead to be replaced or for the last of our wounded to get back to duty. Jones did not even give us until the next Monday to start training at the start of a week.

We worked longer and harder than we had since our first period of training as a unit, back on the world code-named Dancer. Our day started before dawn and rarely ended before dark. By the time the sun came up we had already put in an hour of calisthenics and running. We worked six and sometimes seven days a week. At least once a week we went out on night exercises, drilling in even the most basic squad tactics—over and over. There was never a safe time to slough off because we never knew when the general would show up to watch an exercise. Rumors had him in three or four places at a time, and even the logical impossibility of that wasn't enough to convince some weary soldiers. Raw troops in basic training or in Ranger School don't work as hard as we did.

What the general did, taking part in the training regimen and closely observing the men under his command, his subordinate officers did as well. No one was spared from the rigors of the training regimen, and it was up to every officer and noncom to ride the men under him. As always, pressure flowed the only way it does in the army, from the top down. Anytime someone made a mistake—however minor—there was someone higher-ranking close enough to pounce. I had to run my men as hard as possible, had to jump on any mistake—fast and hard—just like the people over me were doing. I don't like taking that kind of heat, and I don't like holding the torch under other feet.

We got tired and stayed tired. That doesn't help; zombies make more mistakes. There were no passes to get off base, and we rarely had time to get to one of the on-base clubs to soothe our aches with a beer or two. Tempers flared. Noncoms and junior officers had to sit on any outburst before it could get out of control. In three weeks there were two suicides in the regiment, and two unsuccessful attempts. Five men went AWOL. At least fifty applied for transfers. The suicides were the only ones who got out for good. Even the AWOLs were returned to the unit once they were captured or surrendered. They weren't even given the "luxury" of being sent to the stockade.

Brigadier General Montgomery Jones meant business.

It wasn't until Jones had been on the scene a month that we got a weekend off, a day and a half, and then we weren't allowed passes. Sergeants and above could leave base whenever they weren't on duty, but most of us chose not to since our men weren't permitted the same liberty. The few married noncoms whose families lived near base went home. Some hadn't seen their wives since the night we got back from Durestal. That free weekend, most of us were content to simply catch up on sleep and give aching muscles and joints time to recover. The men in our platoon were too tired to fight—or even to bitch.

"I'm starting to worry," I told Tonio that Saturday. We were at one of the bars in the NCO club. "Morale hasn't been this bad since the early days on Dancer." My opinion of Jones had been going steadily downhill. At the start, I could see riding the regiment hard—for a week or two. It's something any new commander might do to establish himself, even without the gaffes that had plagued us. But it was well past time to ease up. Jones wouldn't make us better like this. The suicides alone should have been enough of a clue . . . even for a general.

"I know," Tonio said, after glancing around to make certain no one was close enough to overhear. "I've heard the captain and Herb saying pretty much the same thing." Herb was Company Lead Sergeant Herb Deelock, the top noncom in B Company. "But there's not a damned thing we can do but be as much of a buffer as we can, and try to keep our people from falling completely apart."

"The way things are now, if they put us into combat, the first casualty would be the general," I said. "And there's not a man who would fink on whoever pulled the trigger."

Tonio was frowning as he took a long drink of beer. He didn't want to talk about *that*. There's probably never been a war where some officers weren't killed by their own men, and we both knew that, but . . .

"You think Jones is just out to get himself another star?" I asked when it was clear that Tonio wasn't going to respond to the previous comment. "Does he want to make major general that badly?"

"I don't know what he wants," Tonio said, "and I don't much care. I just hate to see what he's doing to the unit. He says we need more training and discipline to get better, then he rides us past the level common sense should tell him is possible. We're losing ground every day. If we have a major field exercise now, we're so tired that we'll screw up worse."

"And he'll use that as an excuse to ride us even harder," I said, when Tonio gave up talking for another drink. "It won't take much more of that to destroy the unit altogether."

When the noncoms start talking that way, a unit is already in big trouble. I guess Tonio and I were both too tired to realize that at the time, though.

CHAPTER 5

THE NEWS WE RECEIVED AT REVEILLE FORMATION
Monday morning came as a bombshell. Immediately after breakfast, we would be packing field gear to shuttle to central Africa for a major exercise that would last the entire week. Our role would be as the aggressor force attempting to "liberate" the exercise area from the "enemy"—in this case, 3rd Combined Regiment, which was training for its first combat campaign. Our detailed briefing would take place during the shuttle trip.

"What in the hell does the general think he's doing?" I asked Tonio as we walked toward the mess hall. Besides the general dissatisfaction I felt with the way things had been going, I had a bit of a hangover after spending most of the weekend trying to forget how miserable I felt. "And how'd he manage to keep it secret until the last minute?"

"I don't know," Tonio said through clenched teeth. "I heard about it the same time you did." He sounded more than a little miffed at that, as if no one was permitted to keep secrets from him. Well, I imagine he had a hangover as well. We had done a lot of our drinking together, trying to make up for the weeks when we hadn't had time for serious drinking.

"He's just asking for trouble, dropping something like this on us without warning," I said. "The way the men are now, they need to be prepared for an exercise."

• • •

THERE WERE MORE THAN THE USUAL NUMBER OF
snafus getting the regiment loaded, even though we were
taking only the essentials—and leaving Heavy Weapons
Battalion and its self-propelled guns and rocket launchers
behind. We weren't going by ship; the shuttles would take
us to the exercise area. It should have taken ninety minutes
to get the entire regiment off the ground. It took twice that.
The first shuttles to take off spent so much time circling
overhead waiting for the rest that they had to land and re-
fuel, which started the problems cascading.

The shuttle crews weren't the problem. They weren't
part of the regiment, so they hadn't been under the regimen
of training and discipline we had. They did their job. The
problems were all with the men on the ground, and the
mistakes ran at least to battalion level. I guess officers get
worn-out and worn down the same as those of us on the
bottom of the heap.

But for all the problems we had getting started, that
phase of the operation was the high point of the exercise.
Once we hit the ground in Africa, it all hit the fan. The only
good thing anyone could say about that exercise was that
nobody got killed.

Our zone of operations was in a heavily forested, moun-
tainous region—one of the few relatively uninhabited
areas of interior Africa left. Our landing zones were spread
out along a forty-mile arc. Not one unit in the regiment got
from its LZ to its initial objective in anything near the time
that the schedule allotted. In company after company, men
either failed to go as fast as they were supposed to—and
the schedule *was* tighter than it should have been, considering the terrain and the work the regiment had put in over
the past month—or they managed to get themselves "lost"
if their officers didn't keep a constant check on their heading. Apparently, there were more than a few officers who
didn't bother to keep a close eye.

I don't believe that it was—in *any* way—an organized . . . "work action," I think they call it in civilian labor

disputes. If anyone had tried to organize soldiers to do something like that, they would have been guilty of inciting to mutiny. In wartime that's a hanging offense, even in Earth's armies. The porracci army wouldn't have let anyone guilty of that off so easily. They have no compunctions against "cruel and unusual" punishments.

The work slowdown, or however you characterize it, wasn't all that happened. One line company simply surrendered to the first unit of 3rd Combined Regiment they encountered. On smaller levels a number of platoons and squads did the same thing, as did a dozen or more individuals, making no pretense of simulating the fight we had been ferried halfway around the world for.

We landed just before sunset. By midnight, it was clear that the exercise was a total shambles. An hour later, we received orders from regimental headquarters to stand down, to make camp where we were. The exercise was over.

WHERE FIRST PLATOON, B COMPANY, RANGER Battalion was at when the order came was on a thirty-degree slope halfway up a hill that rose a thousand feet over the valley below. There wasn't anything vaguely resembling level ground within a quarter mile.

"We bed down here," I told my men. "Try to find positions where you won't roll to the bottom of the hill in your sleep." We were beyond jokes or gripes—and that showed just how bad morale was. No one asked questions or grumbled about the difficulties of sleeping on the slope. Robbie was the first to demonstrate how it could be done, lying uphill of a tree, feet against the trunk. He staked his pack down with his bayonet on one side and dug the blade of his entrenching tool into the ground on the other.

Once my people were situated, and I had spotted a position for me, I looked around, hoping to spot Tonio, but he had been called off to a meeting. That wasn't unexpected. *He'll get the* word *and come back to pass it on to the squad leaders,* I thought. *Then we'll know just what the hell is going on.*

I sat down, uphill of a good tree, and started to arrange my gear so that neither it nor I would roll down the hill. I took several minutes to get everything just so, wasting time while I looked toward the company command post. I could see the group clustered around Captain Fusik, so I would know when the meeting broke up. Finally, I lay on my side, but kept my eyes open. That meeting lasted more than twenty minutes. As soon as I saw Tonio heading back toward the platoon area, I got up before he radioed for the squad leaders and walked to meet him.

"We head back to the LZs at first light, then return to Kentucky as soon as the shuttles come in," was how Tonio started the conference once the squad leaders had gathered. Even though we were face-to-face, he used the radio, speaking over a circuit that was limited to him and the four squad leaders. "The regiment is in hot water over its head." I knew Tonio. I could tell from his tone that he was deadly serious.

"We've got three hours until dawn," he continued. "I want one squad leader awake, and alert, until then. Forty-five minutes apiece, right down the line, starting with you, Dragon." I nodded. "Platoon sergeants are running the same rotation. So are the officers. Keep an eye on your men. We don't want any problems. Let's keep the rest of the night quiet and peaceful."

No one asked questions. We were to watch our own men. That gave us plenty of hint as to what might have gone wrong on the exercise, but I was still surprised as I learned the whole story—or as much of it as got out—over the next few days.

I had the first watch. I went back to my squad and sat with my back against the tree trunk below my gear, my rifle across my lap. Since this was only an exercise, we hadn't been issued ammunition, just laser simulators, but a rifle makes a dandy club, and if worse came to worst, I did have my bayonet—and my pistol, which I *did* have ammunition for. Not that I dreamed for a second that I might need a weapon—not in *my* squad, *my* platoon, *my* company. But the word *mutiny* kept tickling the edges of my mind.

After forty-five minutes I turned the watch over to Sergeant Chouvana, the porracci leader of second squad, and lay down. Although I was exhausted, I did not sleep, and I'm not certain that I ever closed my eyes—longer than the occasional blink. Not knowing exactly what had happened or what might happen before we got home had me fearing the worst, and it made me too nervous to sleep. Nothing like this had ever happened in my more than ten years in uniform. By the time dawn came and we were "wakened," the only thing I was certain of was that all hell was going to break loose once we got back to Kentucky.

THERE WERE NO EXPLANATIONS IN THE MORNING. Captain Fusik said almost nothing to us, and the lieutenants were even quieter. We got up, ate a battle ration, formed up, then marched back to the landing zone where we had come in. The shuttles started landing a few minutes later. There was no waiting around for an aerial formation. As soon as a shuttle was loaded, it took off. When we landed at Fort Campbell, before dawn because of the time difference, we marched to the company area, handed in our weapons to the company armorer, and were dismissed.

Not one word was said about the early end of the exercise or what was going to happen as a result. The platoon went to the mess hall together for a proper breakfast, then returned to the barracks. No formation, no orders for the day. "Let the men get what rest they can until we hear different," Tonio said, instructions that must have come from Captain Fusik, if not from higher up the chain of command.

After a quick shower, I went into my private room and lay down. I tried to sleep but couldn't. The suspense was all but enough to have me pacing the ceiling like a fly. For a time, I stared at the ceiling, listening, wondering if the men were saying anything in the squad bay—anything they might not want me to hear. Eventually, I shut my eyes and did breathing exercises to relax. I was tired, in need of sleep. An hour later I was still awake, so I got up and paced for ten minutes.

I considered putting a sleep patch on to force rest but didn't. There was no way to know how long this "free" time would last. Once the brass got back we might get called out at any second, and patch-induced sleep might leave me too groggy to respond quickly. Besides, there was that other possibility—the one I was *almost* convinced couldn't possibly happen, certainly not in 1st Combined Regiment—that there might actually be mutiny in the air.

If the history books are right, there hasn't been a mutiny in Earth's army in more than two hundred years, or in the armies of any of the human colony worlds in the Alliance of Light. I had no idea how long it might have been in the armies of the other species. Maybe mutiny isn't so rare among porracci. Their system of fighting for promotion against the guy whose job you want strikes me as close to mutiny.

I DID DOZE, FITFULLY. WE WERE ALL SO FAR BE-hind on sleep that my body finally got past the way my mind was worrying. But I didn't get any *deep* sleep, and I guess I woke up half a dozen times. You don't get much rest that way. It can almost be worse than no sleep at all.

It was past noon when the last units of the regiment got back. We were in the mess hall when someone came in and said that he had heard that the final shuttles had touched down.

"We can expect the axes to start dropping anytime now," I said. My squad was sitting together at one table, a practice Colonel Hansen had insisted on months before—to get the integration of species within Ranger Battalion past the last real roadblock, our tendency to gather by species off duty.

Only a few of my men bothered to look my way. The rest were more concerned with staring at the trays in front of them.

"Look, I don't know what happened on this exercise," I said, tapping my fork on my tray. That drew more eyes. "I don't know what will happen now. We've gone through a lot of crap the last month and more. But we've gone through it *together*."

"Have you heard anything at all?" Toniyi asked. Divotect always seem to have a hangdog expression, but that has nothing to do with mood. It's just the way they're built. Toniyi was perhaps the most taciturn of the men in the squad normally. I was surprised that he was the one who spoke.

"Nothing at all," I said. "I don't think even Captain Fusik knows much. But we'll find out before long. If the general is back, we're sure to hear *something*." I was also certain it wouldn't be anything we *wanted* to hear. Montgomery Jones had come in thinking we were trash, and we hadn't been given much of a chance to show him differently. "Just remember, we're in this together. We've shown what we can do when we're given the chance, no matter what anyone says."

THE MESSAGE THAT FINALLY CAME DOWN FROM regimental headquarters late that afternoon was not what I expected. There was no diatribe about the exercise. There were no threats of punishment, no increase in the already too-heavy training schedule. Quite the contrary, the word that came out of the general's office was that—except for morning calesthenics—there would be no training or work details for the rest of the week. There would be no passes or leaves, and we would still stand the two normal morning formations, but after that we were basically on our own until Reveille the next morning.

"I don't get it," I told Tonio, when he gave me the orders. "Instead of jumping on us with both boots, they're giving us the rest of the week off? What the hell is going on?"

Tonio gave me an expressive shrug of the shoulders. "It's no crazier than the general trying to work us to death for a month," he said. "Maybe the exercise was enough to show Jones the error of his ways." I wasn't certain if Tonio was being serious or sarcastic. Maybe he wasn't sure himself. "I'm going to poke around, see if I can find anything out."

"THEY'RE GIVING US ALL WEEK OFF?" NEVILLE ST. John said, when I gave the news to the squad. Slowly, the other members of the squad got to their feet, moving closer to me. It was the most alive they had acted in weeks.

"Except for Reveille and the morning work formation," I said. "Don't bother asking why 'cause I don't have any idea. My reaction was the same as yours. Don't question it. We're overdue for a break. Let's make the best of it."

"You mean before somebody sobers up and cancels it," Robbie said.

"More or less," I agreed. "Tell you what. Let's all go to the EM club and I'll buy the first round."

A couple of them almost smiled at that.

I ENDED UP BUYING THE FIRST TWO ROUNDS, BUT I didn't have a second myself. I left the men looking halfway animated for a change and headed back to the barracks. Curiosity was racing through my mind so hard that I couldn't enjoy the beer. Tonio wasn't around, but a couple of the other platoon sergeants were, and I started asking questions. A few rumors were beginning to circulate—passed from sergeant to sergeant—a little of what happened in Africa, and a lot of speculation as to what might happen next. The news was fairly reliable. By the time a man gets to be a sergeant he has generally learned to discriminate between idle rumors and those that have a likelihood of being accurate, and a sergeant often has fairly reliable sources of information, an informal network with other noncoms.

The rumor that piqued my interest most had nothing to do with the various shortcomings and misdeeds of our troops during the exercise. It was the flat statement that General Jones had not returned to Fort Campbell. His command shuttle had gone elsewhere, but no one seemed to know where. The order releasing us from training and work details for the rest of the week had come from Colonel Chop, the regiment's ghuroh executive officer.

No one in the regiment saw General Jones the rest of the week. By Friday afternoon, we had heard most of the stories about what had happened during the aborted African exercise, the slowdowns, foul-ups, and so forth. There was an unconfirmed rumor that General Jones had been summoned to Lima, Peru, where the Combined General Staff had its headquarters on Earth.

Also on Friday afternoon, we were told that there would be no formations Saturday morning, and that everyone would be permitted passes from 1600 hours Friday until 0600 hours Monday. That came from regimental headquarters in a written order signed by Colonel Chop.

"Let's not spoil this," I told my squad before anyone could start changing into dress uniform or civilian clothes. "For whatever reason, we've caught a break. Don't give the brass an excuse to lock us on base again." I hoped the advice would take, but the men had a lot of steam that needed to be released.

I HAD A FAIRLY QUIET WEEKEND IN NASHVILLE. I got a hotel room, met the same lady who had given me a good time the last time I was there, and paid an outrageous sum to have her hang with me until noon Sunday. I got my money's worth. I never got drunk that weekend, but I was never completely sober, either. By the time I got on the bus to head back to Fort Campbell, I was feeling more human than I had in quite a while. Mellow.

Most of the squad was back in the barracks before I got there late Sunday afternoon. Only Robbie and Neville were later getting in. Well, they were the only others in the squad who came from Earth. The rest weren't human, let alone Terran. Neville let on that he had gone to Chicago for his weekend. He had a serious girlfriend there—something I hadn't known before—and they were talking about marriage. Robbie had gone no farther than Gavin City, the built-up area across the road from base, but he had stayed until the last of his money was gone.

I can't say that everyone acted the way they had before General Jones came to 1st Combined Regiment, but we were getting close. We were talking among ourselves again. It was a step in the right direction.

WE FELL OUT FOR REVEILLE MONDAY AND WENT through our normal morning exercises and a one-mile run before breakfast. Nothing was said about any change in plans, whether we were going to continue sloughing off or go back onto a training schedule. At 0800 hours, morning work formation was a full regimental job, instead of something done by company or battalion, with Colonel Chop standing on the reviewing stand in front of regimental headquarters. We went through the daily routine of submitting manning reports: "All present or accounted for, sir." Then Colonel Chop gave us the "parade rest" command.

The colonel held a sheet of paper and read. "From: Chief of Staff, Combined General Staff, Grand Alliance. Effective immediately, Colonel Chop"—well, actually, he read his true name in the ghuroh language that tied the tongues of every other species in knots—"is promoted to the rank of brigadier general and will assume command of 1st Combined Regiment."

Soldiers don't applaud or cheer while they're standing in formation, but I'm sure I wsn't the only one who had to stop himself. To my left, I heard Robbie's voice whisper, "I'll be damned. The old bastard's been canned." I glanced along the row but didn't tell him that he wasn't supposed to talk in ranks. An officer who gets himself relieved of command that way has a black mark on his record that will follow him through the rest of his career—and shorten that career considerably.

General Chop handed the paper to an aide—giving us a full minute to absorb the news and turn our attention back to him. I looked around, more than I should have, trying to gauge reaction. I could see men moving a bit, not standing as stiffly as "parade rest" calls for, but I didn't hear any sergeant or officer reprimanding anyone. The officers I could see close by—lieutenants and Captain Fusik—were doing more than a little rubbernecking of their own.

"We return to a normal training schedule this morning," General Chop said. "Let me repeat, a *normal* training schedule, not the . . . accelerated schedule of the recent past. The new schedule has been distributed to each battalion and company. During this first week, there will be no night exercises. We will concentrate on the basics, at a normal pace." I noted that he had used the word *normal* three times in five sentences. He spent a few seconds looking around, then braced to attention, gave us that order, and said, "Dismissed."

AFTER TWO WEEKS, I WAS READY TO CONCEDE that it was for real. We were being treated like soldiers again, and the men responded. It took us most of those two weeks to get our timing back, but we were working like a team and not making so many mistakes. Disciplinary problems dropped back to pre-Jones levels. No information had filtered down yet about just what had happened to General Jones—why he had been relieved or where he had gone.

After a month, General Chop used a regimental formation to tell us that he was pleased with our progress and that he was certain that within another few weeks we would be at the top of our form, better than the best we had shown in our first two combat assignments, "When you showed the worlds just how well we can work together," was how he phrased it.

If was four days after that when the orders came in. The regiment was being sent offworld again. It looked as if it was time for us to get back into the war.

CHAPTER 6

NO, **I** WAS NOT EAGER TO GET BACK INTO COM-
bat. I'm not *that* crazy. I got the usual knot in my stomach
at the thought of what might be waiting. I know the odds,
what can happen. But there was a war on, and I was a career soldier—a professional. There was an Enemy out
there who wanted to destroy peoples, wanted to conquer
every world it could. It had to be stopped. After a time
under a cloud, my outfit was going to be given another
chance to fight, and this time I thought we were ready for
whatever we might face. We had shown how good we
could be, even when we had a lot going against us, before
we learned how to fuse men of half a dozen species into a
credible fighting machine.

We were given seventy-two hours notice of movement,
but were not told where we were going or what we were to
do when we got there. That's a routine security measure.
There was little training between notice and departure, little more than calisthenics each morning . . . and our
"morning" was gradually moved later, to get our diurnal
rhythms prepared for the cycle of day and night at our des-
tination. That was also routine.

Before we went to bed for our last night on Earth, we
could see some of the ships gathered overhead. They were
a couple of hundred of miles out, but they are *huge*—the

largest transports are more than five miles long and over half a mile in diameter. Some of the fighting ships, the weapons platforms with their squadrons of aerospace fighters and banks of rocket launchers, and particle and energy beam weapons, are even larger.

There was a briefing for company commanders and above before we fell out for transport to our shuttles. The rest of us were loaded on trucks and moved to the Fort Campbell spaceport under the supervision of our lieutenants. As soon as the senior officers returned, we boarded shuttles and were ferried up to the transports. It was an orderly operation; no snafus. Ninety minutes after the first shuttle lifted off, the fleet started moving out-system. And Captain Fusik gathered the men of B Company, Ranger Battalion, to give us the scoop.

"The first thing," he started, "is that this is not—I repeat, *not*—a combat deployment." He paused to let that sink in. I felt a mixture of relief and concern, the latter because maybe we were still under a cloud, not considered good enough for combat. The reason for relief should be obvious: my men and I were less likely to become casualties. For the time being, the pressure would be reduced.

"We *have* drawn an important mission," Fusik continued before anyone started asking questions. "The world we are going to is called Unity. You may have seen something about it in the news over the past months." I hadn't, but I don't follow the news closely, except for war news.

"Unity is an experimental Alliance colony world being jointly settled by humans, porracci, ghuroh, and divotect. A few hundred abarand families are expected to arrive shortly. After that—well, we don't know whether any biraunta are going to join the experiment or not." I could understand the why of that, remembering how difficult it had been for biraunta to serve alongside porracci when our regiment was created. Porracci resemble a prehistoric predator from the biraunta homeworld, and they had been terrified of the porracci in the unit.

"What we have shown can be done in the military, Unity

is designed to show can be done by civilians. The Alliance considers this experiment critical to the future cooperation and peaceful coexistence of our peoples. Unity is in what might prove to be a strategically important location in the war, which means that it is possible that the Ilion Federation might decide to invade once they learn about our colony there." Fusik paused, then shrugged.

"Military intelligence feels that there is little chance that the Ilion Federation will be in any position to invade Unity for at least two months, probably longer, and by that time the Alliance will have strong defenses on the ground and in the space surrounding Unity. We are going in as a temporary garrison, due to be relieved in a month.

"I know, this battalion is not designed for defensive operations, not geared toward garrison duty. It's not something Ranger Battalion—or the Regiment as a whole—has trained for. But the Grand Alliance doesn't want to take chances. They don't want to leave Unity unprotected until proper units finish training and move in. We are to fill that gap." He stopped again and cleared his throat noisily—obviously a theatrical gesture to make sure he had everyone's attention.

"It's not a combat assignment, but that does not mean that the high command doesn't believe we're ready for such an assignment. With the importance being placed on the defense of Unity, they want the best available troops there. Us." I don't think the timing was intentional, but Fusik stopped then as the ship started to vibrate—building power for its first transit of hyperspace. The ship made its jump and the vibration and noise stopped. There would be a pause of, perhaps, only three or four minutes while the computers verified our position and the calculations for the next jump, and made sure that the entire fleet was accounted for.

"Unity is a brand-new colony. The first shiploads of settlers have been on the ground for three months. The total population is under ten thousand, fairly evenly divided among the participating species. We have one extended community, laid out similar to the common divotect plan, with considerable space between homesteads. The town spreads out over an area of approximately twenty-five square miles, at the edge of a forested area, but with open savanna to the south and west that can be used to graze animals and be turned by the plow to provide fresh food for the colonists.

"As I understand it, the initial complement of settlers is not merely farmers and their families, although agriculture is always important in a colony's first years. Preference was given to heads of family with military experience, and the colonists are armed with more than the usual hunting weapons. They will be forming their own militia, and part of our duty on Unity will be to give them as much training as we can—another reason why this regiment was deemed appropriate. Ranger Battalion will draw most of the training duty since our makeup is similar to that of the colony, while the line regiments will establish defensive positions around the settled area. This fleet is carrying satellites to give the colonists an outer warning system as well as a few defensive weapons systems. The units that replace us next month will bring in more."

The ship started vibrating again, building up for its second hyperspace transit. I felt surprised; it hadn't seemed like enough time had passed for the things that have to be done between jumps, but they certainly knew what they were doing on the bridge. I guess I had let myself get too caught up in what the captain was saying.

"We'll be going in easy," Captain Fusik continued. "No airsleds, not even hot shuttle landings. I know no one is going to complain about that. Maybe there won't be any bars or any of the other, ah, recreational facilities on Unity that you'd have back home, but we'll get through this month as professionally as possible, get in a little training of our own while we're training the militia. Then, after this assignment is done, we'll be ready for something more active. We'll have earned it."

•   •   •

THERE WAS A LONGER INTERVAL BETWEEN OUR second and third hyperspace transits, and we emerged in normal space farther out from Unity than we would have if we had been going in for a combat landing. I guess that was to make sure we didn't spook the people we were coming to protect. We had a three-hour wait between the end of our last hyperspace jump and getting in the shuttles for our trip down to the surface.

We had video of the world to occupy our minds during that interval, long-range stuff magnified so that we could see a little detail. I could have seen more by unfolding my electronic map, but I watched the show on the larger screens with my men. There were captions to orient us. There were large ice-covered continents around both poles, with most of the readily habitable land on one massive continent that straddled the equator and extended about 60 percent of the way around the world. The colony had been planted near the eastern edge of the continent, in the southern hemisphere. We had been told that the climate would be on the border between temperate and subtropical—warm but not excessively hot. And it was early spring.

"I still don't see how we managed to luck out and draw a month in the Garden of Eden," Robbie said, after Captain Fusik had gone to another briefing. "Things like this don't happen to me."

"If you feel guilty about accepting good luck when it falls in your lap, I'm sure we'll be able to find enough miserable details for you to feel at home on Unity," I offered, trying to stifle a laugh.

"Do me no favors," Robbie said, holding up a hand as if to ward me off. "Whatever you do, don't wake me. If this is a dream—and it must be—let me sleep as long as possible."

We had a hot meal before we were ordered to the shuttles. With conditions undoubtedly at a fairly primitive state on the ground, it might be days before we got mess kitchens set up to provide us with our next hot meal. Unity might not be a combat assignment, but we'd probably be eating a lot of battle rations while we were there.

MY GUESS IS THAT IT WAS MENTAL INERTIA SOMEwhere up the line that sent Ranger Battalion in ahead of the rest of the regiment. We would be the first ones in on a combat landing. You put the spec ops people on the ground to disrupt enemy defenses and make it easier for the line battalions to come ashore. Apparently, somebody didn't want to tax their brains by changing the routine simply because this was different. We would go in first. The line regiments would follow. Heavy Weapons Battalion and additonal supplies would come in at the end of the process. It was the same sort of routine that had us draw a full field issue of ammunition and battle rations before we filed aboard our shuttles—as if this were a combat insertion.

One platoon filled a shuttle. The web seats aren't particularly comfortable, but they beat the accommodations in a sled by one hell of a margin. We strapped in, checked to make certain everything was secured, and waited. The hangar was depressurized, a boom lifted the shuttle away from the ship, then turned us loose—giving the shuttle a push to move it farther from the ship. The shuttle pilot used bursts of inert gas to increase our separation, then lit the rockets, and we started our ride down to the surface of Unity.

"Remember, it's Alliance people here," Tonio said over our platoon channel. "Friends. We land, get out of the shuttle, and move just far enough from the LZ to be out of the way of the rest of the shuttles. I don't know if the colonists are going to be on hand to welcome us, but watch your manners if they are. We don't want them running off to lock their daughters away until we leave." Tonio kept his tone light, almost joking, but we knew he was serious. We didn't want the locals to think we were modern Vikings come to ravage their land and their women.

It was midmorning at the LZ, located a little more than

four miles from the nearest edge of the settlement—far enough that the noise of shuttles landing and taking off wouldn't be overwhelming. Our shuttle dropped us off, turned around, and taxied about a mile before turning and starting its takeoff run. By the time our lander had taken off, we had trotted out of the clearing, and two other shuttles were landing. I could see the next flight of three shuttles on their final approach. It was very military and very precise. The shuttle jockeys knew what they were doing.

As soon as all of B Company was on the ground, Captain Fusik and Lead Sergeant Deelock formed us up and marched us toward our bivouac area—about three and a half miles away. The captain didn't push the pace. There was no hurry. We were all loaded down with a full field load—in the case of the humans that meant close to eighty pounds of gear. Porracci and ghuroh carried even more. Even divotect were expected to carry half their body weight. Biraunta, who only averaged about seventy-five pounds, carried less—both absolutely and also relative to body weight.

We reached our assigned area before the landings were complete—before the last of the line battalions reached the ground, before Heavy Weapons Battalion and the extra supplies even left the ships. According to the schedule, it would be close to sunset before the operation was complete, and even then, there would be more stuff to bring ashore later, like the defensive weapons we had hauled along to set up for the colony.

The last of the day's scheduled shuttles were just moving away from their ships when we got the news. An IFer fleet had just popped out of hyperspace, less than three hours out from our ships. It looked as if Unity was going to turn into a combat assignment after all.

CHAPTER 7

"I KNEW THIS WAS TOO GOOD TO BE TRUE!" Robbie said, after Captain Fusik passed the word.

"You had to crab," I told him, slapping his faceplate down. "Couldn't let well enough be."

"That's right, blame me for being a realist."

There was no sense of distress evident around me, though I must admit that the butterflies in my stomach had turned to lead. Robbie's cracks showed that our morale was better than it had been since General Jones started wearing us down. Whatever happened, we would give a good accounting of ourselves. I was strangely sure of that.

We might need a break or two along the way to come out on top, or to last until our relieving force arrived in a month. We were on the ground, and an IFer force of unknown strength was in the system, heading toward us. Our little month-long picnic was about to be attacked by a swarm of murderous ants, and we didn't have all our goodies laid out yet.

The rest of the loaded shuttles were launched. As many more shuttles as could be loaded with supplies were, and hurried out of their hangars so they could ground before the IFers got close enough to endanger them. My guess would be that maybe the order in which things were supposed to be landed got screwed up, and they started loading up whatever was easiest to get to.

At the same time, our combat ships started moving out to intercept the IFers as far away from Unity as possible. You want to make it harder for the enemy to strike targets on the surface or launch its own ground troops. The optimal outcome would be to make it impossible for the enemy to land, or to destroy all his troop shuttles on the way in.

I don't know that it's ever happened that way, in any modern war. It certainly didn't happen at Unity.

There was no panic on the ground. Our company had reached its assigned bivouac location, but we only stayed there ten minutes after we heard about the incoming IFer fleet. Robbie got in his wisecracks. A couple of people moaned and groaned, but even the grousing was welcome—stony silence would have been chilling. We moved, aiming for a location another four miles away, to establish defensive positions. The new idea was to ring the civilian settlement and cover any places inside it that were open enough for hostile shuttles to land. There were a lot of those. We had drawn one of the longer routes.

The mood was different from what it had been right after we landed—when we were expecting a month of garrison duty and training the local militia. Our pace was quicker, our attention more focused, and we kept biraunta out in front and ghuroh on either flank while we marched—as if there were a chance that the enemy might already have people on the ground. We had also loaded our rifles and grenade launchers, on orders, but we kept the safeties engaged. *Time*: we still had time. How well we used that time might decide the fate of Unity.

We covered four miles in seventy minutes, then formed a rough defensive perimeter while Captain Fusik and Lead Sergeant Deelock scouted around to find out exactly where we would prepare "permanent" positions. We were under the cover of trees—tall, thick monsters of trees—so the IFer ships would not be able to spot us even if their long-range snooping gear was radically better than our own.

The largest of those trees had trunks twenty feet in diameter near the ground and had to stretch over two hundred feet up—not quite redwoods, but grander than most trees you'll see on any world. We were also close to the edge of that forested area, with miles of open savanna reaching out to the south, and a little to the east. It looked as if the wild grasses might range up to ten feet high. It would make it difficult to spot infantrymen crawling through it.

"Be nice if we could burn that all out," I told Souvana, who was standing next to me. "Make it a lot easier to target the enemy if they come in this way."

He grunted his agreement. "They will never let us do that in advance," he said. "We wouldn't want to damage the unspoiled beauty of this place." The translator button in my ear captured his sarcastic tone perfectly.

"It might not burn easily in any case," I said, gesturing out toward the grassland again. "Too green, full of moisture. It would need artificial accelerants. In any case, the wind isn't right. If it did start burning, it might come back in on us."

"There is that," Souvana replied. I turned my head to stare directly at him. My assistant squad leader still thought he was more qualified to run the squad than I was and—by porracci standards—he was probably right because he could take me in one-on-one unarmed combat, and that is how porracci decide those things in their own army. But he had made a lot less noise about his "superiority" since Olviat. We hadn't become bosom buddies, and I didn't hold out any hope that we ever would, but we worked together with a lot less friction than in the early days.

"This is not the role we trained for," Souvana said. "It feels . . . strange to sit and wait for an enemy to come to us. I feel as if we should be doing more, though I know there is nothing useful we could do until the enemy attempts a landing."

This time, Souvana turned to meet my stare. It was rare to hear a porracci—*any* porracci—voice uncertainty. To them, doubt implies weakness. I wasn't sure what I should say, and Souvana seemed to sense my dilemma. "I know, that does not sound like me," he said. "Maybe I have been around humans and the other members of our alliance too long."

"If the enemy does get troops on the ground, we probably won't sit still for long," I said. "We'll go hunting them. That will put us back in a more familiar role. Until then, let's not question our fortune."

He rolled his lips back in the porracci equivalent of a smile. "No, I will not wish away good fortune as Lance Corporal McGraw does. Porracci know how to deal with life as it comes."

FUSIK AND DEELOCK FINISHED THEIR SURVEY. They had covered three hundred yards to either side of where we had set up our temporary perimeter. The lead sergeant gathered the platoon sergeants and gave them precise instructions on where we were to dig in. From a distance, I watched the sweep of his arm as he pinpointed locations for each squad. It didn't take long. Then Tonio came over with first platoon's assignment.

"We'll dig two lines of trenches," he said. "The first will be over here, just back of the end of the trees, keeping as much of this wood as we can for cover—from ground troops, aircraft, or overhead thermal sensors. A slight arc, bowed toward the grassland. Until the line regiments all get in place, we might have as much as half a mile of empty space separating us from the nearest friendly units. Unless something unforeseen happens though, everyone should have time to get into position—and dug in—before the enemy lands.

"Once our positions are ready on this side, camouflaged as well as we can manage, we'll move back eighty yards and dig a second set. That will give us a fallback if we need it, or leave us ready to meet the IFers if they cross us up and come from the other direction." My squad would have the right end of the platoon line—the right end of the company line—on the side facing the southeast, out over the grassland.

I didn't have to worry about anyone goldbricking on *this* detail. Every man fell to with full enthusiasm. That's something you never see on a training exercise, no matter how realistic the planners want it to be. We worked hard and fast to make our positions as secure as possible.

We shoveled out holes and piled the excavated dirt around them. I had Ala and Oyo climb trees to chop small branches to give us some structural support for our slit trenches and help camouflage the positions. Since we had time, we dug grenade sumps at the back of our trenches— deeper holes with the tops angled away from us that we could shove explosives into if they landed beside us, get them down where they wouldn't do as much damage when they exploded. I hadn't forgotten all the tricks I learned back in basic training, though this was the first time I'd actually had a chance to put *that* trick to use.

In ninety minutes, we had both sets of trenches dug and camouflaged. The enemy fleet was seventy minutes from being close enough to launch shuttles with ground troops—*if* our space jockeys failed to slow them. Since our people weren't going to roll over and play dead, we would probably have more time. There was just no way to determine how much.

"Even if the IFers get through relatively unscathed, they won't launch ground troops before sunset," Tonio said. He had gathered the squad leaders in the center of our area, halfway between the lines of trenches. "I haven't heard anything about the fight upstairs, but I imagine it's a doozy."

"Do we have any figures on the size of the enemy force yet?" Sergeant Slash of fourth squad asked.

"Not even the number of ships," Tonio said. "I don't know who's sitting on that. The general and his staff must have some idea what we're facing, but they haven't decided to share it with us low types yet."

I figured that the fact that they weren't telling us how many IFers to expect meant that the odds weren't going to be good. If the invading army looked small, they'd be telling us that we had nothing to worry about. They weren't bragging about how many enemy ships we had blown out of space either.

"I haven't seen anything that looked like a major explosion out there," Slash said, gesturing upward. "Perhaps it is just that this canopy is too thick to see through, or maybe the fighting isn't near enough to the zenith for us to see."

"The navy will not rob us of our work," Sergeant Chouvana, second squad's leader, said. "The enemy will land, then it will be up to us." Although he was porracci, Chouvana sounded only moderately eager to get his chance at the IFers.

"No doubt," Tonio said drily. "But I'm in no hurry, and I'll lead the cheering section for our navy any day of the week. Let them take out as many of the enemy as they can. I wouldn't complain if they blasted the whole IFer fleet. For now, try to keep your men relaxed. Let them get what rest they can. Once the enemy lands, it's hard telling how long it might be before we get a chance to sack out for more than five minutes at a time."

SLEEP, WITH AN ENEMY ARMY OF UNKNOWN SIZE and composition on its way to attack you? It *is* possible. I doubt that many of us actually slept, but we got as much rest as we could, lying in our slit trenches, eyes closed, trying to deal with whatever level of nervousness we were suffering. It *was* different, sitting and waiting for the enemy instead of hunting for them, the way a spec ops squad usually does. Maybe that's the way a turkey feels when Thanksgiving gets close. The nerves would have been a lot simpler to deal with had we been moving, trying to sneak up on an enemy position or the like. That gives the brain something to concentrate on.

Still, it's up to the leaders to put on a good show when

necessary. You have to avoid making your men think you're nervous, or scared, even if you are—*especially* if you are. Give them the impression you see it as all in a day's work, and maybe they will, too. Nervousness, like fear, is contagious.

On other campaigns, we had always had an information channel from the Combat Information Center on one of the ships broadcasting news. We hadn't been given a channel for it this time, but I finally stumbled on the proper frequency. Information was sparse. It was more like eavesdropping on one half of a conversation than listening to a feed that was intended to keep you up to the minute, but I did get some information. There was, apparently, one hell of a fight going on between 250 and 300 miles out, farther west, well away from the settlement. There was no indication that our guys were scoring a major victory, but it also didn't sound as if we were dangling from the tip of the short end either.

I had been listening for twenty minutes before the voice from CIC changed, and we started getting a direct update. I switched channels to tell Tonio that we had a news feed, then went back to listening. The latest estimate was that the IFer force had probably arrived with two regiments of ground troops—double our strength. At least three enemy transports had been hit, with unknown casualty levels, so perhaps they would be unable to attempt to land more than one and a half regiments—a three-to-two advantage for the invaders if all of those troops survived to reach the shore. For defenders, those odds usually aren't bad, as long as you have control of the air overhead—or parity with the enemy's air support capabilities. From what I was hearing, and from what I could deduce, we still had the enemy matched in ships and aerospace fighters.

It started to get dark under the trees well before sunset, but we could still see light out on the grasslands. The enemy wasn't close enough to launch landers to put ground troops ashore, even if they wanted to try in daylight—which I could assume that they did not. *We've still got at least an hour,* I thought, *probably two or three hours from the sound of the fight.* We would have the cover of dark when the battle started on the ground, and an infantryman loves the dark. It gives him a better chance for survival.

LISTENING TO THE CALM VOICE ON THE CIC FEED helped me relax. It helped pass the time and gave my mind something to focus on other than my worries.

When sunset finally reached us, there was still no word of the enemy launching shuttles or sending aerospace fighters down to inflict what damage they could. Waiting can be miserable, but I'll take that to fighting *any* day, and twice if the alternative were to be aboard one of the ships engaged in combat. On the ground, I figure I've always got some control, some chance to survive—no matter what happens. If you're on one of the big fighting ships, one lucky enemy hit can rip open large sections of a ship, exposing the crew to vacuum—and certain death—and you don't have any way to affect the outcome. Fighter pilots have it a little better. They're pretty much in control, wired into their control systems, and their cockpits double as escape pods.

It was thirty minutes past sunset when our last line units moved into the defensive perimeter around the settlement. I made contact with the platoon sergeant closest to my men, to make sure we knew where each other's people were. The company to our right was ghuroh. I had met the platoon sergeant on the end of their area of responsibility, but I can't say that I knew him well enough to pick him out of a group of ghuroh. There is more visible distinction among ghuroh then there is among biraunta, but—for a human, at least—those differences are still minor. I could tell Razor and Claw—the two ghuroh in my squad—apart at a hundred yards, and I can distinguish among most of the ghuroh in our platoon, but that's because I've been around them routinely.

It was just a few minutes later that orders came through for us to start observing "strict" electronic silence, instead of the laxer standard we had been using, simply *minimizing* the use of electronics. That meant we weren't to use our radio transmitters or do active scanning unless we were in contact with the enemy . . . or for some equally urgent reason.

I could still listen to the constant feed from CIC. Our receivers are too passive for a scan to pick them up, and the enemy could *see* our ships. Electronic silence would not hide them the way it will individual soldiers with good visual and thermal camouflage. Something that large can't be hidden by stealth technology, not when the enemy's "eyes"—electronic and otherwise—are as sophisticated as they are in any modern navy.

Wait. Captain Fusik had put us on half-and-half watches at sunset. That meant that 50 percent of the men would be awake and watching at any time. The rest would be sleeping, eating, or just resting. Theoretically. When we switched off, it would put fresh eyeballs on the job. An hour at a time. We did it by fire team within each squad. The four squad leaders in the platoon worked it so there would always be two of us alert.

It lacked only twenty minutes of midnight—the day on Unity was almost precisely identical to the day on Earth, off by no more than three minutes—when we received the warning we had been expecting. The enemy transports were launching shuttles. The estimate (and I had been a soldier too long to put more than minimal faith in the estimates we received in the field) was that the IFer fleet was putting four thousand men in the boats. The first would be landing in half an hour. There was no way to tell yet exactly *where* they would land. Wherever they put down, it would be too damned close.

CHAPTER 8

I HEARD RELAYED REPORTS OF THREE ENEMY shuttles shot down before they went atmospheric—that would mean 150 or 160 soldiers out of 4,000 or more CIC said were coming in. That was scarcely a tally to raise spirits of the men on the ground waiting: 4 percent. If that was all the troops our sky jockeys accounted for, the IFers would still have us outnumbered when they landed . . . unless they were incautious enough to try to land close enough for soldiers with surface-to-air missile launchers to knock more out before the grunts could get out of the box. Most IFer troops I had encountered had been aggressive, but few of their commanders had been that stupid.

I wonder how much stuff we got landed before the IFers got too close to risk more? I thought as I waited for some indication where the IFers would land. I hoped we had put plenty of ammunition, for all our weapons, on the ground before the battle was engaged overhead. We could scrounge food from the land. It might be strange and only partially nutritious for some species in the Alliance, but life is not so different from one world to the next that you're likely to find more examples of plants and animals that are actively toxic if eaten than you are on the world your species originated on. But if you run out of ammunition, the best rifle in the Galaxy turns into nothing more than a club—or a spear if you've got your bayonet. That's why they still issue us bayonets, and why we train hard with them. As long as you have to put men on the ground to take it or hold it, there will still be a use for the bayonet—no matter what some theoretician who has never experienced combat or soiled his hands might tell you.

Overhead, our ships would be tracking every enemy shuttle, and all the enemy's aerospace fighters and ships. The computers would plot courses and feed the information to CIC, with improving estimates of where those shuttles were likely to land. As soon as CIC had an estimate it considered more than 50 percent reliable, the information would be given to General Chop, and it would—eventually—get to us on the ground.

Knowing *why* we hadn't heard yet where the enemy was most likely to land didn't make the waiting easier. Every two minutes, it seemed, I had to wipe sweat from the palms of my hands. I was thirsty, as well—nervous thirsty—but I limited myself to one very small sip of water. If I had started guzzling it the way I *wanted* to, the men closest to me would have seen how edgy I was.

When I figured that an enemy landing was about twelve minutes off—wherever they chose to land—I did a slow tour of the positions my men were in, kneeling beside each to say a few words of encouragement . . . or whatever. I stayed calm, and I made a good show of moving slowly from man to man. The show had its intended effect. My men weren't going to be so keyed up that they would be likely to screw up the minute the shooting did start. And the activity helped me control my own nerves.

I HADN'T MADE IT BACK TO MY OWN HOLE WHEN Tonio gestured, calling the squad leaders to him. I changed course and went to him, ten yards behind the platoon's line. We moved into a tight clutch facing him and lifted our faceplates—as he had.

"It looks as if the IFers are going to concentrate on three

LZs," Tonio said. "Two of them are on this side of the set-tlement, but unless the landers change course radically in the next thirty seconds, neither of those is close to us. It looks as if they're taking care to land far enough out to avoid any danger from missiles fired from the ground. The first shuttles should touch down within two minutes. If the IFers hold to the paths CIC thinks are most probable, they will need at least ninety minutes to form up and get to our perimeter. I know," Tonio continued before anyone could speak, "more waiting is the last thing we need. But I doubt that General Chop will leave all of Ranger Battalion sitting on its butts until the IFers decide to close. Once the IFers land, my guess is that some of us will be sent out to harass the enemy."

"Be better if we had been out *there* waiting for them," Chouvana said, gesturing south and using his rifle as a pointer. "Where we could come up on them from behind."

It was an obvious idea for a spec ops man. Tonio shrugged. "The general didn't ask my opinion."

IT DIDN'T TAKE LONG FOR ORDERS TO COME, MORE or less what we anticipated. The general wasn't going to send *all* of the rangers out, but half of each company was told to start moving—three minutes after the last enemy shuttle touched down. Our platoon was one chosen to go hunting IFers. All four squads started out together, the object being to move two miles south, then turn west to come on the flank or rear of the nearest enemy units. That would depend on how fast they moved from their landing zone, and the precise course they took.

Once we got close to the enemy, we might split up to op-erate independently . . . but that depended on what the IFers were doing. They hadn't been shy about using elec-tronics so far, but that wouldn't make much difference. They were in the open, crossing savanna grass, and they could be seen by our ships. The information was relayed immediately to the ground.

Chouvana's squad took the point. Tonio set a rapid pace, but that was nothing to complain about. Moving fast was a relief after sitting and waiting. We had a lot of nervous energy to work off.

We were out in that high grass, some of it twice as tall as I am, spread out in two lines, trying to stay right in the tracks of the man in front of us. We crunched down grass, but it was resilient. It whipped back to slap faceplates and helmets. At first, that was a little unnerving, but it didn't take long to get used to it. The grass wrapped around ankles and legs, pulled at us, dragged our feet. We rotated positions a couple of times, to put different people up front where the going was toughest, "breaking" a path.

Wading through prairie grass remained disorienting no matter where a man was in the line. The compass readings on our head-up displays were our only sure indication of what direction we were moving in. The only way you could see more than a few feet was directly over the man in front of you, or over the man behind you. The trace sometimes ended one or two men away. Our night-vision systems didn't do much good in that grass. It was rare to see the man on the point or the rear guard. That slightly serpentine track might have been all there was to the world. It was a type of terrain I didn't have much experience with—I don't think there are any tracts like that left on Earth—and it made me uneasy.

After less than half an hour, Tonio gave us a five-minute breather. We needed it. The excess energy we had started out with had evaporated, sweated out by the work of wading through the grass. Even though I had been several spots back in the line, I could feel the strain.

"You ever come across anything like this before?" I asked Tonio—face-to-face, our visors lifted so we could speak without radios.

He hesitated before he nodded. "Once on a training mission in Alaska. Chest-deep snow. That makes this grass look like fog. It was ten below zero, and there was a twenty-mile wind blowing."

I wasn't sure if he was serious, but true or false, the story helped. "I needed that," I told him.

"One lesson I learned then that I should have used here, right from the start. You put the biggest men out in front to break the trail." With us, that meant the porracci. "Let them open the path, tromp it down."

WE MADE BETTER PROGRESS WITH PORRACCI ON the point in each of our two files. We still switched individuals, but there were eight porracci in the platoon, and they all took turns—even Sergeant Chouvana. The porracci squad leader volunteered for the first shift. After that, none of the other porracci could even think about complaining about the duty.

Twenty minutes after we switched the porracci to the point, Tonio received orders to change course ten degrees to the right—more toward the west. CIC had identified the part of our perimeter that the enemy appeared to be aiming for. We weren't going to have time to get all the way behind them, so we would hit from the flank. Not long after, another spec ops platoon would hit the opposite flank. Two platoons weren't going to destroy a battalion or so. All we could do was inflict what damage we could and try to interfere with the execution of their plan of attack. Sowing confusion was more important than piling up a huge body count.

We stopped again about eight minutes from contact to let Tonio and the squad leaders check the latest positions on our electronic maps and talk out the plan of attack, with Tonio making the final decisions since he was the ranking man on the scene.

There was nothing fancy about the plan. Three squads would turn more directly toward the IFers and attack when they got within range, hoping to catch the enemy by surprise. They would get in as much rifle and RPG fire as possible before the IFers could effectively return fire. The remaining squad—mine—would hold to its present course.

If the enemy tried to close with the three squads that attacked, we would hit their counterstrike on the flank, maybe catch them completely off guard and make them wonder just how large a force we had. In any case, the other three squads weren't going to stay engaged with the enemy. They would strike and withdraw, moving directly back along their own track, hoping to draw units of the IFer force after them . . . into the trap my squad would set.

The list of things that could go wrong might be nearly infinite, but under the circumstances, it was a fairly good bet. Spec Ops: this was our bread and butter.

After the conference, the squad leaders briefed their men. I got my squad going first since we had the farthest to go. Time started running all over itself then. Sometimes it seems to go too fast, sometimes too slow . . . and sometimes it seems to do both at once. Perception. I was just as happy that time seemed to be tripping over itself now. I couldn't worry about the results of the firefight.

I put my men down in a skirmish line, and we crawled the last twenty yards to our ambush site, doing our best to avoid breaking down or bending the tall grass; we didn't want to leave huge arrows indicating where we were. During the day it would have been more difficult, but at night, I thought we could get away with it. The enemy on the ground wasn't going to see the tops of the grass moving improperly, and there was only a minimal chance that IFer shipboard observation could detect it.

If I had chosen our positions well, the enemy would pass thirty or forty yards from us when they chased the rest of our platoon east. *If* everything went the way we had it planned.

WE WERE FACING NORTH, WITH SOUVANA'S FIRE team on the left, nearest the enemy's line of march. The IFers were heading almost due north. Tonio would lead the other three squads of our platoon in from the east, hit the IFer force, and withdraw east—hopefully before the enemy could target them accurately. We hoped the enemy would detach at least a couple of platoons to chase them. We would hit the pursuers from the side. How that went would determine what we did next. The more of the enemy we could draw off, the more we would disrupt whatever plans they had, the more we would weaken their assault against the perimeter around the lone settlement on Unity.

Souvana's fire team had planted two electronic snoops to give us some warning. The one possible snag was that the IFers might have a flanking patrol out farther than we allowed for. If they stumbled on us before the firefight erupted, it would really screw things up . . . perhaps including screwing us.

I kept glancing at the time line on my head-up display. The enemy's point squad should have moved past us, but they hadn't tripped a warning from our snoops. The van of the main body should be even with us. Almost as I thought that, I got a signal from the first snoop—a signal that ended abruptly; the IFers had apparently found the snoop and damaged it. *They must know someone is around,* I thought. *They'll be more careful now.*

I adjusted my position, trying to get a more comfortable shooting posture. That snoop had been less than 150 yards from me. Tonio and the rest of the platoon would be moving across in front of us soon. I didn't expect to see any trace of their movement. Our guys were just too good for that.

With the external sound pickups on my helmet cranked up to the maximum, I could hear the enemy moving even though they were a hundred yards from me. The sound wasn't much, just the crunch of boots through the tall grass, an occasional clink of metal on metal. There was an orderly, slow cadence to the movement—men hiking cross-country, not taking any great care to be silent.

They don't know we're this close, I thought. If they had known, or even worried, that we might have troops near enough to strike, they would have been a lot quieter. But they had silenced one electronic snoop, perhaps both . . .

since I hadn't heard a signal from the second one. Maybe word of the snoops hadn't yet filtered through to everyone. The average level of ability in the IFer armies is high. Man for man, the tonatin—who resemble Neanderthals from Earth's prehistory but who are larger, and perhaps smarter, than modern humans—are at least the equal of any of the the other sentient species in military ability. I wasn't sure of the makeup of the IFer battalion we were about to hit. Still, the tonatin dominate their military, both in numbers and influence. There were undoubtedly tonatin in the invasion force.

I heard the pop of grenade launchers firing, quickly followed by automatic rifle fire. That all came from north of us, aimed toward the IFers. The rest of the platoon was a little farther west as well as north of us. They put up a real fusillade for about forty-five seconds—and it took half that time before the IFers started to return fire, and at first that was uncoordinated and wild.

"Pull back." Tonio spoke only the two words over the platoon frequency. My men knew that the order did not apply to us, only to the squads that had exposed themselves by firing at the enemy. We hunkered down. I did everything but hold my breath, wanting to be as near perfectly silent as possible.

While the other squads started pulling back, my men and I waited. The safeties were off on our weapons. Fingers rested over trigger guards—not *on* triggers, because that might lead to premature firing. Fifteen seconds after the others began moving east, Tonio gave a cease-fire order, which also just applied to the squads with him. They wanted to break contact, at least temporarily. It would give them a chance to move away from the track they had been on, out of the direct line of fire. Tonio was going to move north, but not too far. When we hit any pursuit from the south, he wanted to be in position to contribute as well, and maybe to slow the enemy down enough to let me get my squad clear of imminent danger.

If the IFers took the bait and followed the three squads

that had hit first. We could hear men moving in our direction, crashing noisily through the grass, running—parallel to the line we had established. The IFers were incautious, but they might have gotten away with it if we hadn't been lurking.

Still, they *should* have anticipated a secondary ambush. *We* would have looked for one. Maybe it was the fact that we were so near that threw them off. We had set up far too close for safety, trusting that the audacity of it might give us a break. It had. Little things can make all the difference in combat.

I could tell when the first IFer troops came even with our positions. They were at forty yards out, about where we had hoped they would pass. I let the enemy point get to the east end of our line, then gave the command to fire . . . and opened up before the word was all the way out of my mouth. I moved my rifle muzzle back and forth, spraying bullets as if I had an endless supply, keeping my point of aim low—cutting a lot of grass. Kiervauna and Razor each emptied a clip of RPGs among the IFers. The rest of us were rather spendthrift with rifle ammunition.

My estimate was that the IFers had sent two platoons out to retaliate. Between the rifle fire and the RPGs, we must have caused at least thirty enemy casualties in twenty seconds. We really didn't have to see them to score, as long as we kept our rifle fire low.

Once the enemy started returning our fire we were too close to withdraw without letting them mow us down the way we had them. I called Tonio, and asked, "What now?" There was no need to observe electronic silence while we were engaged. The enemy *knew* where we were. Tonio didn't reply immediately, but it was only fifteen seconds later when the other squads engaged with the enemy again. Almost simultaneously, we heard that the Ranger platoon on the far side of the enemy strike force was making its first attack, though we couldn't hear that firefight over the noise of our own piece of the ruckus.

"Move southeast," Tonio said. "Now." Sure, we were

speaking in the clear, but we never needed verbal codes. Our electronics systems scrambled everything. Even if the enemy could lock onto one of our communications channels, it wouldn't do any good. Each channel alternates frequencies, and the encryption algorithm is secure enough that by the time the scheme could be deciphered it couldn't possibly endanger us.

I relayed the order to withdraw over my squad frequency, and told Souvana to start with his fire team, while the rest of us provided covering fire. We pulled back like that—fire and maneuver—while the rest of the platoon hit the IFers. Once I had my squad far enough from the enemy patrol to break contact, I informed Tonio. Then all of us quit firing at the enemy and moved. My squad headed due south. The other squads would move east, then south.

Our goal now was to get behind this enemy force—a little more than one battalion in strength, about the same as the other two major portions of the invading disposition— and hit them again. We had been uncommonly lucky for an encounter at such close range. There hadn't been a single casualty in the platoon. If anyone wants to call that a miracle, I won't argue.

CHAPTER 9

TWENTY MINUTES AFTER WE BROKE CONTACT, I
stopped my squad—putting the men in an impromptu defensive perimeter. We needed the rest but, more than that,
the stop was to give the rest of the platoon time to reach us.
I loaded a fresh double magazine in my rifle, then took a
sip of water to get the sandpaper feeling off my tongue. I
scanned the command frequencies for anything about conditions close by, then went back to the CIC channel to listen to the constant feed from there.

It appeared that the augmented IFer battalion had resumed its march north, more slowly than before. CIC
could not be certain if *all* the enemy soldiers were moving
north. There might be patrols searching for us and for the
platoon that had hit them on the other side. We were going
to have to remain on our toes.

We knew *that* without hearing it from two hundred
miles away.

AFTER TEN MINUTES, I GOT MY MEN MOVING
again, but we didn't go far. I just wanted to make sure we
didn't stay in one place too long. We shifted our position—
carefully, trying to avoid leaving impressions in the grass
that would show where we had gone—by less than two

hundred yards before we set up another tight perimeter. We were still waiting for Tonio and the other squads to get to us.

I had known that none of my people had been badly hurt in our brief firefight, but it really wasn't until this second stop that I went from man to man and learned that no one had even been scratched or had his fur singed.

"At least we have shown the fools in the high command that we still know how to fight," Souvana whispered, when I stopped to check on him. He wouldn't have dared say that in the porracci army, but only 20 percent of our senior officers were porracci. He could always rationalize that he was talking about the other 80 percent.

"Don't get too cocky," I told him. "We're not out of this yet by a long shot."

"But we have shown that we have lost none of our edge," Souvana said. "It can only give added confidence to those of us who require it."

I snorted softly, glad that Souvana couldn't see the grin on my face. He obviously didn't feel that he was one of those who needed something to boost his confidence. After I finished my rounds, I got back in my own position and waited, not certain whether we would stay there until the rest of the platoon reached us or if we would move once more.

I'll give them ten minutes, I decided. *If they haven't reached us by then, we'll move again.* I took another sip of water. Then I took several deep, slow breaths. I had a lot of adrenaline pumping through my system, and I needed to calm my heart rate.

Eight minutes had passed before Tonio's advance scout—a biraunta from third squad—flashed a narrow-beam blue light in a prearranged code to let us know they were there. I returned the countersign—a different pattern—and warned my squad so that no one would mistake our people for the enemy.

Tonio brought his people in. We expanded the perimeter to make room, and Tonio told them to take ten minutes. He came over to where I was sprawled and dropped to the ground next to me. "We did good," he whispered. "All of us. We hurt the enemy and got away without losing anyone. I see you've still got all your people." He made a rather weak gesture around us.

"Not a scratch in the lot," I said. "How many IFers you figure we put down for good?"

He shook his head. "We didn't try to take a count. I'll leave the guessing to the brain boys."

"Hell, they're just going to ask us," I said. "We must have taken out more than a platoon between us."

"Doesn't do much to help the odds though," Tonio said.

"Okay, so what do we do now?" I asked, surprised that he sounded so glum. Tonio is never a font of exuberance in combat, but this was extreme even for him.

"Catch our breath," he said. There was a pause before he continued. "Head farther south, then turn west. Go a quarter mile, then turn north again. Hit them from behind before they reach the main perimeter."

"Gonna be hard," I said. "Unless they stopped cold after we hit them, they can reach the perimeter long before we cover that much ground. CIC says they're still moving, just slower. The way I've got it figured, they can be in position to assault the perimeter in an hour—all three units of the invasion force."

"We've got people out to slow them down more, and land mines. That should give us time. If it looks like it won't, Colonel Hansen said we'll try to bring in a few fighters to hit them from the air."

I started to say something but stopped when Tonio waved me off. "Let me be for a minute," he said.

I gave him his minute—several. Tonio had his faceplate up, so I could see that his eyes were closed. *Who are you?* I wondered. I had known Tonio for years, and I had never seen him like this. Even on Olviat, after he had been seriously wounded and was still in pain, he hadn't been this . . . detached. It worried me.

"What's wrong with you?" I asked, softly, after five minutes of silence. "I've never seen you like this."

For a moment, I thought he was going to ignore me. I wasn't going to let him off, though, and I was about to say something else when he opened his eyes and turned his head so he was looking at me.

"Maybe I'm just getting too old for this shit."

"Come off it. This is the Dragon. You're not that much older than me, and you're as fit as I am. We haven't had to push ourselves, and the only action we've seen might have been target practice. Talk to me. What's going on between your ears?"

"I really don't know, Bart," he said. The way he said my name, I realized he was serious. "Earlier, before we opened up on the IFers, I looked at the men closest to me and . . . just for an instant, I was looking at cadavers in uniform, men who were already dead and just hadn't fallen down. Gaunt, drawn faces, skin that barely covered the bones, the smell of bodies that have been lying in the sun for days. I squeezed my eyes shut, shook my head, and everything was back to normal. But I *saw* that, smelled that, just as sure as I see you now. It's crazy, and it scares the crap out of me. What comes next—ghosts clanking their chains?"

"Don't let it wear you down. You know what it is," I said. "Post-traumatic stress. We've both seen a lot of death, come close to dying more times than anyone should have to. We've got every right to our ghosts. You and I have both had to have our brain boxes tinkered with before. Just hang on until we get back to the rest of our people. You'll talk to one of the doctors. He'll ask questions, make you talk about things you don't want to talk about. They'll run their tests, maybe shoot a few extra nanobots into your blood. In no time at all you'll be on top of your form again."

It is lousy timing, I thought. *Detached from the battalion, several miles from any real help, with close to a thousand enemy soldiers between us and the nearest friendly doctor.*

"Hard telling when we'll get back to the rest of the regiment," Tonio said. "What if I snap out here, maybe in the middle of a firefight or while we're waiting to spring an ambush? I could get a whole lot of us killed."

"Don't borrow trouble. You haven't snapped and you won't."

"I don't *know* that, Bart, and neither do you."

No, I didn't, and for all my faith in Tonio I knew that something like this could catch any of us at any time. Medical science hasn't penetrated *all* the secrets of the sentient brain or figured out how to keep it from going completely nuts once in a while. Chemical balances can be monitored, adjusted when necessary, but not all problems can be traced to simple, physical causes. Maybe our war would be the one that gave the doctors enough information to patch up a few more holes in the treatment of psychological disorders. I wouldn't hold my breath. None of that was going to help Tonio right then and there.

"We don't have many options right now," I said. "One, we go on the way we planned and try to deal with anything *if* it comes up. Two, we head back toward the perimeter, give up on our mission. Three, you break electronic silence to tell Captain Fusik what happened to you and pass the buck."

I *thought* I knew Tonio well enough to gauge which option he would choose, but I held my breath until he confirmed it. "We'll go on," he said after a short hesitation. "Stay close to me, Bart, and put me down fast—whatever it takes—if you see that I'm starting to lose it. Don't let me screw the platoon."

"I won't because you won't," I told him. "And your ten minutes are more than up."

Tonio pulled his faceplate down, got to his feet, and gestured for everyone else to get up. Second squad took the lead. First squad, mine, followed, and Tonio took his position ahead of me. We had a lot of ground to cover and not nearly enough time to do it.

• • •

IT WAS HARD TO CONCENTRATE ON THE NEEDS OF the march. Tonio had given me more to worry about than I needed. My eyes and thoughts kept drifting to him. We finished the southward leg of our move and turned west. It wasn't until we had crossed the route the IFers had taken north that we took a break—about two and a half minutes—just long enough for the squad leaders to cluster around Tonio while we checked our maps, and our biraunta scouted around for any indication of land mines or snoops.

Maybe a thousand IFers had moved north, in four columns with 150 yards between columns. Our job would have been easier following one of those trails. Enough men had walked the ground that most of the grass had been beaten into submission. We did not take the easy way. It was safer to find our own path, between the traces left by the second and third columns. When we saw the occasional lateral trace through the grass—perhaps where couriers had gone back and forth—we were especially careful, in case the IFers had left nasty presents for anyone who might be following them.

We still made reasonable time, and from the reports I heard from CIC, the three enemy strike forces had all been slowed considerably. It would be close to dawn—at the earliest—before they could reach the perimeter we had set up to protect our colonists. We would have time to catch up with the IFers we had been assigned to harass, and we should make contact while we still had a little darkness to play with.

Tonio showed no signs of distress. No matter what he was feeling inside his head, on the outside he appeared as competent as ever. When there was a chance for us to exchange a couple of words, he would say, "So far, so good," and I would nod or give him a couple of equally bland words of encouragement, as if I didn't have any doubt at all that he would be fine.

The night lacked forty minutes of sunrise when one of our advance scouts signaled for the platoon to stop. The

IFer rear guard—a platoon of tonatin—was two hundred yards in front of us. Tonio gathered the squad leaders to lay out how we would hit the enemy this time.

"If the rear guard is tonatin, it's almost certain that the rest of this outfit is tonatin," Tonio said. "The IFers haven't shown any tendency to mix species within a unit the way we do. That means—porracci and ghuroh sensibilities aside—we're up against the best the enemy has to offer." Neither Sergeant Chouvana from second squad nor Sergeant Slash from fourth voiced any objections, though I'm sure both had them.

"I want us in a single skirmish line, with the ends forward of the center. Minimal safe separation between men and fire teams. We hit the rear guard with everything we've got, then move before the commander can rotate new troops back to face us. When we break contact, we'll come back toward the east. I don't want to get too far out of position since we don't know where our spec ops squads on the other side are, and we don't want a friendly-fire situation. Get back to your men and let's get moving. It's going to be light soon."

SECOND SQUAD WAS ON THE LEFT, THEN FIRST, third, and fourth. Tonio stayed with my squad, close to me. That wasn't according to standard doctrine. There should have been more separation so the same grenade or burst of rifle fire wouldn't take out the two senior noncoms in the platoon, but I knew why Tonio wanted to stay close. Besides, even if Tonio and I both went down, there were three other sergeants in the platoon, and any of them would be qualified to lead the survivors away.

We spread out and started moving forward, working through the tall grass. Since each man had to break his own trail, it was slow going. And the tonatin ahead of us weren't standing still waiting. They were also moving—away from us. We needed fifteen minutes to close the gap to 120 yards. At that range, the few seconds' advantage we had should be decisive.

"Down! Fire!" Tonio broke radio silence to issue the commands on the platoon channel. Since everyone had been anticipating the orders, they were executed smartly. All four squads operated together—eight men with grenade launchers, thirty-three with automatic rifles. The enemy's rear guard was approximately equal in size, but they were looking the other way until they heard the first shots . . . and the first casualties had already fallen.

Our attack lasted only fifteen seconds—sixteen grenades, perhaps a thousand bullets. Not many rounds came back in our direction. Our onslaught was too heavy and too accurate. I don't know that we killed every man in the enemy rear guard, or even that we *hit* everyone, but I do feel safe in saying that the rear guard platoon effectively ceased to exist.

We reversed course and dropped back a hundred yards before we turned east and made the best speed we could in that direction. Once more, we had emerged from an ambush without suffering a single casualty. We put distance between us and the enemy before they could detach troops to chase us. We moved quickly for three-quarters of an hour, which took us east of the path of the enemy's right flank, before Tonio gave us a break.

"If we could hit them like that another three or four hundred times, we'd have this crew licked," Robbie said, while we were sitting. "Trouble is, how long can our luck last?"

I was still trying to get enough breath back to be able to take a swallow of water, so I didn't try to reply. I blinked once or twice. Even shaking my head was too much of an effort. I shifted my gaze to Tonio, about five feet from me. He had his forearms resting on his knees, his head hanging forward.

It's just that he's tired. We all are, I told myself. *We've been on the move a lot of hours, and the grass is murder.* But after what Tonio had told me earlier, I had to worry.

But then, I worry a lot, most of the time. Maybe too much—Tonio had told me that more than once over the years. "You're not happy unless you've got something to worry about," was how he put it one time. Maybe there was some truth to that.

The break lasted only five minutes, hardly more than enough to let us catch our breath. We were all tired. We had been on the go for a day and a night. None of us had managed any *real* sleep since we left Earth. Before many more hours went by we were going to have to remedy that. Or turn into zombies who couldn't think fast enough to survive.

We had just gotten back to our feet and started east again when we heard the news—relayed from CIC. Two of the three enemy elements had reached our perimeter around the settlement. The major ground battle had been joined.

CHAPTER 10

I WAS A LITTLE SURPRISED THAT THE IFERS HAD gone into the attack at dawn. I know—we had been moving to slow them down, to make sure they couldn't reach our perimeter while it was still dark, but fighting a daylight battle on open ground is anathema to modern armies. Maybe darkness is no certain protection, but it does give you slightly better odds of survival. It would *not* have surprised me had the IFers set up defensive lines far enough out for relative safety and waited for nightfall to assault our perimeter, maybe tried softening the perimeter up with artillery or air strikes in the meantime.

Perhaps the general commanding the invading army didn't like the odds of sitting in open grassland for twelve hours, even out of rifle range. Our artillery had a much greater reach, and if the IFers moved back until they were out of range of the remote-controlled howitzers and rocket launchers, they would be too far away to make it back in one night. And our Ranger Battalion had been giving the enemy quite a bit to think about. The enemy had to expect more attrition with nothing to show for it if they waited.

So maybe I shouldn't have been surprised that they attacked as soon as they got within reach. Our artillery hadn't been active during the night. I wasn't privy to the reasons, but I could guess a couple of possibles. The general might be worried about running out of ammunition for the heavy weapons when we might really need them. The other is that once the howitzers and rocket launchers start operating the enemy could track them and start counter-battery fire. At this point, the enemy might not know—for certain—that we had heavy weapons on Unity. They would worry that we had them, but until they were spotted—or started firing—the enemy would not *know*. That was an advantage for us, as was the possibility that they could not be certain how many troops we had. Of course, the IFers hadn't used any heavy weapons fire either. I assumed they had brought self-propelled artillery and rocket launchers, though they must have expected to face only civilian colonists.

Half an hour after dawn, Tonio had a call from Captain Fusik. We were to make our way back to our lines. Other spec ops units would continue the harassing raids. We were going to be given a chance to rest. *If* the enemy attack didn't get so hot that every man had to be put into the lines.

Tonio led us another half mile east—that much farther from the enemy and the fight—before we turned toward the settlement. We moved at a modest pace and took several rest breaks. After as long as we had been on the go, we had little choice but to ease off.

"I wish the captain had given us the option of finding a place out here to sack out," I told Tonio during one of our breaks. "Save us that much walking and have us closer to getting back into action after we got some sleep."

Tonio shrugged. "Yeah . . . but I'm kind of glad we're going in, too."

I had forgotten about that. I was that tired. "Look, you're okay," I told him, very softly. "We've been back on the attack and got out. You didn't come unglued. You're not likely to now. A little sleep, and you'll be as good as new—at least, as close to that as either of us old farts is likely to get."

"Maybe. Still, I'll feel better once I talk to one of the doctors. Maybe I haven't done any more hallucinating, or whatever it was, but I can't forget what I did see. I'm almost afraid to shut my eyes, knowing those faces will be there, staring at me."

I've seen the faces of the dead myself, those who had died around me in previous fights, back to the start of the war. It's not pretty.

IT WAS PAST EIGHT O'CLOCK BEFORE WE PASSED through our lines and walked to the reserve area a couple of hundred yards behind the secondary trenches. The fighting, such as it was, was farther west, not directly in front of our section of the perimeter. Some of our people had been shifted closer to the action, but Captain Fusik simply told Tonio that our platoon was to get a meal and then sack out, that he would give us as much time as possible. We didn't even have to stagger our sleep. There was no requirement for half-and-half shifts, or even for sentries.

Tonio left me in charge of the platoon. He talked with Captain Fusik for several minutes, then Tonio went off with the captain. I could guess what their conversation had been about, and where Tonio was headed. As he disappeared behind a clump of trees, I sent the thought, *Hurry back,* after him.

IT WASN'T UNTIL I WAS SITTING ON MY BUTT, reaching for a ration pack, that I realized how exhausted I was. Pulling the strip to open the pack and heat the entrée was almost too much effort. I started yawning and had trouble stopping. I came close to putting the meal away for later, but you have to eat when you can. Later, there might not be time. Eating was a slow chore, but I forced myself to finish the meal.

The spot the captain had found for us was in a thickly forested patch, with a slight rise in the ground between us and the perimeter. We were far enough back that only enemy artillery or air attack could pose an immediate threat.

I had my pack and web gear off, but close. I used the pack for a pillow. I kept my helmet and body armor on. I wasn't comfortable, but that didn't matter. My guess is that I was asleep in ten seconds. I couldn't even spare the energy to worry about Tonio. Or anything else.

IT WAS NEARLY THREE O'CLOCK THAT AFTERNOON before I woke. I could hear rifle fire and the occasional pop of a grenade, but *very* distant, almost at the edge of audibility.

After debating for a minute or two whether I should try to get back to sleep, I sat up and looked around. Most of my people appeared to be sleeping. The two biraunta were on their feet though, about twenty yards from the rest of us, having a fairly animated conversation—in whispers. Their tails were going like crazy—twitching from side to side or coiling and uncoiling. Hands were busy, too. Biraunta put a lot more than voice into conversation.

Field sanitary facilities had been erected, so I went to wash and take care of the necessary. Then I looked for Tonio. I was relieved to see that he had returned, but he was sleeping, so any chat would have to wait. I wouldn't wake him to ask how he was feeling. The fact that he was back meant that the doctors hadn't found anything too seriously wrong between his ears.

Captain Fusik's command post—under an eight-by-eight sheet of camouflage tarp stretched between trees—wasn't too far away, so I went there to let the captain know I was awake. Fusik was sitting on a folding stool with his electronic map open on his lap. The faceplate of his helmet was tipped up, out of the way. When he saw me he waved for me to come "in."

"You and your men did a damned good job last night— the whole platoon," Fusik said. He sounded calm, almost relaxed. That meant that either the battle was going pretty good for our side, or he was a better actor than I gave him credit for.

"That tall grass is a real bitch, Captain," I said. "Grabs at you like an unlicensed whore who's afraid you'll make off without paying her."

A small grin played across his face. "I'll take your word for that," he replied. "According to my wife, I shouldn't even know what the word *whore* means."

"How's Tonio—Sergeant Xeres—sir?"

"He's fine. They found a slight imbalance in brain chemicals, aggravated by . . . conditions. The doc gave him something to counter it."

"He was real worried it might make him screw up while we were out there, sir. But he didn't hesitate. He just warned me to be ready in case something did go wrong."

"I know. He told me. Xeres is one of the best noncoms I've ever served with."

"You won't get any argument from me, sir. I've known him too long. Any idea when we're going to be going out again, or what we're going to be doing?" First things first: I had needed reassurance about Tonio more than I needed to know what work lay ahead. "I haven't even heard anything on how the fight is going since just after we got in this morning."

Fusik stared at me, as if he were deciding how much he should say. "It's nothing spectacular. The IFers haven't really tried to breach the perimeter yet. They're digging in beyond the limit of RPG fire. Trying to give their people enough cover to get through the day, I imagine, waiting for nightfall, the way we would. They *can't* be thinking siege. That would be crazy."

"Captain?" I said after a couple of quick, involuntary blinks. "Maybe it's not so crazy."

"What do you mean?"

"Something I was thinking before. Maybe the IFers thought that all they were going to find here was colonists— civilians without military weapons or training. We might have come as much of a surprise to them as they did to us.

Maybe they didn't come *prepared* to fight soldiers. Maybe they sent an MR to tell their command that we had troops here when they spotted our ships. Maybe they're expecting reinforcements as quickly as they can be sent. If many of those 'maybes' are true, they might dig in to wait—a few days, maybe a week or more. Don't you think?"

The captain gave me a long stare, his brows knotted in a frown—the kind you get from thinking too hard. "They *did* send out two message rockets within fifteen minutes after they popped into normal space." He stared toward the tarp overhead—still frowning—before he shook his head, almost violently. "I'm *sure* the general and CIC have taken that possibility into account." Hesitation. A subtle change in the nature of his frown. "Still, I'll pass your idea along, in case they missed it. Thanks, Dragon. Maybe you've plugged a hole nobody saw."

I like praise as well as anyone, I guess, but I felt sheepish. "Well, Cap, you know how it is. My head's on the line as much as anyone's, and I want to keep it attached."

His frown disappeared as he laughed. I didn't learn about it until much later, but when the captain passed along the things I had mentioned, he made a point of saying that I was the one who spotted the possibility, along with a lot of the sort of lather you dress up a recommendation for promotion with. Not every officer I've served with would have done that. More than a few would have taken credit themselves.

IT WAS NINETY MINUTES BEFORE SUNSET WHEN the word was passed to get everyone up and fed. We would be going out as soon as it was full dark. We had a chance to replace the ammunition we had expended, but we were also told to be more careful with ammo until we knew when—or if—we might be getting more. Tonio called for the squad leaders to brief us on the night's mission. I didn't get a chance to talk with him privately, but he gave me a thumbs-up before he started the briefing.

"The job tonight is intelligence," he started, when all four squad leaders had arrived. "We loop around to the enemy's rear and see what we can learn about troop dispositions and what arrangements they've made. If we find evidence that they've established travel routes between their LZs and the lines, we'll plant a few mines and snoops. We'll plant snoops on the side, too, to let us know if they try shifting to their right. Now, for the fine points. The platoon will exfiltrate together, but we'll separate into squads once we get into decent cover, so we can cover more ground. Slave your maps to mine."

I focused mostly on the mission for my squad. All I needed to know about the other squads was any point where we might stumble over each other. Tonio didn't play favorites. We might be best friends, but he gave my squad the longest route. I tried to take that the best way—that he had more confidence in me than in any of the other squad leaders. But that long route meant that we would be out the longest, and would have to cross the areas of operation of each of the other squads and—coming back—we would have to be on the lookout for the snoops and mines they were going to plant.

That can be tricky, but it's not as ridiculous as it might seem. The snoops would register the friend or foe signals of our gear—and all they could do is tell the observers where we were. The tricky part was the mines. We would have to spot them for ourselves and either avoid them or use a temporary disarming signal. The former is considered preferable, since even a low-powered disarming signal might be picked up by an enemy scanning for electronic emissions.

You might be thinking that if *we* could spot the mines soon enough to avoid them, then the enemy could as well. To a point, that's true, but we knew about where to look, and the enemy wouldn't be certain that there were any mines to look for . . . until some of their soldiers got caught by them. My men and I had all been through the same training that the men in our other squads had. That would give us a definite edge looking for the minuscule signs that a special operations man would leave.

THE SQUADS THAT HAD BEEN OUT HARASSING THE enemy during the day filtered through the perimeter just following sunset. We had moved nearly half a mile east of where we had come in that morning, farther from the known positions of the nearest IFers. That should make it easier for us to get out without being spotted. A quick conference with the leaders of the returning spec ops squads gave us some assurance that there were no enemy patrols close, but we knew better than to take those assurances for gospel. You don't take any chance of underestimating the enemy. That's a cheap ticket to a toe tag.

By the time the briefing was over, the night was as dark as it was going to get. There was moderate cloud cover—not nearly complete, but enough to lower visibility a little for anyone not equipped with a night-vision system. It was time to move out. We went through the lines of a ghuroh company, with them at full alert in case we ran into trouble immediately.

We slipped out as if we knew there were eyes watching from the other side, one squad at a time, staying low, disappearing into the tall grass as quickly as we could. That meant a little running since the line troops on the perimeter had done what they could to give themselves decent fire zones during the day, trampling down the grass, cutting some, and so forth. There had even been a couple of attempts to burn firing lanes, but the grass had too much moisture. None of the efforts to clear lanes had been *completely* successful, but the IFers would have a hard time sneaking closer than eighty yards without being spotted . . . even if they got past the electronic snoops and mines planted farther out. We knew where the mines in *that* string were located. They were spotted on our electronic maps.

Once we were past the area where the grass had been disturbed, and past the mines and snoops the troops on the perimeter had planted, Tonio stopped the platoon long enough for all the squads to gather. Then we started moving a few degrees east of south, at what amounted to a fast walking pace—difficult enough in the tall grass. Tonio was going with second squad for this operation. They had the next-to-shortest route, and Tonio would be better able to direct things if any of the squads got into trouble and needed help.

Even with the grass grabbing at us, we moved in almost perfect silence. In the first hour there wasn't a single word spoken in the platoon.

After an hour we stopped. It was time for the platoon to split into squads. I led my people out first, heading almost due west. The other squads would leave at intervals of three or four minutes. As we started out, I glanced toward Tonio. He raised his right hand and gave me an okay sign with his fingers. He couldn't see my answering grin. I gave him half a wave, then turned my attention to the front.

As I did whenever possible, I put a biraunta in front. There weren't any trees for them to get up in, but the biraunta were shorter and thinner than the rest of the species. They created less disturbance in the tall grass. Ala was on point first since I had Souvana's fire team in the lead. We would switch after a time, so that the duty—and the special dangers up front—would be shared. I was at the front of the other fire team, which basically put me in the middle of the formation, where I could deal with difficulties at either end, and Kiervauna was our rear guard.

This is the way we were meant to operate, I thought, after we separated from the rest of the platoon. A single spec ops squad behind enemy lines. Our mission this time was reconnaissance. We would plant a few land mines and electronic snoops, but unless we got unlucky, we would not be doing any actual fighting. Our orders were to avoid contact if possible. Unless we stumbled over sleeping IFers, or bumped into one of their patrols, there was every chance that we could avoid engagement.

After thirty minutes, Ala stopped and waited for us to

reach him. That had been prearranged. My fire team moved into the lead, with Oyo going out on point. Kiervauna was next—twenty yards behind Oyo—and I dropped back to the last spot in the fire team, which allowed me to remain at the center of the formation. We hadn't seen anything yet but the trace where the IFer force had moved north from its landing zone. We weren't yet to the area we were to investigate—though we would report on anything we saw along our course.

We went farther west than the platoon had gone the night before, near where the Rangers had hit the enemy on the other flank. We were also farther south. If our estimates were right, we were two miles south of the IFers facing our perimeter, and about the same distance from their LZ. There were a few enemy shuttles on the ground—perhaps enough to evacuate serious casualties—but most had returned to their ships after landing their troops and supplies.

Once I knew we were where we were supposed to be, I gave the squad five minutes to rest. But we couldn't flake off. We went into a complete perimeter, in case an IFer patrol happened by. It was a dead certainty that they *would* have patrols looking for the likes of us. Even the densest commander could not fail to do *that*. Twice we had crossed what might have been the tracks left by patrols, but we had not seen anyone.

I had been fairly loose through the early part of the mission, not relaxed, but not wound spring-tight. But once we reached our operational area, my nerves tightened up. I felt hyperalert, aware of every sight and sound within reach of my eyes and ears. With my external sound pickups cranked to their maximum setting, my hearing would be extremely acute. I could hear some of my men breathing . . . and wished they would be more silent. If I could hear them, an outsider might also.

•　•　•

WE CRISSCROSSED OUR AREA IN A PRECISE PAT-
tern, using compass headings and elapsed distance readings. We planted our snoops and mines, and recorded the
various tracks through the grass we found. The video of
that—noncoms' helmets have built-in cameras—would
give the computers and intelligence analysts a lot of raw
data. It was nearly time to start back when we had our only
alarm.

Razor was the first to hear the approaching patrol and
gesture for us to go to ground. The patrol wasn't coming
directly at us, so we didn't have to worry about them literally stumbling on us unless they changed course. They
were going to come precariously close. I lay flat and motionless, and held my breath. I could hear breathing, but
this time it was coming from the IFer patrol rather than my
men. I couldn't hear anything else from the IFers until they
were within fifteen yards, and then it was only the sound
of the grass against their uniforms, a soft swishing noise.

The way I was lying, I could only see with one eye, and
not very much with that. My rifle was in the grass at my
side, my hand over the receiver. It would only take a fraction of a second to bring the weapon up and start firing . . .
if that became necessary. I saw movement through the
grass. The point man for the enemy patrol was ten yards
from me. On his present course he might come with five
yards of Razor.

If we stayed absolutely motionless, I figured the odds
were—by an optimistic stretch—thirty-seventy that we
would escape detection. Not good odds in my line of work,
but I've been on the short end of worse. Our uniforms and
helmets provided decent thermal camouflage, but not perfect, and the uniforms of the porracci and biraunta did not
cover near as much of their hide as the rest of ours did.

Six IFers—tonatin—passed, moving in good order, eyes
scanning, weapons at the ready. None of the tonatin I could
see gave any indication that *he* saw anything out of the or-
dinary. Except for the man on point, who was watching

where he put his feet, the rest were scanning farther out to either side, over our heads—for the moment. I had held my breath so long by the time the sixth soldier moved past my field of vision that it was uncomfortable, but I was afraid to take another breath because it might be too noisy—enough for the enemy to hear.

The ninth tonatin came into my field of view. *How many are there?* I wondered. Was this a squad, a platoon, or more? How long could our luck hold? How long could I hold my breath before automatic reflex made me drag in air? I couldn't take a chance on the last. I forced myself to empty my lungs very slowly and softly—at least enough to leave room for fresh air. It was difficult. I could feel the strain in my face and temples. For an instant I thought I might pass out before I got in new air.

Twelve tonatin. Fourteen. There was still no indication that any of them had seen us, but if they were *really* smart, and disciplined, they might go past without taking action, figuring to loop behind and take us by surprise—at less risk to themselves. It's what I would have done. There were no more tonatin coming into view. The last I could see was passing Razor. *Maybe a trailer, some distance back?* I wondered. *How far back? How long can I afford to wait?*

I couldn't wait *too* long, in case the enemy patrol had seen us and was going to try to catch us from behind, but if we moved too soon, that hypothetical trailer—or someone in the number we had seen go past—might see or hear something and give the alarm . . . most likely in the form of a burst of rifle fire.

There's no sure-fire formula for a problem like that. It comes down to instinct . . . and luck. I watched the seconds tick by on my head-up display. We needed to give the patrol at least three minutes to get far enough away that they might not hear us move. If a trailer hadn't happened by in that time, there probably wasn't one coming.

Three minutes . . . and twenty seconds. I got up on hands and knees, enough movement to draw the attention of my men. Then I used my hands to gesture. The enemy patrol had been heading north-northeast. We would head northwest for fifty yards before we turned east again. It was time to start back to rendezvous with the rest of the platoon. We had used our allotted time. And then some.

The next fifteen minutes were the tensest of the night for me, knowing that an enemy patrol was in the area and not certain just where they were. We turned east and moved with far more care than speed. When we crossed the patrol's track we were especially careful, but the tonatin had moved far enough that we couldn't see them—which meant they couldn't see us.

It was another fifteen minutes before I had Ala, on point, pick up the pace. We couldn't race because there might be other enemy patrols about, but we had to go a little faster, both to put more distance between us and the tonatin who had almost discovered us and to reach our rendezvous with the platoon so we could get through our lines before dawn. If we missed that rendezvous, we might have to spend the entire day hiding in the open, and I did not relish that possibility.

We were out of our area of operations and halfway across where fourth squad had been working when we heard gunfire to our east. One of the other squads in the platoon had run into trouble.

CHAPTER 11

SINCE WE HAD BEEN IN STEALTH MODE, WE HAD done no broadcasting on any radio channels through the entire mission. Use the radio or active electronics only when you're in direct contact with the enemy, or when you don't care if they can pinpoint your location.

I started moving my men toward the gunfire instantly, before I heard the call from third squad's leader. They had run into a strong enemy patrol—a full platoon. In the IFer army, that runs to sixty men, occasionally more. Two men from third squad were dead. Two others, including Aytah, the biraunta squad leader, had been wounded too seriously to move on their own.

My squad was closest, but I wasn't certain we could reach third in time to do anything but count the dead. I unfolded my map long enough to get a fix on Aytah's position, then changed course to a more direct route. It looked as if we would need six or seven minutes to get there. I didn't know if Tonio would try to take second squad in to help. They might be too far away. With the need to preserve electronic silence, I couldn't ask for instructions. I had to make the decision whether to try to help third squad. I never considered *not* going. Only a direct order would have stopped me.

Aytah and his men were putting up as much of a fight as

they could. From Aytah's occasional comments, it appeared that the IFers were in no hurry to finish them off. They were moving to encircle the squad, but staying 150 yards out. At that distance, they could pick our people off at leisure, while minimizing their own casualties. I doubted that the IFers would *complete* the circle. That would raise the danger of hitting their own people. It was more likely that they would attempt only a semicircle, leaving men on the ends to prevent our people from escaping through the gap.

When we were five hundred yards from the IFers, I split my squad into fire teams. I took the left side. Souvana had the right. We spread out into a skirmish line and moved in. Our grenade launchers theoretically had an operational range of 250 yards but were reliably accurate only to two hundred. In the tall grass, our rifles wouldn't let us actually target the enemy at that distance, and we couldn't be too wild for fear of hitting our own people. At least the bulk of the IFer platoon was on our side of Aytah's squad.

We would start with RPGs at two hundred yards, and close with the enemy—until they turned their full attention against us. Then we would have to go to ground, work in as we could—on our bellies. If Aytah's assessment of the strength of the patrol was correct, we would still be heavily outnumbered unless we were extremely lucky with our first RPGs.

You do what you have to.

Third squad was still putting up *some* resistance when we got within three hundred yards. I slowed my people to avoid giving ourselves away before we got into RPG range. We paused long enough for me to tell everyone what we were going to do. Then we moved forward.

Into the attack.

A SOLDIER HAS TO USE HIS BRAIN, BUT THERE are times when you have to ignore that little voice telling you that what you're doing is stupid, suicidal. If people couldn't get past that voice, there wouldn't be soldiers. Some folks might consider that a good thing, but I'm no philosopher. I'm a soldier, and as long as somebody else has soldiers trying to do nasty things to my people, I'll shut that voice off when I have to. There's a more insistent voice telling me that fighting to maintain your freedom and what you believe in is better than being a slave to whoever has the will to make you do what *he* wants.

There weren't any really brilliant ways to attack this problem. If we wasted the time to try something fancy and relatively safe, we would have failed before we started. The rest of third squad would be dead. Maybe they would all be dead anyway, but we had to try to help them . . . or live with the knowledge that we hadn't. Pick your nightmare.

We stopped at two hundred yards from the nearest enemy targets. There was still a little return fire coming from third squad, so somebody was still alive there. I held a fist up, looked to either side to make sure my grenadiers, Kiervauna and Razor, were ready, then brought the fist down and forward. The two men with grenade launchers each quickly scattered a four-round clip. The rest of us opened up with rifles, careful to aim low so that any rounds that missed the IFers would hit the ground and not our own people.

We moved forward then, running. The fire teams moved farther apart. Except for the men with the grenade launchers, we kept firing on the move. Razor and Kiervauna needed a few seconds to reload. We covered maybe twenty yards, then went to ground before the IFers turned their fire in our direction.

"Still four of us alive," Aytah said on the platoon frequency. "We're all hit, but we can keep fighting."

"Hang on," I said. "This is Drak. We're coming in." He didn't give me any phony plea to stay away. We had opened fire. The enemy knew we were in the neighborhood, so we were committed. When no one else spoke, Aytah would also know that it was only my squad involved, and he would know that the odds hadn't changed all that much.

Some IFer fire was coming close to us by the time we got within 160 yards, but we were giving more than we received, and we had a lot more targets to shoot at. I couldn't trust my estimate too much, but I thought that we had cut down a fair number of the enemy with our initial volley of rocket-propelled grenades—plus whatever third squad had accounted for before we arrived. Maybe the odds were no more than three to one against us now.

We couldn't move much closer, and it wouldn't take the IFer commander long to decide that there were few enough of us that he could take us the way he had taken third squad. The enemy commander might turn his attention completely toward the new threat, shift soldiers to flank us. They might already be on the move. Spec ops doctrine called for us to move somewhere, even if it wasn't closer to our objective. *Don't stick around long enough for the enemy to pin you down. Stay mobile.*

Move left or right? It was a toss-up unless we spotted which side the enemy was going to try to get at us from. I hadn't seen any shift in the direction of fire. If there were tonatin on the move, they weren't shooting. There was another danger—that the enemy was moving fresh troops toward this fight. We might have no way to know about that until they started potting us. That was another reason not to stay put.

Since I was on the left side, I decided to move that way to try to outmaneuver the enemy. My fire team moved twenty yards—without firing—while Souvana's team stepped up their rate of fire. Then we took over, covering them. We had to keep up some fire, or the IFers might choose to finish off third squad while they waited for us to get back into the firefight. But shooting meant that the IFers could track our movements.

No plan is perfect.

"St. John is down," Souvana reported. "Dead."

"I hear," I said. The gritted teeth weren't particularly because of what Souvana said. Details could wait. At the moment I could only register the fact that we were one man short. Any reaction would have to wait until after the fight. I didn't even think about the fact that our "perfect" record on Unity had been broken. My squad was no longer unscathed.

I felt something tug at my backpack—a not-unfamiliar sensation. A bullet had struck it, but not me. Again, you register the fact but keep moving. Thinking about how close the round had come was something else that had to wait. I'd come a lot closer than that, more than once.

It was my team's turn to move again, so I scuttled forward and left, getting only a couple of feet closer to the enemy. We weren't trying to close with them. You don't want to *think* about that unless you have clearly superior numbers and no way to finish the job more economically. Charging into the teeth of the enemy might made for dramatic video, but actors don't pay the same price soldiers do. All we wanted to do was get somewhere we hadn't been, make it that little bit harder for the enemy to concentrate their fire effectively.

The tonatin started to move, parallel to us, north, toward the rest of their people. At first I wasn't certain if they were trying to keep in contact with us, or if they had something else in mind—like breaking off the engagement and getting back to their own kind. There was only one way to test that. I reversed course, shifting south, then east.

The tonatin kept going north.

I DIDN'T WAIT TO SEE IF THIS WAS A RUSE. AS soon as I was sure that the tonatin were trying to end the firefight, I turned my people toward third squad. We got in and started patching the wounds—doing what we could to stop the bleeding and get extra medical nanoagents into them, trying to reverse the damage before it was too late. There were only three men—Aytah, an abarand named Zhirie, and a ghuroh named Mace—still alive, and I wasn't certain that any of them would last until we got them to better help. I radioed on the platoon frequency, to let Tonio know we would be carrying casualties—and to have someone inside our perimeter alert the medical staff for action once we got the wounded back.

Once the immediate first aid was finished, we picked up the wounded men and moved east. We left most of the wounded men's gear behind, everything but guns and ammunition. My two ghuroh carried Mace. Souvana picked the biraunta up and cradled him in one arm, leaving his other arm free to use his rifle. Robbie carried Zhirie. Abarand are not a whole lot heavier than biraunta, and their bones—originally built for flying—are not particularly dense.

The rest of us positioned ourselves to protect the wounded and the men carrying them. Kiervauna took the point. Having a porracci break the trail helped the rest of us get through the tall grass. I kept watching for the IFers to come at us from the side. I was so focused on that that I hardly noticed the strain of that fast march.

We had traveled for twenty minutes before Tonio and second squad met us. We took a couple of minutes to catch our breath, with second squad taking over security. Then we picked up our wounded again and headed for the perimeter. It was within minutes of sunrise when we crossed that line. Private Mace died before the waiting medtechs could get him into a medtank.

THE STRANGE THING ABOUT THAT NIGHT WAS THAT the IFers had really not *tried* to take advantage of it. They had probed, feinted, sparred, but had not pushed any of their assaults hard. Most of their troops had fallen back, just out of range of our rifles and grenade launchers and dug in before the morning was half-over. We had assumed that was to get through the day without serious casualties so they could attack in the dark, but they had staged only a couple of probing attacks against our perimeter during the night, while we were out behind them. The IFers hadn't really tried to break our defensive line or open a full-scale fight.

I didn't need a bank of computers and years of training as an intelligence analyst to make a damned good guess at what that meant. The IFers were expecting reinforcements and were simply going to wait for them to arrive.

"That's my guess too," Tonio said when I mentioned it to him. We were back away from the perimeter again, eating breakfast and getting ready to sack out for a few hours. I had reported to Captain Fusik on the firefight and the rest of the patrol, told how St. John had died. "Nothing else makes sense. Captain thinks so too."

"How about CIC and the general?" I asked. "Is there any official word?"

Tonio just shook his head.

I had gone back to listening to the continuous feed from CIC after we got in, but there had only been current situation reports, and with so little going on, those reports had been repeating every ten minutes, so I had shut the channel off. Nothing really significant was going to be broadcast over a generally available channel.

"Anybody said anything about requesting reinforcements for us?" I asked next. "If the enemy has more men and ships coming, we're going to need help if we're going to have any chance to stop them." I couldn't help but remember that we had been told that 1st Combined Regiment was being sent to Unity because no other troops would be available for a month. A month without help was starting to look like a death sentence.

"Nobody's told me anything," Tonio said. "As far as I know, it's wait and see. Look, while we're talking, let me cover something else. There's no way we're going to be able to reconstitute third squad until we get replacements, and that's not likely here. So, when Zhirie gets out of the medtank, he'll be reassigned to your squad to cover your open slot. Sergeant Aytah will be attached to company headquarters—for now."

Tonio's qualification on Aytah's reassignment was clear.

Temporarily meant until there was an opening for a squad leader elsewhere in the company . . . until one of us got killed or too badly injured to continue. "I hope he gets to sit on his tail until we get home," I said, fervently.

I DIDN'T SLEEP AS WELL, OR AS LONG, AS I HAD the day before. After three hours I woke up and couldn't get back to sleep. I had lost another man. I hadn't known Neville St. John as well as I knew most of my other men. He had always kept a little apart. He worked as hard as anyone, but when we weren't working, he didn't mix as freely. That's not uncommon with men who come into a unit as replacements for soldiers killed in action. The bond is rarely as strong as in the original team.

Still, he had been one of *my* men, my responsibility. That means something to me. I had his face in my head, memories of little things, as if he wanted me to reassess everything he had done during his time in the squad. I didn't fight it. That has never worked. If I tried too hard to suppress the memories, St. John might end up as another of the "ghosts" who haunt me during my bad stretches. I know, that's one of those post-traumatic stress things. Every so often mine rear up and bite my brain until I have to get help. Nightmares, voices in my head . . . sometimes hallucinations, sweat, the shakes. That's part of the price some of us pay . . . and I have no idea what makes some soldiers immune.

Once I gave up on sleep, I walked around for a few minutes. I switched the CIC radio feed on. There was still nothing new—nothing significant. There was some fighting going on in space, but even that was sporadic, as if the IFers also didn't want to risk ships and fighters until they got reinforcements. It was the same on the ground, minor engagements, long-range exchanges of rifle fire, desultory clashes between patrols. Men were dying, but not in wholesale quantities.

So much for the "soft" assignment Unity was to be. We might have it easy for a few days, but I knew it couldn't last.

CHAPTER 12

WHEN PRIVATE ZHIRIE REPORTED TO ME AFTER his hours in a medtank, my squad was back to its original mix of species. We had been without an abarand since Jaibie's death. I talked with Zhirie for a few minutes. He wasn't a total stranger. No one in the company was after all the time we'd had in training. I gave Zhirie his assignment to the squad's second fire team, then introduced him to Corporal Souvana and left them together.

It's strange, in a way. I had been with 1st Combined Regiment since its foundation, well over a year before. Maybe I was just too used to having all the other species around, at close quarters. Most of the time I was no longer struck with the differences among us. The things we had in common were—usually—more important. We were all soldiers, teammates, fighting alongside each other. We worked together, fought together, ate together, lived together, slept together. Sleep, nothing else; I hadn't heard of any instances of interspecies fooling around in the regiment. It was only at odd moments when something happened to make me blink and really see the uniqueness of the situation, the differences.

There were only five of us in the squad who had been together since the beginning—Souvana, Kiervauna, Claw, Oyo, and me. Five individuals, four species. Half the squad. The rest had come in as replacements, and—with the single exception of Robbie McGraw, who I had known before he joined the squad—I wasn't as close to any of the new men as I had been to those whose places they had taken. More than that, I really didn't *want* to get that close. That had nothing to do with who they were or what their qualifications were as soldiers or sentient beings. It had everything to do with the fact that we were in a war, and getting close to people just makes it harder to handle their loss. And the memories of those they came in to replace. It's different at the start, when the whole unit is new. Then, you don't have much choice, but, after that . . .

It was hard not to recall the pessimism I had at the start, the feeling that the experiment couldn't possibly work— and how totally wrong I had been. We were a good outfit, and diversity made us better. Each species brought something to the mix. Porracci were large, strong, and had a social background that emphasized individual prowess. Ghuroh had more of a packhunting ancestry and tradition; teamwork was their forte. Biraunta were smaller than the other species, more accustomed to hunting through stealth than power. Divotect . . . well, there was nothing particularly martial about their backgrounds, but they had risen to the needs of self-preservation as a species. In the face of a series of invasions that seemed designed to drive them to extinction, they were doing what had to be done. Then there were the abarand, like Zhirie. In many ways, I found them the hardest to understand of the species in the Alliance of Light. They were far from the most numerous, and as individuals they were probably the most fragile, the least well adapted to warfare, but they hadn't let that stop them from joining a crusade they saw as philosophically unavoidable.

The humans? Well, we certainly had the military tradition. Some folks think it's hardwired into our genes, but I don't know enough about that stuff to have a valid opinion. On the other hand, maybe someday there'll be a war that we'll stay out of, but I wouldn't hold my breath waiting.

We were on both sides in this war, for a variety of reasons. But then, except for the divotect, every species in the Alliance of Light was also represented in the Ilion Federation. Maybe it has something to do with sentience itself, rather than "human" nature—this thing we have for getting involved.

IT WAS NEAR NOON WHEN WE HAD VISITORS TO the company area. The bulk of the group was clearly civilian, which meant that they had to be from the colony, but they were accompanied by Lieutenant Colonel Josiah Wellman of regimental operations, two junior staff officers and a squad of enlisted men. Big shots—especially those who aren't too secure with their positions—need their entourages. The colonists were all men, of three species. The group headed to the company command post, where Captain Fusik was.

Since Wellman, my personal nemesis, was with the group, I stayed away and did my best to act invisible. I could put my curiosity on hold. It occurred to me that the visit might have something to do with the local militia we were supposed to train while we waited for our relief. I also guessed that the colonists might be looking to start their training despite the current situation—not that I could see much value to that. With the enemy on the ground, we weren't going to teach anyone enough to be any real help in a few days, which might be all we would have before the IFers got reinforcements and pushed the attack. All that putting poorly trained civilians into the fray could do was get them killed.

It was two hours later before I found out that my guess had been correct. I would have liked to blame Wellman for such an . . . ill-advised decision, but he couldn't have had the final word. The locals must have insisted, and the general and his staff had gone along.

"These people are not totally raw civilians," Captain Fusik said while he was briefing the company's lieutenants and sergeants. Someone had let out an audible groan at the news that we had been chosen to start training the local militia. "The men are all veterans, of various armies or militia units. Selection for Unity was based largely on those qualifications. They've all had weapons training and small units tactics. Some were career soldiers. A few were officers. What these people haven't had is training as a unit, and they don't have military experience working with several species simultaneously."

There were other things the local militia did not have, such as combat experience or youth. Most had been civilians for at least half a dozen years, some far longer. None had served in the war. All had families; that is a given when you're talking about settlers on a new colony world. And the youngest were well past the age at which they would have been accepted for basic training by the armies of any of the species. On the other hand, they were all in good physical condition. Even with labor-saving devices, opening a colony on a raw world requires a lot from a person. And they certainly had incentive—protecting their families and themselves.

A month might be enough for us to turn them into a credible militia, a *home defense* unit, not an offensive military weapon. But we didn't have a month. We would be lucky to get three or four days before it all hit the fan.

"YOU'VE GOT TO BE KIDDING!" WAS ROBBIE'S REaction when I explained our assignment to the squad. We had been given twenty minutes to get our stuff together to move farther from the perimeter. Our company would be setting up in the center of the rather spread-out colony settlement—in the thirty-thousand-acre "park" around which they had built their homes—and we would start training our people the next morning.

"We'll do our best," I said, and I repeated all the pluses Captain Fusik had laid out about them all having prior military service and so forth. "Maybe we can't make Rangers out of them, but we can give them enough unit training to be a credible home defense force. That's what they want, to be able to contribute to their own defense, to help protect their wives and children."

The men of Unity had weapons—rifles, pistols, shotguns—and ammunition. Those had been part of the original colony supplies. They also had a couple of tons of explosives—not land mines or anything sophisticated, but the raw explosives that might aid in construction work for a new colony. There were many ways to convert those charges to military use, and there was a squad from our battalion quartermaster section working on that.

We marched toward the village, with the locals in front, in loose military order—as if they had done some drilling on their own but weren't going to be very serious about drillfield soldiering. There were a few females out to watch us arrive, mostly human, and rather more children. I noticed that the kids were mostly separated by species, with a *lot* of distance between groups. The integration wasn't complete on Unity.

Our officers and platoon sergeants were introduced to the colony and militia leaders. We set up our shelters under the trees at the edge of a piece of grassland about five acres in size. This grass had been mowed to less than four inches. Some of the field had been well trampled, as if the colonists used it for social gatherings.

The colonists were making it easier for us. Rangers don't normally haul tents, just pieces of tarp that can be used either as a ground cloth or overhead to keep weather off. But the Unitians had enough tents for everyone—mostly low two-man jobs, similar to those some human armies have used for centuries. It was clear that most, if not all, had been put together in the colony, just for this purpose. If they were waterproof, that would gain the sympathy of a lot of men who were used to getting wet and staying wet when it rained on campaign.

Areas had been marked off for each platoon, so there had been some coordination before we made the hike, and there were latrines dug. There was even a field kitchen—one of ours—being set up. All the comforts of home.

"Best behavior," I said when I had my people gathered. "Nobody gets out of line, not even half a step. Behave the way you would if your mama was watching." I didn't know how apt that line would be with the other species. I didn't know what porracci or ghuroh mothers—or any of the rest—might expect or accept from their sons. But it sounded good, and if it needed explanation, well, Robbie and I could handle that.

The conference between the locals and our officers and platoon sergeants lasted twenty minutes. Then Tonio came back to the platoon and called for all of us to gather around.

"The locals have nearly three hundred men organized into two militia companies," he said. "The way it works out, each of our platoons will have two platoons of Unitians to train—two of our squads to each of their platoons. They'll be with us twenty-four hours a day. We'll divide responsibilities, put one squad to actively teach the locals and use the other squad as simulated opposition, or whatever."

I was about to remind Tonio that we only had three squads in the platoon but he held a hand up in my direction. "I know what you're going to say, and, no, I haven't forgotten that we're shorthanded. First and second squads will each be assigned as trainers. Fourth squad will handle the other half of the duties for both groups—with an assist from one of the squads in third platoon if necessary. Let's not go looking for problems that might not show."

He paused and looked over both shoulders before he continued. "We don't plan to start working until tomorrow morning, and if the IFers decided not to wait, we might be called back into the lines before we have a chance to get started here. This afternoon, while we lay out the details of the training schedule, it's going to be mostly a get-acquainted sort of thing. You'll meet the men you're going to work with, get a chance to find out what sort of training and experience they have. I know, this isn't the way we'd do it at home, but . . . this is their home, not ours."

THE UNITIANS HADN'T CARRIED THE INTEGRATION of their militia as far as we'd carried it in Ranger Battalion. Each militia platoon was made up exclusively of one species. The one we would be training was human. A few of them looked surprised at the makeup of the two squads that were going to teach them the ropes.

"I don't see what you're so surprised at," I told the Unitian platoon sergeant, a man named Ewan Casper, who appeared to be fifty years old. There was as much gray as brown in his short-cut hair. "Isn't this what Unity is supposed to be all about? Showing that the races can live together in total harmony?" His nod was a bit on the reluctant side. "Well, that was the goal of the 1st Combined Regiment—and the three additional combined regiments that have been formed since we showed that we can work together on the closest levels. In Ranger Battalion, we've carried that as far as it *can* be carried, and it works." I don't know why I put so much emphasis on that, why the word *work* came out so many times in just a couple of sentences.

Ewan Casper smiled. "It's good to know, but we're still feeling our way around here, getting to know each other, learning the ways of each group. Not everyone has arrived. We're about equal in numbers with the porracci and ghuroh. The divotect contingent is considerably smaller. Their one militia platoon is, ah, undermanned. A shipload of abarand settlers is supposed to be coming within weeks, but whether they will come at all now isn't certain. My guess is that they'll wait to see how the fight turns out, rather than try to land in the middle of a battle. And I don't know if we'll ever have biraunta." He gestured toward Oyo, as if I might not know he was biraunta. Maybe he just didn't want to hash over why biraunta might not join the experiment on Unity. I assumed that he was referring to the fear of porracci that biraunta start out with.

"Well, we'll try to make sure you get the chance," I said. "You've got the integration down to the platoon level, and that's good for starters. Each species has something unique to offer. Using all the abilities together gives us a decided advantage against the IFers." I wasn't just being a commercial for the project, but while I was talking I discovered how deeply I believed what I was saying.

"GET AS MUCH SLEEP AS YOU CAN TONIGHT," I told my men after we had an early supper—a hot meal, served in a pavilion manned by local women of all three mammalian species. The divotect came by, but weren't part of the operation, so far as I could tell. It looked as if the iguana-like divotect were running into the same prejudices on Unity that they faced everywhere else. Or maybe they simply didn't feel comfortable enough with the others to press the unification. Unity had a long way to go to live up to its name. Our "recruits" had gone off to their homes, for a final night with their families before moving into shelters similar to those provided for us.

"Maybe we'll go into our training routine in the morning and maybe we won't."

"You think the IFers will strike tonight?" Souvana asked.

"I think it's possible," I said. Then I grinned. "From what I've seen, tonatin are almost as aggressive as porracci, and I doubt that porracci would be waiting around for help."

Souvana grinned back and clicked his teeth. "You can bet that we would not wait to share the glory with those who came too late," he said. "One night we might wait, just to lull the enemy. Then we would drive for their heart, and try to do it from an angle they did not expect."

"Well, in case the tonatin have been taking lessons, we'll keep our own sentries posted, one man at a time. That way, no one loses too much sleep if I'm just paranoid and they don't attack. Keep your helmets on and your receivers active." There was no need to warn them to keep their rifles close. Away from our home base, that was a given. "If we do have to move in a hurry, I don't want to lose even a second. This is still a war zone, despite the civilians hovering around." The hovering had stopped before sunset. After the meals had been served and the kitchen cleaned, the civilians had gone, except for three who would serve as liaison if we needed anything during the night.

I HAD TROUBLE GETTING TO SLEEP, EVEN THOUGH we were far enough from the front line that we were in little danger from the enemy, even if they started a full-scale attack on the perimeter. Not *zero* danger, because the IFers might have spec ops squads like ours, but the danger level was moderate. I kept the CIC feed on, volume so low it was little more than background noise. There were apparently harassing raids going on, as on previous nights. Some of our spec ops squads were working behind the enemy, and the IFers were throwing occasional probes against our lines—feeling each other out. There was no indication of anything major though, but there might not be until the minute when it was actually launched.

There was also no indication of new ships entering Unity's solar system—but that's a good news, bad news thing. There were no enemy ships coming in to increase the odds against us, but there were also no friendly ships bringing us help. Before we landed we had been told that the Alliance of Light needed a month to get troops to garrison the world permanently. Whether the presence of an enemy army would accelerate that timetable was beyond my knowledge.

At some point, I did finally slip into sleep, but it was not an easy slumber.

•   •   •

IT WAS TWO-THIRTY IN THE MORNING WHEN **I** WAS wakened by a sudden increase in traffic on the CIC channel—and by a change in the tone of the voice reading the updates. The IFers had launched a serious assault against our perimeter. One of the three segments of the IFer army was pressing against the north side. That was nearly four miles from my squad. The terrain outside the perimeter on that side was not so uniformly wild grass. There were trees, more cover for an attacking force, and the IFers were taking advantage of it.

I doubted that there would be any major shuffling of our forces. The general could hardly weaken the perimeter elsewhere to reinforce the section under attack. That would just give the enemy commander another spot to attack. If reinforcement *was* needed, it would likely be our company, or one of the other Ranger companies, that would be moved. Since we were the ones sitting on our hands, relatively, my guess was that we were the ones who would get the job. If it became necessary.

Since no orders came, I should have gone back to sleep, but there wasn't much chance that I would be able to without a sleep patch, and using medical assistance to get to sleep would make it more difficult to react if orders came later. So I lay on my bedroll, my head at the end of the tent so I could see a small patch of sky through the leaves of the tree that sheltered the tent. At least it wasn't raining.

I listened to the radio. I tried to figure out what wasn't being said from what was; a guessing game any soldier would understand. The information circuit wasn't going to have the latest news—or necessarily everything that was going on. It was only going to carry what the general and his staff thought we might need to know. So I thought, trying to read between the lines. I worried about what might come next. I fidgeted more than I should have, no longer even moderately comfortable. But getting up and pacing wouldn't have been any better, and it might have telegraphed the message that I was worried to my men—

never a good idea. So I just lay there, trying to rest even if I couldn't sleep.

It made the night stretch longer than it had any right to. After an hour that felt like ten hours, I decided that the fact that we hadn't been ordered to move to help our people on the north side was good news, the best I could expect . . . short of an unlikely announcement that the IFers had decided to surrender or had all just lain down and died. The general must not be worried about the attack—not enough to want to bring in more people to hold off the IFers.

I never did get back to sleep, but I wasn't spending much energy, so I guess I did get some rest. It would just have to be enough to get me through the following day . . . and however much longer it might be before I got another chance at sleep.

CHAPTER 13

IT LACKED ONLY A FEW MINUTES OF SUNRISE when I got up and shuffled to the latrine. I could see clearly under the trees without my helmet's night-vision system. There were a few birds chirping in the trees, but I couldn't see what they looked like . . . not that birds really interested me. Unless they were sitting on my plate and well-done.

I wasn't the first man up. There had been movement around the tents for half an hour or more before I rolled out of the sack. There were cooks, civilians from the colony, putting together a hot breakfast—an unexpected luxury. When I finished my business in the latrine, I went back to the squad's area, rousted my people, and told them to get their shelters squared away and get ready for the day.

"Don't leave any combat gear behind when we start working," I told them when I had them all on their feet. "There's major fighting on the north side of the settlement. Don't count on sticking with the training regimen for long. This *is* a combat zone in case you've forgotten. The enemy might crash our party anytime. And even if the IFers don't drop on our heads, if the general gives a yell for us, I don't want to waste time waiting for you clowns to come back here to collect your unmentionables." *Let the translator buttons sweat over that one,* I thought, grinning. As far as

I knew, the only other species in the unit that wore underwear were the abarand.

We had to use our mess kits for breakfast. The kitchen facilities didn't offer trays or silverware. We weren't going to grouse about that when we were actually getting a hot meal on campaign. Nor were there tables and chairs. We got our food and moved off to sit on the ground while we ate.

I kept looking for Tonio to show up, but he didn't. I didn't spot any of our officers or the other platoon sergeants either. I could make the easy guess that they were in a briefing, but I didn't see that it made much difference. If we were going to be hurried over to join the fighting, we probably wouldn't have had the luxury of that hot meal. It would have been battle rations and maybe about ninety seconds to wolf them down. I wasn't going to borrow trouble.

The sun was fairly up by the time we finished eating. There were low clouds in the west, but overhead it could hardly have been clearer. "They can't mean for us to fight today," Robbie said, gesturing at the sky. "Weather's too nice. If we were going to fight, it'd be rainy as hell."

"You can die as fast with the sun smiling all over you as with a thundercloud taking a dump on your head," I said. "The enemy can see you better, and that stupid grin on your face would be a perfect target." Maybe I sounded a little grouchy, but I hadn't been up long enough to stomach all that good cheer.

"Yeah, Sarge, well, all you have to do is lift your faceplate and give the enemy a look at that ugly kisser of yours, and they'd run so fast their toes would get home ten minutes before their butts."

I didn't try to make sense of that.

THE IFERS WITHDREW FROM THEIR ATTACK ON THE north side at about the time our militia trainees reached our camp. From the secondhard reports I heard, the IFers fell back in disciplined fashion—a planned withdrawal, not a retreat, and certainly not a rout. They had apparently done what they set out to do and got out of range of our perimeter.

Our militiamen marched, after a fashion, into camp, but their order was no better than I would have expected. They did not have proper camouflage uniforms, battle armor, or any of the other gear that regular soldiers would have. I hadn't expected anything more than what I saw. Sergeant Casper marched his men up to where my squad was standing. He told his men, "At ease," then came over to me and flipped me a casual salute, which I returned reflexively.

"Second platoon, Unity Militia Company One, all present, Sergeant," he said. "For a bit, earlier, I thought we were going to have to jump right into the fight. Bit of a noisy wake-up this morning—in the night, rather."

"It's not a game, Sergeant Casper," I said, as softly as I could and still be certain he would hear. I didn't want to put him down in front of his men, but what I wanted to tell him was to just shut up. He was being cheerful, treating this as a lark, and it was going to be anything but that.

"That noisy wake-up, as you put it, was men dying, and some of them came a long way to try and keep you and your fellow colonists alive and free." It wasn't a slap in the face or a bucket of cold water, but my words did have the intended effect. Casper got a more sober look on his face instantly.

"Sorry, Sergeant," he said. "I know your lads are doing this for us."

Not for you, for ourselves, for the regiment, and maybe for all the other people who might get squashed if we didn't do it, I thought. That wasn't something I could tell Casper, not then and there, with all his men watching. On top of everything else, it would have sounded hokey, like a plea to buy government bonds to pay for the war. Besides, I wasn't all that sure I knew all the reasons why *I* was there.

"I know this is new to you, Sergeant," I said, still speaking very softly. "But it isn't new to us, and we've all lost friends in this war. Unfortunately, it looks as if you and your people will join us in that before too long."

The color went completely out of Sergeant Casper's face. But he didn't get angry or resentful. He met my stare. His eyes narrowed a bit, then, very slowly, he nodded. "Once more, Sergeant, I'm sorry," he said. "We'll give this our best, and if it means dying to keep our families free . . ." He shrugged. "Now, how shall we start this?"

Maybe you'll work out after all, I thought . . . *if we have time to do you any good at all.*

WE WORKED THEM FOR TEN HOURS, HOT AND heavy, with rest breaks short and few. I lectured on small unit tactics, then put them through practical drills; the exercises were longer than the lectures and probably did them more good . . . once we pointed out where and how they screwed up. We gave them training in unarmed combat—with all the little tricks we had come up with to help minimize the disadvantage humans were at against several of the other species. We even had them fire their weapons. Before doing any shooting, we had to alert everyone up and down the command structure so we wouldn't set off any alarms of enemy patrols inside our lines. We had to give the militiamen a chance to sight in their weapons and get used to them, but we didn't want to waste ammunition. Neither their stores nor ours were bottomless. But we had to make sure they were familiar with the weapons, and the only way to do that is to fire them.

One day's training wouldn't make them soldiers, and it wouldn't even make up for all the years they had been out of service—especially since none of them were *combat* veterans—but it might buy them a few extra seconds of life if they got thrown into the fight. I hoped that the settlers had more good sense than to try to take a hand in the battle. Maybe with two or three weeks we could give them enough training to give them a halfway-decent chance of surviving a fight. *If* they had professionals at their sides.

By sunset, our trainees were dragging. I was feeling the effort of the day, so they had to be *really* hurting. A few of the militiamen were ready to skip supper to go flop on their bedrolls. They were camping near us now, not going home to their wives and children. I didn't let anyone miss the meal. They would need every bit of nourishment they could get to keep up with the pace. Robbie and I stayed with the militia platoon until we had seen them finish their battle rations.

Then we got our own food. The rest of the squad had already eaten, so Robbie and I sat by ourselves, and I situated myself more so I could watch the militia platoon than my own squad.

"We're never going to have time to turn them into soldiers before this place gets too hot for all of us," Robbie said. "They'd be better off if we didn't try. We'll teach them just enough to let them think they can be heroes . . . and they'll be dead before they learn better. If we hadn't started this cock-up, it'd be easier to convince them to leave the fighting to us."

"If they get into the fighting, a lot of them will die," I agreed, "but we weren't given any choice, so it's up to us to give them everything we can, in whatever time we have. We don't have to turn them into Rangers, just give them enough that maybe they can hold a piece of the line with professionals on either side. It's their world, and once the professional soldiers are gone, it will be up to them to hold it, and protect their families. Maybe if they have to fight for Unity themselves, it'll mean more to them—and their families—down the road."

"Well, you can't say they're shirking," Robbie said, looking toward the tents of our militia platoon. "They've taken everything we've thrown at them. I've got to give them that much." He got to his feet and stretched. "Unless you're planning to work them tonight, I'm going to bed."

•   •   •   •

A FEW MINUTES AFTER ROBBIE WENT TOWARD HIS tent, Sergeant Casper walked over to me. Casper was limping, but he didn't say anything about that, so neither did I. I gestured for him to have a seat, and he sank to the ground awkwardly. He looked as if he ached all over.

"I thought I knew what hard work was," he said, after a couple of soft groans. "Until today." There was clear pain in his face.

I smiled to ease what I had to say. "The work's only going to get harder, but after a couple of days you'll get used to it. You'll sweat your fat out, build muscle, and all the rest."

He nodded, a minimal gesture that also suggested how badly he must be aching. "I was not seeking a reduction in the load," he said. "I know it's necessary, and I recall what it was like when I went through recruit training. That was more than thirty years ago."

"You have my sympathy, but that's all I can offer, except maybe a pain patch to help you through the adjustment stage."

"I'm already wearing two patches. They only seem to help if I don't move a single muscle. But I will bear whatever I must to help defend my family and this colony. Not one of my men has suggested quitting, though there were a couple of times today when I thought a couple of them were simply not going to be able to continue."

"That says a lot for your dedication," I said—because I felt that I had to say *something*.

"We all knew that it might come to this. We were carefully screened before we were permitted to be part of this settlement. We're here because we *want* to be, because we believe in what Unity stands for."

"We'll do everything we can to help you," I promised. "That's why we're going to work you until you think you can't move another step."

"I know." He struggled to his feet and limped back toward his people and his tent.

* * *

THAT NIGHT, THE IFERS ATTACKED IN ALMOST THE same place as they had the night before, but they used more men. CIC's estimate was that they had increased the assault force by 15 percent. They came earlier and pressed the attack until nearly dawn, then withdrew. The night after that, they attacked on the south side of our perimeter, but toward the west end, almost as far from where we were training the local militia as the first two attacks. The spy-eyes in the fleet had done a fairly decent job of tracking the movement of IFer units, but that kind of surveillance is rarely perfect.

"They play games with us, Sergeant," Toniyi said, while we were at breakfast the morning after the third attack. This time, we had been alerted for possible movement two hours before dawn, but the order to move had not come, and the enemy had withdrawn once more. "They toy with us, attacking, then pulling back without committing to a breakthrough." Our divotect rarely spoke unless it was absolutely necessary, so he had everyone's attention. There was a sibilant quality to his voice that gave it a distinctive sound, as with all divotect, but that is a quality of the language as much as the physiology of their vocal apparatus. It's a massively difficult language for humans to learn to speak—or understand readily.

"Like a cat plays with a mouse before she kills it," Robbie said. "I think Toniyi is right. These attacks aren't meant to break through or even to inflict maximum casualties. They're playing with us, strutting their stuff, trying to rub our noses in it."

"Which might mean that they expect their reinforcements very soon," Souvana said. "Tonatin have acted like this in other places, but only when they are certain they will have clear superiority when the real battle begins."

"It might be wise to disrupt their playing," Kiervauna said. He sat as far away from Souvana as he could without leaving the squad altogether, but he looked at his fellow porracci without blinking. "If we do not respond, it gives them a psychological boost, reinforces their delusions of superiority."

"Shall I give the general a call and tell him he can put his staff on the perimeter, that we've got the campaign scoped out for him?" I asked, my voice not quite as sarcastic as my words. I happened to agree with the others. It looked too obvious to be anything else. And I wasn't at all certain that the tonatin had only "delusions" of superiority. There was a damned good chance that they were superior.

"That should not be necessary, Sergeant," Toniyi said, and he sounded perfectly serious. He had completely missed my sarcasm. "If the likes of us see this so clearly, some of the general's proper advisors must also be able to see it and will make proper plans to confuscate the enemy." I don't know what divotect word Toniyi used, but *confuscate* was how my translator button rendered it. I wasn't even certain what it meant . . . or if it was a real word.

"Good. I would hate to interrupt our training schedule unnecessarily." Our militia trainees were still game, giving it everything they had, and each day they had more to give, especially once they worked off their morning stiffness. They were still a long way from being truly proficient at anything, but they were making strides, and I planned to ease off a little on the hard physical stuff and get more into the thinking part. The physical conditioning would continue, but it had been necessary to overemphasize it the first couple of days, because some of the locals were *way* out of shape. Some had burned enough calories and sweated out enough body water to lose ten pounds in two days.

THERE WAS MORE THAN DEDICATION BEHIND THE way I pushed the trainees, something I was slow to recognize. The other companies of our Ranger Battalion were *involved* in the fight, one way or another. Platoons and squads were taking turns patrolling outside the perimeter, harassing the enemy however they could. *We* were sitting in the middle of the regiment, teaching, as safe as anyone could be anywhere on Unity . . . while others were fighting and dying. At some point, that started grating at my brain. I don't consider myself a hero type, but there was a more important job to do than playing drill instructor for over-age retreads, and I figured that I was at least as good at that job as the people who were doing it.

Maybe it's crazy, but that's the way my mind was twisting. After the first day of the training regimen, every time I saw Tonio or Captain Fusik I wanted to tell them that, to ask for some other squad to be given our job so we could get out and "contribute" to the effort. The only reason I didn't was because I could recite the lecture either of them would have given me about how every duty was important, and we were doing a *blah, blah, blah* service as we were. And so forth, probably with a reminder that our turn would come, and that sooner rather than later Unity was liable to get hotter than any of us wanted.

It took a couple more days for circumstances to start warming up, but it did look as if that hell-heat was on its way. More IFer ships were spotted heading toward Unity.

CHAPTER 14

THERE WAS NO PANIC IN THE VOICE FROM CIC when he reported the news, and I didn't sense any panic on the ground. We had expected the enemy to reinforce their assault force quickly. I thought I heard relief in the voice from CIC, though that might have been my mind projecting its own relief that the situation wasn't worse. There were only three new enemy ships, and they were all small. Two were weapons platforms. The third was a transport that could carry no more than a single battalion of soldiers. So even though the news was bad, it wasn't nearly as bad as it might have been.

According to CIC, the new ships had emerged from hyperspace nine hours out from attack orbit. I guess their captains were being cautious, wanting to be far enough out that they could bug out in a hurry if the situation on Unity had been settled in our favor. It meant that we would have that much longer to get ready to meet the new enemy force, and it gave our fighting ships that much longer to damage or destroy the enemy ships before they could land troops.

It was just before sunset when the new ships appeared out of hyperspace, which meant that it would take them until nearly dawn to get close and land any shuttles, even without the opposition they were sure to have from our fleet. That meant that we wouldn't have to worry about the enemy hitting the ground before morning. I wasn't at all surprised when Captain Fusik called the company together, before supper.

"I know some of you have been itching to get back into the fight," he started. I felt a thump of anticipation in my chest. "Well, our time has come. General Chop has decided that since it appears that the enemy is about to commit another battalion of troops to the battle, we need to try to account for at least that number of enemy troops already on the ground." I guess that's the kind of math a general needs to know.

"Our 1st and 2nd Battalions will target the nearest enemy battalion, pushing out on the south side of the settlement, to inflict maximum casualties and make it more difficult for the enemy to use the same LZs they used for their initial landings," Fusik continued.

"Ranger Battalion will operate outside the perimeter. A Company and B Company will both target the same enemy-reinforced battalion as the line companies, from opposite flanks. C and D Companies will do what they can to keep the enemy from redeploying troops to interfere and to make certain that the enemy can't use the opportunity to breach our perimeter elsewhere while we're engaged on the south side. Our heavy-weapons battalion will also be committed to the fight." That was a minor surprise. So far, the howitzers and rocket launchers had remained silent, hidden. They could contribute a lot to this sort of action.

"We'll be moving through the perimeter in less than an hour, and we'll have no more than forty-five minutes to get in position and start harassing the enemy before our two line battalions advance behind an artillery barrage. Grab a quick meal and check your equipment. We'll form up to move in twenty minutes."

"Sir, what about the militia we've been training?" Tonio asked. He was standing close to the captain.

"They will move into the perimeter to help shore up our defenses," Fusik said. "They'll be well dispersed, a single

Unitian platoon attached to a company of our line troops. I have reservations about using them, but the reports I've heard on their progress are encouraging."

WE HAD A FAST MEAL—BATTLE RATIONS, NOT HOT food from the field kitchen. I told my men to fill their canteens while they were checking their gear. There wasn't time for much more. The noncoms and officers had less time than the men. We spent a couple of minutes in an additional briefing, by radio, with our electronic maps open and slaved to the captain's so he could show us just where the action would be. Then it was time to go.

For a change, I felt anticipation as well as that edge of fear that you always have when you know you're going into combat. My first reaction to the captain's news had been, *We're back in the action at last,* and that bothered me a little—my reaction, not the news. Getting back into the action meant that my men and I would be facing the possibility of death again, and that's something that should never be a matter of excited anticipation, or even relief from boredom. At least I didn't have too much time to think, to worry about what might happen. This would be more than the harassing raids we had staged the first couple of nights. This time we were going to try to really cripple a third of the enemy force on the ground. Once you start something like that, you can't be certain where it will go, or that you'll be able to end the action when you want to. If we were still engaged when the enemy put his reinforcements on the ground, it could all get very ugly, very fast.

I GUESS **I** WASN'T THE ONLY ONE WHO FELT THAT anticipation. We formed up and moved toward our staging area behind the perimeter, and it felt as if we were marching more quickly than usual. We had a few minutes to wait when we got to our jump-off positions. It wasn't quite dark enough for us to attempt moving through the perimeter into no-man's-land. We would exfiltrate a platoon at a time, then regroup once we were far enough out.

Unusual for Ranger Battalion, we would be operating as a unified company, rather than as independent spec ops squads or platoons. It would be up to us to hit the right flank of the enemy unit that General Chop and his staff had marked for destruction. Our battalion's A Company would target the other flank. We were to hold the enemy in place and try to get far enough out to keep them from simply retreating south to escape. Heavy-weapons battalion would contribute to that as well, putting enough fire into the area at their rear to make it too risky for them to attempt.

It was a nice plan—on paper. If everything went exactly according to the plan, that enemy-reinforced battalion shouldn't have a prayer. But nothing *ever* goes perfectly in combat, and the enemy probably had pretty plans on paper as well.

WE HAD BEEN ON UNITY NEARLY A WEEK. THE savanna south of our perimeter had taken a beating. There were large sections where that ten-to-twelve-foot-tall grass had been flattened so thoroughly that it no longer sprang back. There were other patches that had burned, leaving a covering of dark gray and black, with new shoots of green already starting to poke through. Out to nearly two hundred yards there was much less cover than there had been the first two nights, when we had been able to operate almost invisibly. It wasn't that easy now. There were still a few patches with cover, but it was that much easier for the enemy to concentrate his surveillance as well.

By the time we were all through the line, we had used more time than had been allowed for in the operational plan. We regrouped and hurried to get to our assigned positions. It was fairly clear that we wouldn't be there when the big rocket launchers and howitzers opened up. We might not be there when our line battalions started moving toward the enemy.

With all the hurry, there was no time to think about anything but the needs of the moment. I couldn't worry about what we were rushing to, I just had to do everything I could to make sure my men and I got there as quickly as possible—without tripping a land mine along the way or stumbling over an IFer patrol.

When I heard the heavy guns, we were five hundred yards from where we were supposed to be. The heavy thump, thump of the howitzers carries a long distance when there are no competing noises. Then came the overtones of the rockets, higher-pitched and longer-lasting, whining overhead. They would reach their targets more quickly, which is why they didn't start firing until after the self-propelled guns had. The goal was to have all the hell hit the ground at the same time—time on target, they call it. This was a pattern bombardment, trying to saturate the area where we thought most of the troops in that enemy unit were.

Heavy-weapons battalion had twelve howitzers and twelve rocket launchers, all remote controlled. Those weapons are too inviting as targets to risk men with them. The controllers would operate from a safe distance. Each self-propelled gun and rocket launcher would move immediately after firing each round, to make it harder for the enemy to target them with counterbattery fire—if the enemy had any artillery. We still didn't know that they did, but we couldn't assume that they did not. Since the IFers had apparently only expected to find civilian colonists on Unity, our people *thought* there was a better than even chance that the IFers had not brought heavy weapons. But . . .

There were half a dozen volleys from the howitzers and perhaps three rounds from each of the rocket launchers in the initial barrage. The explosions were closer than the firing points. Once the shells and rockets started hitting, some within three hundred yards of us, we no longer had to worry about making noise that might give *us* away on the flank. We were moving at the double, spreading out into skirmish lines, angling closer to the enemy while we continued moving farther south.

I checked the time when I could spare half a second from making certain I didn't trip. We were past the area where the grass had been flattened, and at the speed we were moving it would be all too easy to get some of that grass wrapped around an ankle or leg, get snagged, and fall. I had seen several men stumble, and a couple had gone to a knee before catching themselves. I hadn't seen anyone go flat on his face yet, but I couldn't see all our people.

Finally, signals came along the line to slow the pace. We were too close to where the enemy might be for running. If the tonatin soldiers were trying to get out from under the barrage—and even tonatin are not habitually suicidal—we might encounter them any second. We slowed to a walk— a *slow* walk—which gave us a chance to catch our breath and get our heart rates back down near normal.

First platoon had been in the lead. We had covered the most distance and were farthest south. But we were thirty yards more to the east than the other platoons, not as close to the enemy flank. Fourth platoon, on the other side, was the first to encounter the enemy, a single squad. There was a brief exchange of rifle and grenade fire. Both sides were apparently surprised. The tonatin fell back and went to ground. Captain Fusik halted the company. Where one enemy squad had been, others would probably not be far away.

If the line battalions were on schedule, they would be crossing the perimeter now, starting their advance toward the IFers while heavy-weapons battalion continued with more selective fire missions, a creeping barrage designed to hit the IFers nearest our advancing troops. How many causalties our 1st and 2nd Battalions took would depend on how effective the bombardment was. The explosions of heavy shells and rockets seemed to be almost continuous now, but with the rounds spaced so that each explosion was distinct. We were really putting everything into this effort, as if we weren't worried about running out of munitions. Nothing had been said to us about conserving ammunition, either.

Fourth platoon finished off the squad they had stumbled on. We all started moving southwest again, very slowly now, using three platoons to cover one as it advanced. Since we were the farthest back, we were the first to move. *We go as far as we can,* I decided—assuming that would be the plan. Since we were not in contact with the enemy, electronic silence was in order.

I got to my feet when Tonio did and gestured for the squad to move with me. We advanced twenty yards, running bent almost double to minimize the target we presented, before Tonio signaled us down. Second platoon rose from the grass and started forward. They started from fifteen yards east of us, but only got a yard or so beyond our positions when IFer rifle fire came toward them, obliquely, from almost due west. Second platoon went down while the rest of the company opened up with rifles and grenade launchers on the source of the hostile fire.

After thirty seconds, third platoon rushed forward while the rest of the company continued firing. They got level with fourth platoon, maybe seven or eight yards ahead of first and second platoons. There was no longer hostile fire coming toward us. I don't know if the IFers had moved away or just to one side. Second platoon got up. They had barely started to move when we came under fire again, this time from our left, farther south. That meant closest to us. I got my men turned. It couldn't be the same group of troops as the last time. They couldn't have covered that much ground so quickly.

With enemy fire coming in on our left flank, it was awkward for first platoon, especially my squad. We were the only ones who could return fire without firing over—or into—our own people, and the other platoons needed time to move into better positions. Under fire. I heard a scream, behind me and to my right—one of our people—but I couldn't look to see who had been hit. I knew it was no one in my squad. The scream, quickly ended, had not been that close.

"This is at least a platoon on my flank," I said on the channel that would connect me to the officers and sergeants in the company. "Out two hundred yards, maybe a little more. It might be the tip of a breakout."

When more gunfire erupted to our southwest, that seemed even more likely. There had to be close to a company of IFers, maybe considerably more. "They're trying to get out over here," I said on the same channel, "and I don't think we can stop them."

It was nearly a minute before I got any response. Captain Fusik came on the all-hands channel, and said, "Keep your heads down. Help is on the way." He didn't have to spell it out. The artillery was going to send at least a few rounds our way.

It took less than thirty seconds before the first shells whistled overhead. We were flat but we still tried to duck. The kill radius from one of those shells is—theoretically— fifty yards, but it can be greater if the terrain is flat, there isn't much heavy cover, or if the shells explode a little too high. They are set to explode just before they hit the ground, ideally a yard or two before impact, to spread the shrapnel over the widest possible area.

We didn't have all the guns and launchers working our sector, but I'm certain that at least four shells and two rockets went off south and west of our location, between two and three hundred yards out. If there were more, the explosions overlapped too perfectly for me to distinguish them. I had cranked the volume on my external sound pickups down as soon as the captain gave his warning; I didn't want to destroy my hearing. Even so, the noise had been nearly deafening. Afterward, there was a moment when I couldn't hear anything but the ringing in my ears. It might have been a minute or more after the final explosion before I could hear Captain Fusik shouting over the radio.

"Up and at 'em! Let's finish this."

We started toward the area that had just been devastated by our artillery. There were several small fires smoldering, and a lot of smoke—a bluish haze hanging low to the ground. The air carried a powerfully acrid smell, the kind that makes your nostrils want to fold and pull your nose inside your head. I stumbled a couple of times in the first few steps. I was trying to clear my ears and get rid of the ringing. It might take hours before it disappeared completely, but I could hope it would fade enough to let me hear things around me—noises that might affect my chances at survival.

Ten yards. Twenty. There was no gunfire coming toward us. The rest of the company shifted around until we were at the point of a shallow wedge. First platoon was in front, but not by as much as we had been at the start. We had covered about eighty of the two hundred yards I had estimated had separated us from the enemy before the artillery barrage when we started taking a little rifle fire from off on our right, and at a considerable distance. Most of the hostile fire was well over our heads. Whoever was doing the shooting must not have actually had us in sight. Fourth platoon turned and moved west to take the new situation in hand while the rest of us kept moving south, maybe south-southwest.

We reached the edge of the area our artillery had pounded. All of the shells and rockets had hit within a circle with a radius of no more than two hundred yards. Inside that circle, there was no grass left standing, except for some that was badly bent. Much of the grass was burning . . . and there were no live IFers in view. We saw bodies—more commonly, *parts* of bodies—scattered all over the place. Some of the bits of uniform and flesh were burning, or smoldering. The little tongues of flame were an eerie greenish orange through my night-vision system, giving the area a weirdly surreal look. There were a few wounded men on the ground, most with limbs missing or gaping holes in their guts.

I didn't bother to yell for medtechs to treat the enemy casualties. None of the ones I saw had any chance of surviving long enough to reach a medtank. They had already lost too much blood, even if there was enough left of their internal organs for repairs. Besides, we weren't going out into the middle of that blackened circle. It would have left us in the open, exposed, and there might be enemy soldiers close enough to target us.

We moved around the edge of the area, staying far enough back in the grass—what there was of it even away from the total destruction—to give us *some* cover, some concealment if not protection. We had moved far enough out from the perimeter around the settlement that a lot of the tall savanna grass remained relatively undisturbed, except where soldiers had trampled it or where heavy gunfire had mown it short or plowed it under. Fourth platoon had dealt with the last batch of enemy shooters and was moving along on the flank.

We didn't bother trying to get a body count. An accurate census would have been nearly impossible, given the intensity of the artillery fire. I did try to estimate—for my own satisfaction . . . or morbid curiosity—how many IFers the artillery had put down for the count, and tried to reassure myself that no one in that circle was suddenly going to start firing at us. I was confident that there were at least forty or fifty bodies—bodies with enough left intact to prove what they were, or had been. There could have been twice as many dead. A heavy rocket or a 225mm artillery shell going off close sometimes leaves nothing large enough to recognize.

The company moved just west of south until we were 150 yards south of the far end of that blackened circle, then Captain Fusik turned us more west. By that point, we should have been behind virtually the entire IFer-reinforced battalion, at the corner, where we could make it difficult for them to move either south or east. *If* our intelligence was correct and current. The platoons spread out, leaving gaps of as much as eighty yards between them, so we could cover more of the area.

Then we started moving in, toward where we assumed most of that IFer unit was. If things were going on schedule, A Company should be doing the same thing on the other side, and I knew from reports on the radio that 1st Battalion and 2nd Battalion had advanced two hundred yards from our perimeter, meeting the enemy head-on and pushing them back. Heavy-weapons battalion had slowed its fire considerably. Now, it was only firing selective missions, when definite targets had been pinpointed by observers in our ships or troops on the ground. Conservation. Someone had finally recalled that we did not have endless supplies of munitions to draw on.

YOU SEARCH FOR INFORMATION CONSTANTLY, near and far, during a combat mission. You look, listen, and smell, trying to be aware of everything going on all the way around you—out as far as your senses can reach, because danger can come from a long way off. The mind speeds up, processing what eyes, ears, and other senses feed it. Some of this is training, but more comes from experience . . . and instinct. Some people fit naturally into this life. Others can't get the hang of it at all—and usually don't last long, unless their luck is extremely good. A moment of inattention, a fraction of a second, can be fatal. Reflexes that aren't quick enough. Bad luck.

Luck does play a part, perhaps a big part, in who lives and who dies in combat. Many soldiers are superstitious because—consciously or not—they recognize that their lives might depend on luck. We train hard to minimize our reliance on the fickle lady, but even the best soldier can have Fate roll craps for him. Ability, training, and good leadership aren't always enough.

Half of our second squad had their luck run out all at once that night on Unity.

•   •   •

THERE'S NO WAY TO KNOW EXACTLY HOW IT HAP- pened. We were moving toward the enemy but we weren't under fire. Apparently, someone in second squad tripped a land mine. Most likely, the mine was out of sight under flattened grass. It could have been one of ours as easily as one of the enemy's. An entire fire team was killed, if not instantly, then before anyone could get to them. Maybe they had been clustered too close together. It's easy to say that after the fact. But it doesn't make much difference now—certainly not to *them*. Five men were dead before the medtechs reached them.

The rest of us moved on. You try to put the dead out of mind. After the battle is the time to remember the dead— assuming you don't join them first.

CHAPTER 15

OUR COMPANY WAS INVOLVED IN ANOTHER HALF dozen brief firefights before dawn—skirmishes that served mostly to keep the enemy from breaking free on the side. None of those scuffles escalated into lengthy confrontations. We inflicted casualties and suffered them. In my squad, we escaped any deaths or serious wounds. Kiervauna took a bullet in his left side, but it was a clean wound that did not involve any major organs. Once the bleeding had been stopped, he continued moving with the squad. I couldn't see that his injury slowed him at all.

The reinforced IFer battalion—casualties had certainly reduced their numbers below those of an unreinforced battalion by then—was able to move south, squeezing between us and A Company. We slowed them, inflicted casualties, and made sure they could not simply outrun 1st and 2nd Battalions. Our line battalions were taking heavy casualties, but they were still moving south.

By dawn, our artillery had almost completely stopped taking part in the battle. It was—from what I could gather by eavesdropping on the CIC channel—becoming more difficult to identify good targets, and the battle was becoming too fluid, with opposing units getting mixed up, too close together, to be certain that we wouldn't have friendly-fire casualties. I would guess that there was more worry about conserving ammunition for later use as well. Fire missions, when they did come, involved only a few rounds or rockets, carefully targeted for the most urgent need.

The incoming Ilion ships? One of the weapons platforms had been disabled by particle beam weapons and rockets; it was drifting, apparently out of control. The lone troop transport had been damaged but less severely. Its speed had been cut by nearly half. It would be at least another three hours before it could get close enough to launch troop shuttles—if it was going to be able to launch them at all. That wasn't certain. Long-range damage assessment isn't perfect.

SUNRISE. WE TOOK A MUCH-NEEDED BREAK, TAK-ing advantage of the fact that we weren't in contact with the enemy just then. There hadn't been many chances to sit and rest during the night. We had been on the move much of the time, and—all too often—involved in exchanges of gunfire. There certainly hadn't been time to sleep or eat. We had been on our adrenaline rushes so long that it didn't do much good any longer. That's bad. Your mind slows down. Your senses slow down. Your reactions get sluggish. It wasn't much comfort to know that the enemy had to be suffering similarly—maybe worse since we were forcing them to retreat, and making that retreat as difficult and costly as possible.

I closed my eyes, maybe for the first time in eight hours. I doubt I had even blinked often in those hours. I've had people tell me about the impossible stare I wear in combat. My eyes were burning and dry. I had a buzzing in my ears, maybe just the remnants of what the initial artillery barrage had caused, maybe another symptom of exhaustion.

Even ten seconds with my eyes closed seemed to help. I opened them and took a drink of water. The best beer in the Galaxy never tasted that good.

"How much longer you figure they're gonna keep us

moving?" Robbie asked. He had crawled over from where
he had plopped originally. Crawled. We weren't in a safe
zone, and Robbie was smart enough to remember that.

"No idea," I said. "We could be a long time at this."

"We've been on the go more than twenty-four hours."

I closed my eyes again, but not for long. I had blocked
that out of my mind, the fact that we had put in almost a
full day training our militia platoon before we started this
mission. It made me feel twice as tired to be reminded of
it. "I wish you hadn't said that," I said.

"Zhirie is really dragging, Sarge. I don't think he can
keep it up much longer. Abarand just aren't built for this
kind of strain."

"Ala and Oyo can't be in much better shape," I said,
turning to see where the biraunta were. They weren't built
for endurance either. For that matter, we were pushing it
for most of us. Our ghuroh and porracci hadn't shown any
sign of weariness that I could see, but they were the only
ones who looked as if they could go on indefinitely. I could
even see signs of exhaustion in Toniyi, but that was probably only because I had more experience with divotect
than most of the people in the platoon did. This was the
second time on this campaign that we had been kept on the
go for a full day or more, and there hadn't been that much
time to catch up on sleep even while we were in the middle of the defended area training the colonists' militia.

"You gonna ask somebody?" Robbie asked.

I stared at him for a long moment. "Are you in that bad
a shape?" I asked then.

"Yes, and so is everyone else in the squad, including
you. The way we are, we're gonna make mistakes, and
that's gonna get people dead." He met my stare without
blinking or looking away.

"Sometimes you've got to keep going anyway," I said,
after a considerable hesitation. "I'll talk to Tonio, see what
he says."

"Thanks, Sarge." Robbie crawled back to his position.

I started moving toward Tonio. I couldn't use the radio

since we weren't in contact with the enemy. Tonio was sitting hunched forward, arms on his legs, looking for all the world as if he were asleep. He turned his head before I got to him, so I knew he had heard me coming.

"Let me guess," he said, and I could tell from his voice that he was as tired as I was, "you're upset because you didn't get your soft-boiled eggs for breakfast."

"They'd have to be soft-boiled because I haven't got the energy to chew anything harder," I said. "How much longer you figure we're going to keep this up?"

"I already asked the captain. However long it takes to put these IFers down to stay. Or until they surrender, if you believe in miracles. There's no one to relieve us and we can't take the pressure off now."

"We're going to need a little time, regardless. I've got a couple of men about ready to drop. We can't handle much more, Tonio, and that's the bare truth."

He let out a deep breath. "I know, Dragon. I know."

THE CAPTAIN GAVE US TWENTY MINUTES. IT wasn't nearly enough, but it helped. We couldn't sleep. Hell, with the enemy maybe within spitting distance, we took our lives in our hands just to close our eyes for ten or fifteen seconds. I won't speculate on how many people did fall asleep—to be wakened by the man next to them as soon as they were noticed.

Twenty minutes. The captain was the first man back on his feet. Lead Sergeant Deelock was next, hardly half a second behind him. After that, it was a rather general thing, lieutenants and sergeants, and the rest. I took a good look at each of my men, trying to assess their condition, trying to perk them up one way or another—a word of encouragement, a barb about ability, whatever.

"Just remember, the IFers have to be hurting as much as we are," I told some of the men. I don't know if it helped. They could see and hear that I was as tired as they were. That might have helped more.

We formed up and moved out. We needed to get farther south to make sure that the IFers couldn't turn east to escape the continuing fight. We were getting close to the IFer landing zones, moving slowly because that was the only way we *could* move, but the IFers weren't breaking any speed records either.

IT WASN'T EVEN FIFTEEN MINUTES AFTER OUR break that we hit trouble again. Once more, the IFers were trying to turn east, and this time it looked as if they were going to run right over us, no matter what it cost them.

We saw them coming before the shooting started. The two or three seconds warning—broadcast over the company channel by some anonymous voice—gave us a chance to dive for cover. Or fall down. It was getting difficult to tell the difference. Several enemy RPGs exploded, all short, out far enough that they didn't do too much damage. Then there was general rifle fire, and it seemed clear that we were facing superior numbers—not overall, but right at that spot facing us.

There was no need for a specific command to return fire. Our instructions were to return fire immediately unless we received contrary orders. Spray the enemy line. Work your sights back and forth across a twenty- or thirty-degree angle, enough to ensure overlapping fields of fire. Keep your aim low, *consciously* low. Many soldiers tend to shoot high, especially on full automatic. Besides the obvious fact that you're not scoring hits if you fire high, you don't have any indicator out there to show you your error. If you're shooting low, your bullets will kick up dust or grass, or whatever is on the ground. Then you adjust upward. A bullet in a foot will slow an enemy down. A bullet through the knee can take him out of the fight. He either stays where he is or needs a couple of comrades to carry him.

Gunfire can be a better stimulant than caffeine or drugs, especially if that gunfire is coming your way. For a time, at least, it can speed reflexes. But it's not perfect, and the effect doesn't last forever. In time, mental dullness can return. The mind doesn't register the continuing threat as effectively. Soldiers do stupid things. That makes heroes, but it also makes dead men.

"Stay down," the captain said on his allhands channel. "They've got to come to us if they want to get out on this side. Hold your ground, and make your shots count." Yeah, the captain knew what shape we were in or he wouldn't have wasted air with that kind of talk. I did my best to tune him out.

I emptied a magazine and ejected it with one hand while I reached for a loaded magazine with the other. For the life of me, I couldn't have told how long this particular firefight had been going on. It was an infinite *now*. I jacked a shell into the chamber and went back to firing, stopping for a few seconds when a yawn threatened to get out of control.

When this batch of IFers opened up on us, they were about two hundred yards away—about as far as anyone could see anyone else through the thick grass. We had gone to ground and stayed put. The IFers were attempting fire-and-maneuver tactics, still coming toward us. They were moving slowly and taking heavier casualties than they were inflicting, but they *were* moving, and it looked as if they might have the numbers to roll over us in time. If you don't mind losing people, and you have enough numbers to replace the dead and wounded, you can overrun almost any oposition.

Finally, our people put a couple of artillery rounds along the enemy skirmish line. That took maybe ten or fifteen of them out of action and left a gap in their line, but there were more tonatin moving forward to take the places of those who had fallen. A few yards to my left, Kiervauna suddenly rolled over onto his side, facing me. He grunted loud enough for me to hear it over the sound of my rifle. When I glanced his way, he was trying to slap a field dressing over a fountain of blood spurting out of his right arm, a couple of inches above the elbow.

While I wondered how Kiervauna had gotten next to me in line—as my assistant fire team leader, he should have been a couple of men farther away—I started crawling toward him. He was never going to get that arterial bleeding stopped one-handed. He was fumbling badly, and it looked as if he might be ready to pass out from loss of blood. His left hand did drop away from the wound as I reached him, and the gauze pad dropped as well.

It took me nearly a minute to get the bleeding stopped and a hypo full of blood-building nanoagents injected into Kiervauna. He was unconscious but alive, and his vitals were encouraging. Unless he got hit again, or we were forced to leave him behind, he had a good chance of recovery, even if we couldn't get him into a medtank. The medical nanoagents I had pumped into him, along with those already resident in his system, would speed the replacement of blood. With a human, it might take an hour or two to get the process far enough along to get him mobile again. I wasn't certain about porracci. I thought Kiervauna would recover more quickly. If he got the chance. That might depend on how the battle went.

I wiped the blood from my hands and moved a little away from Kiervauna, ready to get back into the action. The nearest IFers were 120 yards away, but they were having trouble getting any closer. We were meeting them with overwhelming rifle and grenade fire, and at that range it was almost impossible to miss. There wasn't much grass left standing between us, and the haze of heavy gunfire didn't do much to hide anyone. But they kept trying, and they kept dying.

I emptied another magazine and switched to a fresh one. After that, I only had one more full magazine for my rifle. I knew a lot of our people had to be in that kind of shape. Some would be a lot closer to empty. I just hoped that the IFers were as badly off as we were. I told myself that they *had* to be getting short on ammunition—they hadn't had any more luck landing supply shuttles than we had—but I was afraid that might prove to be wishful thinking.

"Be careful with your fire," I said on my squad channel. "This close, go for the aimed shot when you can, don't go wild with auto-fire unless they get a lot closer. We don't have anyone hauling ammo for us." Yeah, any veteran soldier should have known what the situation was, but it's up to noncoms and officers to make sure they remember.

A single artillery rocket exploded, maybe forty yards behind the frontmost IFers. Some of them went down, thrown forward, maybe just from the concussive force of the blast. If we were lucky, it might have taken out a good batch of IFers moving up to take their turn at the van.

Whatever, there was noticeably less enemy fire coming our way after that rocket exploded. The firefight did not end, not immediately, but I didn't see any IFers getting up to try to charge forward. That one rocket seemed to make more of a difference than all the earlier rockets, artillery shells, grenades, and rifles. There's no logic to it, just a lot of clichés like *the straw that broke the camel's back* that come to mind.

"Cease fire!" The order came from Captain Fusik on the all-hands channel. "Let's see what's going on," he added. "Unless we get a general advance again, noncoms will take care of any single enemy soldiers or units of less than squad size. We've got to conserve ammunition."

There was something very close to silence along our stretch of the battle. Once my ears got used to that, I could still hear gunfire and grenade explosions from farther off, to the right, but nearer than on other occasions. The main fight, the one involving our two line battalions, had obviously moved a lot closer to where we were. I wasn't quite so certain, but I thought I could hear gunfire directly west of where we were, but at longer range, the other flank of the battle, perhaps. I didn't put a lot of faith in that, though. It's too easy to make mistakes in that kind of situation.

Maybe this is getting close to the end, I thought—hoped. I was breathing heavily, and took a moment to get it under control. I was also sweating so much that I felt as if I were swimming inside my uniform and boots. I switched my radio to listen to the CIC channel. I might pick up news faster there than waiting for something from the captain or Tonio. The first news I heard wasn't particularly good. The other IFer units were pressing attacks against the perimeter around the Unity settlement, obviously trying to take the pressure off the third of their people we had targeted for destruction. According to CIC, our perimeter was still holding. There was no information about whether the partially trained militiamen were involved in the fighting.

WE REMAINED FLAT—WEAPONS POINTED TOWARD the enemy, waiting for whatever might come—except for the men tending our wounded, and even they took care to stay low. No one made a start at moving those wounded farther from the line. There was no place to take them, and just moving them would have exposed more people to enemy fire. I checked with my men to make certain that there weren't any additional casualties that I didn't already know about. Then I crawled back to Kiervauna to check on him. He was still unconscious, but his vital signs were stronger. A medtech came over and also did a check.

"He'll be okay if we can get out of here soon," the medtech assured me. "But the captain said not to try moving anyone yet."

I told him I understood, and moved away from him and Kiervauna. That was still tactical thinking: don't cluster together in case the enemy starts coming toward you, starts firing and trying to overrun your position. Tactical thinking. But there was nothing going on at the moment and reaction started to set in. The adrenaline of the firefight drained away. Exhaustion returned, reinforced by the extra tension and exertion of the last . . . I don't know how many minutes. I wasn't sure when it had started, so I couldn't tell how long it had lasted.

It was all I could do to keep my eyes open. I found myself with my head down, helmet faceplate touching the ground, only seconds from falling asleep. It took an act of will to raise my head to look toward where the enemy was—or had been. I saw absolutely no evidence of activity, not even medical personnel trying to attend to the IFer wounded. I scanned as much of our front as I could, slowly, looking for any indication of what the enemy might do next. It was only after I had assured myself that I couldn't see any developing threat that I started looking to either side, toward where the rest of our people were. There was only minimal activity on our side, medtechs working on the wounded, noncoms checking on their men.

Fifteen minutes, maybe twenty, had passed since that last artillery rocket blast had seemed to signal an end to our part of the battle. My mind was near total numbness. Even simple movements were difficult to make, as if my body were not receiving clear instructions from my brain. I started to yawn, then had difficulty containing it. My eyes, dry for so long, started watering as well. I had to lift my faceplate enough to get a hand in to wipe the tears away.

The sound of more distant gunfire—maybe it was starting to fade as well, I'm not sure—was almost a lullaby. Sleep was trying to claim me and I needed time to recognize that, which made staying awake even more difficult. It was a near thing. Sleep can be insidious, its own need greater than any possible residual danger. It makes your mind lie to itself. I forced myself to start moving, crawling from one man to the next, checking to make sure they were awake. That was as much to keep myself awake as to make sure my people weren't asleep.

THERE WAS NO SUDDEN END TO THE BATTLE. AT some point, there was a major decline in the level of fighting, but it took another thirty minutes or more before all of the shooting stopped in the sector we had attacked. Small units or individual soldiers kept fighting in some cases, either not getting the word that the fight was over . . . or deciding to ignore it. There was no general surrender of the remnants of the battalion we had put under all the guns we could bring to bear. By battalion or company, by platoon or squad, the enemy surrendered or was destroyed.

Those of us on the flank were maybe the last to hear that the battle was over. CIC was slow to broadcast a general announcement. We heard first that the diversionary IFer attacks on our perimeter around the colonists had ceased, that the other two major units of the IFer invasion force had withdrawn, out of range of rifle and grenade fire. The perimeter remained intact. The IFers had not reached the colonists. Then we started to hear about surrenders of individual enemy units, and a lowering of the level of fighting. By the time CIC made the announcement that the battle was over, we already knew it. And it was much later before we learned that our line battalions had withdrawn to our original perimeter around the settlement.

Kiervauna regained consciousness and announced that he was "fit," though he was still obviously in pain. I had to order him to lie still. "The fight seems to be over, so rest," I told him.

It was another ten minutes before we had orders. Captain Fusik told us we were going back to the perimeter—the two Ranger companies and 2nd Battalion. Any cleanup on the battlefield would be left to 1st Battalion; two companies were going to make a sweep of the area before they followed the rest of our forces back to the settlement.

We had a long walk ahead of us, carrying our wounded, but at least we knew that we had a chance for sleep at the end. Sleep was more important than food—to me, and probably to the majority of us. Keeping any sort of "proper" military order to the march back was probably impossible, and Captain Fusik didn't insist on it. He just told us to make certain that we didn't lose any stragglers along the way. That put squad leaders at or near the rear of the squads. I guess the captain assumed that sergeants would be less likely to straggle. I was too exhausted to be touched by his faith.

We had been on the move for nearly two hours before we reached out perimeter and passed through, with regular troops and militiamen manning the positions there. We kept going, all the way back to where we had been camping while we trained the militia before we stopped.

"Make sure everyone eats before they sack out," Captain Fusik said on a noncom circuit.

TOTAL OBLIVION. BECAUSE OF THE CAPTAIN'S order, I choked down most of a battle ration pack—as tired as I was, it tasted dry as sawdust even when I took a drink of water with each bite of food—and watched to make certain that my men were also eating. Then I lay down and closed my eyes. I took off my pack and web harness, but nothing else. I think I was asleep before I stopped moving. I did not dream, or did not recall any dreams. When I woke, after sunset, I still felt drained, exhausted. I was awake for ten minutes or more before my brain sloughed off the sluggishness of sleep. I got to my feet and wandered off to the latrine, then came back to the company area. There were few people up and about—mostly men who had wakened for the same reason I did, the need to make a short trip.

Tonio was still sleeping. So were Lead Sergeant Deelock and Captain Fusik. I didn't see either of our lieutenants. I guess they were also still sleeping, though one of them might have been awake, on duty, somewhere close. He wasn't at the company command post—CP. I went back to my tent and gear and sat in the opening of the tent. I still felt tired, but no longer sleepy. My brain was functioning. I switched back to the CIC radio channel, wondering what was going on, whether the IFers had managed to land the troops on that crippled transport, whether there was any significant military activity going on anywhere around our perimeter.

The IFer reinforcements were still in space. The transport was still considerably too far out to launch shuttles. Apparently, they weren't trying to get close enough for that. They were maneuvering to stay away from our weapons ships and aerospace fighters. I wasted time trying to guess whether the enemy was still debating whether to continue contesting Unity or if they were simply waiting for additional reinforcements. Since I had no way to know, it *was* wasted time.

It was almost as hard to decipher from CIC's comments just how costly our victory on the ground had been. They weren't likely to come right out and give casualty figures; *that might be bad for morale* is their usual position. You have to read between the lines and factor in everything they don't say to make a guess there. I assumed that it had been a costly fight. Head-on attacks usually are. I did have a fairly good idea how badly B Company, Ranger Battalion had suffered, because I had seen some of the casualties and had talked with some of the other sergeants on the way back. We had lost fourteen men killed in the company. There were a few men who had been wounded so badly they would need extensive time to recover. Most of the other wounded, including Kiervauna, had been certified for duty again. For 1st and 2nd Battalions, all I could gather was that they had suffered serious numbers of men killed, likely more than ten percent.

I could get no idea at all of casualties on the perimeter from the various IFer attempts to divert attention from the third of their force that we had caught on the south side. There was no word on 3rd or 4th Battalion, or on the militia unit we had put into the lines. CIC simply said nothing about that part of the fight, just an announcement that the perimeter had held, that no enemy troops had penetrated the line.

In return, we had virtually destroyed an augmented enemy battalion—killing, wounding, or capturing almost every tonatin in the unit. Maybe some IFers had escaped, but we had collected close to two hundred prisoners, including those few enemy wounded who had been recovered and treated. That unit may have numbered close to a thousand soldiers at the start of the battle.

The brass would call that a significant victory. General

Chop did use those words when he broadcast congratulations to the regiment. When news reached the newsnets on Alliance worlds, the commentators and news readers would say the same thing, probably in even more glowing terms. Regret would be expressed regarding the casualties in our army, but the number of our dead would soon be almost forgotten—except by the families and friends of those who had died.

CIC did not suggest that the contest for Unity was near an end.

CHAPTER 16

IT WAS PAST TEN O'CLOCK THAT NIGHT WHEN
Lead Sergeant Deelock passed the word for the company's
sergeants to gather at the command post. The company
was concentrated in a fairly narrow area, with the CP tent
at the center, so it didn't take long. Captain Fusik was
there, along with the only two lieutenants we had left, Junior Lieutenant Spike, a ghuroh, and Senior Lieutenant Druvauna, a porracci who had been assigned to us only after
we got back from Durestal, where Lieutenant Trivauna had
been killed. As an SL, Druvauna was the company executive officer. I hadn't had many dealings with either officer
in the short time they had been with us. At least they had
given me no trouble. Most times, that's all I ask from any
officer.

"For the time being, at least, our duty training the local
militia has been suspended," was the first thing Captain
Fusik said. I was puzzled that he would start with that. If
he had left a space for anyone to speak, I would have asked
how the militia had fared, but he simply kept talking.

"Frankly, I don't know what's coming next. We have no
orders to mount patrols or take a place in the perimeter.
The scouting duties have been left for our C and D companies, I imagine because they weren't part of the major
fight last night and this morning. I didn't ask questions be-

cause I didn't want to invite a change in orders. We need the rest. We *do* have to put the men to a little work tonight, cleaning weapons and replacing the ammunition we expended. I know how close we came to running dry out there. If the IFers had been able to hold out for another thirty minutes, we would have been down to bayonets and clubs.

"Cleaning weapons and passing out ammunition is the first priority. We should have done the latter as soon as we got in yesterday afternoon. As it turned out, we got away with the blunder. But get it taken care of as soon as you get back to your men. You all know where we've got the ammunition stockpiled. We'll run this by platoons, as quickly as possible.

"Once we have full loads of ammunition and clean weapons, make sure everyone eats another ration pack. We used a lot of body reserves out there. Everyone needs to get food in."

"Captain?" I said, when he left a pause long enough for the word.

"What is it, Dragon?" He still sounded tired, too.

"The militiamen we were training. Is there any word on how they did? Did they suffer any casualties in the fighting on the perimeter?"

"*Light* casualties is what I was told, specifically one killed and fewer than ten wounded. The militia is still manning the perimeter tonight. From what I've been able to gather, they acquitted themselves well in the fight. That may be why the general decided to keep them on the line rather than bring them back here for more training. You all did a good job with them in the time you had. I'm proud of the company, everyone. And I made that clear when I talked with the colonel."

"I wasn't worried about that, sir, just how our people did, and—more important—how bad they were hurt," I said.

Fusik smiled. "I know that, Dragon."

"Sir, do we have any new information at all on the overall situation here?" Tonio asked. "Any news about reinforcements for us? Or intelligence on what the enemy will do next?"

"No news on reinforcement or relief for us," the captain said. "Nothing newer than what we were told before we left Earth, that it was going to take a month to get troops here to relieve us. I don't know that the IFer invasion will change that. We have to be prepared for the chance that it won't. There are thousands of guesses about what the enemy might do—none of them worth spit. We'll know what the enemy is going to do when they do it. We simply need to be alert for any possibility. I do want to emphasize one thing. After the fight we've been through, it's clear that the enemy does not have any heavy artillery on Unity—no big guns or self-propelled rocket launchers. They would have used them if they did. And we did not lose a single one of our SP weapons. Not one.

"I'm not going to hold you any longer. Get back to your men and do what has to be done. Ammunition. Clean weapons. Eat. Sleep. Let's keep a minimal watch, two men per platoon and rotate them every hour. Unless something comes up, we should have the whole night to catch up on our sleep, maybe a fair share of tomorrow as well, if we're lucky."

BY MIDNIGHT, ALL THE WEAPONS HAD BEEN cleaned—and inspected. We all had at least four fresh hundred-round magazines for our rifles. We had eaten. I was feeling less exhausted than before, and I wasn't ready for more sleep yet, though some of my men were already sleeping—notably Zhirie and the two biraunta. They had been moving like zombies despite the amount of sleep they had managed earlier.

I sat cross-legged in the opening to my tent and listened to the CIC feed. There was really nothing new, just repeats of earlier status reports, sometimes in slightly different language. Even the fighting between the two fleets in space had apparently been suspended sometime the afternoon before. Each side was staying close enough to make it difficult for the other side to land supplies—or reinforcements. Other than that, everyone was just trying to keep out of the way of the enemy's ships and fighters. I guess we were all catching our breath, getting ready for the next act.

THE HIATUS LASTED THROUGH SUNSET THE NEXT day. There was no fighting—except for a few squad-sized skirmishes between patrols that ended as quickly as the participants could disengage—but there was considerable activity, especially in the IFer army. They had to reorganize, move troops to plug the hole left by their losses of the day before. CIC estimated that the enemy was simply trying to put a perimeter around our perimeter, to make it more difficult for us to sortie without being spotted.

"They have to be waiting for more reinforcements," I told Tonio. We were eating an early supper together—hot food from the field kitchen, which went down a lot easier than the battle rations we had been eating. There had been no new orders for us, B Company, Ranger Battalion. As far as either of us knew we weren't going out on patrol that night . . . which was okay with me. "More men and probably heavy weapons as well."

"That's what I've been thinking," Tonio said. That was no surprise. I'm sure most of the people in the regiment must have had the same idea. It was the topic of the day. "Those ships that did come in must have also brought news that there were more reinforcements coming. They're just biding their time, trying to avoid another disaster like yesterday. My guess is that if we went out and tried to pin another batch of them down, they'd run as fast as they could to keep out of the box."

"I wonder if the general feels that way, too. If he does, he's liable to want to put it to the test."

"Wouldn't surprise me," Tonio said. "But I'm not going

to make the suggestion. If it comes, okay, but there's no point in asking for trouble."

I DIDN'T FEEL AT ALL BAD WHEN WE LEARNED THAT the general was going to test it, because C and D Companies of Ranger Battalion got the call this time. They exfiltrated on the northeast portion of our perimeter, trying to make it look as if they were going to do what we had done the last time. Our company got moved to that section of the perimeter, to make the enemy think that we were getting ready for another attack between the two Ranger companies on the flank.

Within minutes after we reached what would have been our "jumping off" position behind the perimeter if an attack was really on the schedule, the IFers started pulling back, and they concentrated on the Rangers who were out beyond the perimeter. Our Rangers did not press, the way they would have if we had really been going to try the same sort of encapsulation. They withdrew, spending some time zigzagging around out in the open before they came back through the perimeter. We got up into the perimeter to support the movement, to make sure they would be able to get back in safely.

C and D companies lost as many men in that feint as A and B had lost in the real fight two nights earlier—just to see if General Chop's guess about enemy intentions had been correct. Maybe, on some level, it was worth the sacrifice. I didn't think so, but I've got a far different perspective on values than any general does. In the hour before dawn, we moved back to our previous bivouac. The experiment was over. We all figured it was almost a certainty that the enemy was waiting for additional reinforcements—and knew they were coming soon.

THERE HAD BEEN CONTINUING WORK ALONG THE perimeter around the settlement on Unity. Almost from the beginning, the soldiers manning the front line had been improving their defensive positions, digging foxholes and slit trenches for the men, piling dirt ramparts in front of them, putting camouflage tarps overhead, planting land mines and electronic snoops farther out. Although we prefer mobility, there are times when you simply have to dig in and do the best you can. On Unity, our primary mission was to protect the colonists, not to hunt and destroy the enemy. As the days had passed, the perimeter became more solid, with connections between positions, deeper holes, and carefully registered fields of fire.

We had help from the locals, civilians as well as the militia. Secondary lines of defense were built in case the outer perimeter became untenable. It was beginning to look like something from the first of Earth's "world" wars, when the major armies had been bogged down for years in a system of trenches, with defensive weapons so clearly superior to the available offensive weapons that movement was virtually impossible. Of course, there were millions of soldiers involved in that, not the few thousand facing each other on Unity.

Even a noncom has to know a lot about military history these days. I could give you a rundown on basic tactics in most of the major wars since humans started keeping written records—and on a few wars humans had not been part of.

"This world is important to the Alliance. They will find some way to reinforce us," Souvana said, sounding supremely confident—about the way he sounded when he was assessing his own physical prowess against anyone else's. We had been sitting together, a little off from our men, and I had been bringing him up to the minute on the news I had learned. "This is the jewel we wish to hold up to the Galaxy to show just how well we can function together. No matter what it takes, the Alliance cannot afford to risk losing it."

"I hope you're right, but I'm sure the Alliance has a fallback position in case we can't hold Unity. Politicians always have a fallback, something they can say is just as important. They can plant another colony and use that as their example."

"There are porracci citizens here. Our politicians do not sacrifice civilians because the military cannot do its job." He sounded very certain of that. I *tried* to share his confidence.

WE FINALLY MOVED OUR BIVOUAC FROM WHERE we had set up to train the Unity militia. Our new positions were in the secondary line of trenches and dirt bulwarks behind the outer perimeter, and we were put to work improving them. It was an ass-backwards situation, with the line troops in front of the Rangers, and I heard a lot of grousing about that . . . but I think the complaints were a cover for the real gripe, doing physical labor. No soldier enjoys that kind of work.

After two days of digging holes and reinforcing them, the complaints got more specific, the expletives considerably more colorful. I told the men that this was not makework, that before we finished on Unity, the defenses we were building might save our butts and various other vital portions of our anatomies, but that didn't stop the complaints.

"We should be out there, doing what we can to beat the enemy now," was the general tenor of what the men told me when I suggested they should quit bitching about the work. Even Toniyi, normally the least aggressive man in the squad, started to sound bellicose.

It was noon of the third day when Captain Fusik finally told us to stand down, that we had done everything necessary to get the secondary line of defense finished. He also told us to get as much rest as possible that afternoon. That was as good as telling us that we were going to see action that night. Even I was ready to say, "About time."

Later that afternoon, there was more information—good news followed by bad news. The good news came when a new Alliance of Light fleet appeared out of hyperspace, bringing reinforcements and resupply. The bad news came fifty minutes later when another Ilion Federation fleet winked into normal space, coming in.

One way or another, the easy days on Unity were about to end.

CHAPTER 17

"WE'RE GOING BACK TO DOING WHAT WE'RE SUP-
posed to do best," Captain Fusik said. He had called a
meeting of the company's officers and sergeants half an
hour after we got the news—about the new enemy fleet.
Apparently, General Chop had not taken long to decide
what to do. Of course, there was a chance that we might
have a new commander, if the general in charge of the reinforcements outranked Chop. Either way, a decision had
come quickly.

"It's going to be up to us to establish and secure the LZs
for our reinforcements," Fusik continued. "The current
schedule is for the transports to launch shuttles at 2240
hours, less than four hours from now. The new Alliance
fleet is going to push through to a launch orbit regardless
of what the enemy does. The escorts and our ships already
in-system will coordinate to do as much as possible to neu-
tralize the enemy ships. The object is to get our people and
equipment on the ground before the new IFer ships get
close enough to launch their force."

Not only had our fleet come out of hyperspace nearly an
hour ahead of the IFers, they had emerged in normal space
at least an hour's travel time closer to Unity, cutting safety
margins to the bare bone. All our people had to worry
about was that portion of the enemy fleet that was already

present and was close enough to intercept them. But our reinforcements would have support from our ships that had been on station since the beginning of the operation.

"Exfiltration will likely be more difficult tonight than before," Fusik continued. "After the major fight the other night and the subsequent feint we carried out on the north side, the IFers have gone to as complete a line around us as they could manage. That line is extremely thin, but there is a chance—hopefully a *slim* chance—that they'll have time to concentrate superior numbers before we get past their observation points and away from their major units. We'll deal with that however we have to, including support from heavy-weapons battalion. The general would prefer to save HW to cover our reinforcements when they land, so keep that in mind. I'm not going to ask for artillery support unless it is absolutely necessary. Now, slave your maps to mine."

Fusik spent the next few minutes going over the maps with us—our route out, where we were going to establish LZs for the incoming troops, and so forth. The plan was for the new men to come down in two widely separated locales, to make it that much more difficult for the enemy to hit them hard in the vulnerable seconds just before and after touchdown—before the troops could get out of the box and contribute to their own defense. The enemy did not have so many troops on the ground that they could do much in two widely separated locations simultaneously. If they tried, our line regiments could roll out and over them.

"The rest of the regiment is going to give us as much diversionary help as possible, but don't expect too much. The enemy will almost certainly recognize it for what it is, and the tonatin are clever enough to ignore the diversion to go after the real threat. Us."

MY HEART WAS BEATING FASTER, BUT THAT'S NOT unusual with action pending. We were going to get back into the fight after the days of working inside the perimeter. If nothing else, we had caught up on our sleep and put a few pounds back on our bones. As usual, I made a point of spending a minute or two with each of my men, doing what I could to gauge their mental condition. I offered encouragement, reassurance, support, whatever I could. That's an important part of a noncom's job. It's not all a matter of yelling.

As soon as it was dark we moved toward our jumping-off point behind the outer perimeter. I wondered just how much heat we might run into. Sliding through the enemy's line had been easy each of the previous times. The trouble had come later, after we had regrouped for whatever the mission was. The captain had said we couldn't expect it to be so easy this time. The IFers were doing everything they could to cover the entire perimeter. Where they couldn't put people, they would have electronic snoops. They would be especially nervous about movements on the ground since they had to know about the new Alliance ships coming toward the planet.

Both new fleets were continuing in. The IFers were coming in awfully "hot," according to CIC, trying to close the gap between the reinforcing fleets as quickly as possible, but there was no way they could overtake our ships before the shuttles were on their way in. They probably would be unable to shave more than six or seven minutes from the lead our reinforcements enjoyed. It would still be close to two hours after our ships reached launch orbit before the IFer task force did. There was already fighting going on among the ships that had already been in the system. We were trying to make it difficult for the IFers to contest the landing. They were trying to get into position to attack our reinforcements.

CIC said that there was no way the IFers could succeed. I was keeping my fingers crossed—mentally, at least. You live a lot longer if you expect the worst.

IT WAS TIME. WE SLIPPED THROUGH THE PERIME-
ter a platoon at a time, while troops in other sections of the

line opened fire on the enemy positions, trying to divert attention. My squad led first platoon out, staying low but moving fast. We got across the open area in front of the perimeter without challenge, but Oyo spotted—and destroyed—an electronic snoop. By that time, of course, the snoop had done its job, letting the IFers know that someone was moving through.

The rest of the company experienced sporadic, and mostly wild, enemy fire, the bulk coming from extreme range. There wasn't much, and we didn't lose anyone in the process. We didn't even lose any time. Our rendezvous lasted less than a minute after the final platoon reached it. Then we moved out again, pushing hard for the site chosen for one of the LZs.

We were halfway there when we saw a brilliant burst of light twenty degrees above the western horizon—a massive explosion in space, a ship destroyed or seriously damaged. There was no immediate word from CIC about the incident. The ship might have been theirs or ours. It was later when we learned that it was one of our ships, a weapons platform lost with all hands except the fighter pilots who had been on missions at the time. Four hundred and thirty-two dead, humans, ghuroh, and abarand.

I took a long look as the point of light expanded, then faded. I may have said a short prayer. We kept moving.

TEN MINUTES LATER, WE CAME UNDER FIRE FROM the right. Since my squad was on that flank, we were told to handle the situation. An enemy patrol had caught up with us—come in on an intercept course, rather. It appeared to be no more than a single squad, not enough soldiers to stop the company, even briefly.

I sent Souvana's fire team to the left of the enemy patrol while I took my team on the right. We had the IFers pinpointed. Their gunfire gave them away. There was still some standing grass around the location, but it was not complete. The IFers were at the edges of one patch, using it for concealment . . . with minimal success.

My people moved low. I don't think the IFers spotted us until we were within fifty yards—maybe a fraction of a second before we opened up on them from both sides, with RPGs as well as rifles. The fight didn't last long, under a minute. A few tonatin managed to withdraw, leaving their casualties behind. We did not bother pursuing them. They weren't important. I led my people back to our position off the company's right flank, thirty yards from the main column.

That was the only encounter we had with the enemy before we reached the LZ. Captain Fusik posted us around the area. We planted land mines and, farther out, electronic snoops. One squad from each platoon was delegated to patrol beyond the circle of snoops. This time, my squad lucked out. We were in the final line of defense around the edge of the landing zone.

There was no question of actually digging in, but we made a few minor improvements to give us a little advantage if we had to stand off an attack before the shuttles started to land. Then we settled in to wait.

WHILE WE WAITED, WE OCCASIONALLY SAW MORE fireworks in the sky—all well to our west. That was the direction the shuttles would come in from. That was where the bulk of the ships were.

D Company's Rangers had gone out north of the perimeter around the settlement to secure the second landing zone. From what I heard on the radio, they ran into more trouble than we did, but they reached the area they had been sent to secure half an hour after we were in position. I listened for any hint about the response of the IFers on the ground. All CIC reported were small-scale movements. The enemy was choosing to concentrate on keeping their line around the settlement intact.

Close to us, there was absolutely no sign of enemy activity on the ground or in the air. None of the electronic snoops spotted anything. None of our patrols ran into the enemy. There was no sign of enemy fighters overhead. We really didn't expect aerospace fighers until the shuttles were coming in—if then. Both sides had been concentrating their small fighters to protect the big ships and to attack enemy ships. Ground support would be far down on the list of priorities.

We remained alert, waiting, watching the time lines on our helmet displays. The minutes passed too slowly, as expected. I could at least help the time pass by moving along the squad line now and then, settling in next to one man after the other—theoretically to make certain everyone was awake and alert, point out avenues to watch, and to offer a whispered word of encouragement where necessary. We were fairly well rested going into this mission, so I wasn't really worried that anyone might fall asleep or be daydreaming.

My squad had a stretch of about forty yards to cover on the west side of the designated landing zone, so that put a little more than three yards between men. The separation wasn't uniform though. You don't make things any easier for the enemy than you have to. Each platoon covered one side of the LZ, so there was a *lot* of space between squads and platoons. We were counting on our electronic snoops and the outlying patrols to plug the holes, so to speak.

Before it was time for the shuttles to be launched from our incoming ships, each of my men had snuggled in among the grass as best he could. A couple had scraped away a few inches of dirt—not proper slit trenches, but enough to give them just that little bit of advantage with the scraped dirt piled up in front of them. Even three or four inches *can* make a difference. And we arranged the grass, where we could, to give us a little camouflage as well—concealment.

Ten-forty at night: 2240 hours. There was no way for us to see the shuttles launch, and there was no immediate announcement by CIC. Since there was no report that they *hadn't* been launched, we assumed that they were on schedule. That would mean they would be coming in for a landing in little more than twenty minutes if their pilots made "normal" hot-combat approaches. *Normal* means that pilots accelerate toward the ground until the last possible second, then reverse thrust on their rockets and jets to avoid plowing straight into the dirt. It's always an uncomfortable ride for the passengers but far preferable to coming in slow and safe when there might be enemy weapons waiting on the ground.

I saw Herb Deelock, the company lead sergeant, moving along the line, running from one platoon to the next—not short sprints by any means. He stopped and knelt next to Tonio, then got up and started trotting toward the next platoon, on the south side of the LZ. Tonio got up and went from squad to squad.

"Keep your eyes open. The shuttles should be approaching. Touchdown should start just after 2300 hours." Eleven o'clock. Then Tonio moved on to the next squad. I passed the word to my men. By the time I finished, we were within ten minutes of the first landing.

It wasn't until thirty seconds before the first shuttle touched down that we saw anything—the flare of rockets mostly occulted by the fuselages of the incoming landing craft. There was the bright glare that served, in part, to silhouette those craft. Then, when the first shuttle was almost on the ground, we heard the roar of its rockets.

"On your toes now," I said over my squad channel. With the shuttles committed to the LZ, I wasn't at all worried about giving away our position by using the radio. The enemy ships would know precisely where our shuttles were landing, and that news could be relayed to their troops on the ground as quickly as they could triangulate our location from electronic intercepts. "Our people will be coming on the run once they get out of the box. Stay down until you hear differently."

There might be a tense moment or two when the incoming troops detected us. They *should* know we had the LZ secured, *expect* to find us guarding the area, and they *should* be able to read our electronic friend-or-foe codes. But there was no reason to tempt Fate in the form of a nervous soldier who might be too on edge to pay attention. This was one situation where friendly-fire casualties were all too possible. I had *seen* it happen on one other occasion, and had heard of several more.

It was in those last few seconds when I realized that Captain Fusik had never said how many reinforcements were coming in, or how many shuttles we could expect at the landing zone we were protecting. No one had asked during our briefing. *I hope the captain knows, at least,* I thought as the first shuttle came in and braked to a stop, with its engines racing at full power to stop the craft.

The shuttles came in quickly, sometimes separated by less than a second, fanning out to put some lateral distance between them. As quickly as the men piled out of a shuttle, the crew buttoned up the hatches, and the pilots taxied to the eastern edge of the LZ. They gave their passengers time to get out of the way, but not much more than that. There was a pause before any of them started taking back off, but none of the landing craft stayed on the ground any real length of time.

"I guess they figure the odds are more in their favor in space than down here," Robbie said on a circuit that only connected him to Souvana and me.

"Can the chat," I ordered quickly. "Pay attention to what you're supposed to be doing. Watch your front."

The first dozen shuttles made it in without difficulty. Then a couple more came in, with some indication of hunters in the air after them—three rockets that missed their targets, ground explosions behind them. We had still seen no indication of enemy activity on the ground. I think it was the fifteenth shuttle that broke the string of luck. At least one enemy fighter had come in locked on its tail. The fighter loosed two rockets—the lines of fire behind them were almost blinding—and both hit, just as the shuttle's wheels touched the ground, ninety yards from where I lay. The shuttle hadn't come to a stop yet, so the men aboard had no chance to get out of the box.

The shuttle exploded. Bits of fire and wreckage arced up and out, falling back to the ground as much as three hundred yards away, well past us. I swallowed the lump in my throat and watched as two shoulder-launched surface-to-air missiles were launched from one of the other platoons in our company. Neither exploded, so that enemy fighter escaped.

"No rockets!" Captain Fusik ordered over the all-hands circuit. "Too much chance of hitting one of our shuttles. And we've got fighters in the air, too. Leave the enemy fighters to them." No one in my squad was carrying a rocket launcher, so I didn't have to repeat the order for my people.

The first reinforcements reached our position. One company rendezvoused just behind my squad. Tonio went and talked to someone—probably the company commander or lead sergeant—then returned to his position in the line.

There was an explosion almost directly overhead—up two or three thousand feet. It had to be a fighter—a shuttle wouldn't have been that high if it was coming in to land—but I had no way to know if it was ours or theirs. Fiery debris came down—too slowly, it seemed. Most of it was a few hundred yards west of us, but some came close enough to be alarming.

A few seconds later, there was another explosion, low and west of us. I couldn't be certain, but I guessed that it was another of our shuttles—more men who didn't have a chance to get out of the box. Later, I learned that it had been one of the shuttles bringing in a self-propelled howitzer with its remote crew. That meant that only the gun's crew and shuttle's crew died. In *that* blast.

From first shuttle to last, it was under twenty minutes before all our troops, heavy weapons, and supplies were on the ground. There were even several tracked vehicles, trucks—also remote-controlled—to carry the supplies. We had two-thirds of 2nd Combined Regiment, less the men in the two shuttles blown up as they made their approach and two other shuttles that had been destroyed in space before they got near the ground. The rest of that regiment, and the porracci 3rd and 4th Firestorm Battalions, had landed north of the settlement—less similar casualties. Altogether, about three hundred men did not survive the trip in.

"Hold your positions and stay down," Captain Fusik told us on our company channel. "We'll cover the shuttles until they get out, and the rear of the reinforcements as they move away from the LZ, then strike out on our own. We're going to hang around and wait for the enemy to try its landings."

THE LAST SHUTTLES GOT BACK INTO THE AIR, burning for orbit with their throttles wide-open. The men and machines of 2nd Combined Regiment did not linger near the LZ either. They moved west and north—not directly toward the perimeter we had established. They were going to try to engage the enemy already on the ground and—with a little luck—be in position to contest the landing of the enemy reinforcements. Of course, we had no idea where the IFers would try to put their people on the ground. They might well settle on LZs that were too far out for us to get to them in time.

I wish there had been some way for me to get a bet down on that.

AS SOON AS 2ND COMBINED HAD MOVED OUT OF sight—which didn't take long because their people were almost as good as we are—Captain Fusik brought our company together, and we started moving east and a little farther out from the settlement. I guess the idea was to get troops in as many different positions as possible, to increase the chance that some of us might be able to hit the

IFer reinforcements as they touched down. No one had thought it necessary to share the overall plan with me, and there's probably a reason why I wasn't the general running the operation, but I figured that the new units might split into several parts and spread out as well.

We moved at a steady clip, past the LZ, skirting it so we weren't too exposed. Then we turned more to the south, that much farther from help if things went sour. The last estimate we had heard was that it would be a little past one in the morning before the enemy could land . . . *if* they pressed in and launched shuttles immediately, the way our people had. Since we wouldn't be able to tell for certain *exactly* where the IFers would land until a minute or so before they touched down, we couldn't be sure that anyone would be close enough to get in a few shots before their troops got out of the box.

At one o'clock, we were four miles from the LZ we had secured for 2nd Combined Regiment, more than eight miles from the perimeter around the settlement—a long way from any help on the ground. That was nagging at my mind more than it should have—spec ops troops are used to operating alone and sometimes with even less hope of help—but it wasn't dominating my thinking. I wasn't as nervous about it as I had been about . . . everything earlier. It was just a factor that had to be taken into consideration.

CIC made an announcement over the information channel when the enemy started to launch shuttles—with an estimate that the IFers were going to try to land approximately two regiments of troops, including those on the ship that had been damaged days before. I tried not to think about the possibility that one company of Rangers might have to take on two full regiments—perhaps as many as ten thousand men—alone. If we were able to use our customary hit-and-run tactics, that shouldn't be a problem. Get in and out, attack the fringe, and be somewhere else before the enemy can respond. Large formations of troops are slower and a lot more difficult to maneuver than smaller formations, and if we broke down into single-squad teams, we could move *quite* rapidly—especially if we knew our butts and other anatomical favorites were on the line.

Captain Fusik stopped the company as soon as we heard that enemy shuttles were on the way. We were back observing electronic silence, so he didn't actually say anything over the radio, but I thought I understood his reasoning, and even if he had different reasons for stopping, the ones I could think of were good enough. Until we had *some* idea where the enemy was going to land, it didn't make sense to move any farther—since we might find we had been going in the wrong direction. We would wait for more information. Maybe they would try to set down right in our laps, give our people with the rocket launchers a chance to pop a couple of the boxes before they opened up. Of course, if that happened, we might be trying to set records for long-distance running once we got those first shots off.

The voice from CIC was unusually loquacious once the IFer shuttles were launched, giving numbers and information on the shuttles, and the number of aerospace fighters we had trying to intercept them. Sprinkled in with that there were updated estimates on where the IFer shuttles might attempt to land and how far from touchdown they were. Until those shuttles went atmospheric, the possibilities were too broad to be of any serious use, so I didn't bother trying to check them on my map. When someone gives an area that is more than a thousand miles in diameter, what's the point? We knew that the IFers would land somewhere within hiking distance of the settlement. I doubted that they would put down so far away that they couldn't get into position near the settlement by sunset the following day. There was nothing else on Unity worth risking so many troops for.

By the time the lead shuttles were within a mile of planetfall, I could figure out that they weren't going to land close enough for our company to intercept, and it looked as if none of our troops would be. The IFers appeared to be coming in ten miles south of us, and we were probably farther south than any other Alliance troops on Unity. What wasn't clear was how far east or west of us those shuttles might land.

THE IFER REINFORCEMENTS ENDED UP LANDING ten miles south and three miles east of us. We saw some of the fireworks as our fighters attacked and their fighters tried to protect those shuttles. I saw a couple of aerial explosions and the trails of many rockets. We heard blasts.

Captain Fusik signaled for the platoon sergeants to come to him. That conference lasted two minutes. Tonio called the squad leaders in our platoon to him when he returned.

"There's a stand of tall timber three-quarters of a mile east of here. We get in there and wait, out of sight, until we know what route those troops are going to take. What we do then depends on them."

Yeah, I could figure that one out. If the IFers came close enough for us to reach them, it would be up to us to harass them until we could bring more troops to bear. That's the kind of operation that can get hairy as hell—one short-handed company against close to two regiments. We probably wouldn't be outnumbered by more than sixty or seventy to one.

CHAPTER 18

NIGHT AND FOREST. BOTH ARE FRIENDS OF THE infantryman. Both offer concealment. Trees offer more *physical* barriers to infantry weapons than darkness—and certainly more than tall grass. The forested area we headed for only covered about two thousand acres, so it wouldn't give us a *lot* of room for playing hide and seek, but it was better than being out on the open savanna. A blade of grass, even if it's twelve feet tall, won't stop a bullet or grenade shrapnel.

My worry was not going into the forest, but the near certainty that we would have to come back out before long, perhaps in daylight, when the savanna would offer minimal concealment. I listened to the feed from CIC with a new intensity, waiting for the armies to sort themselves out, listening for any clue about where the IFer reinforcements would head, for any hint about what my company might be ordered to do. Yeah, I'm so low on the chain of command that I shouldn't have to worry about anything more than obeying orders—there are always higher-ups to do the strategic thinking—but I'm intelligent enough that my mind has to work at questions like that.

It was two-thirty in the morning when we reached the cover of the trees. Patrols were sent to scout the area while the rest of the company set up near the southern and western edges—in the cover of the trees but where we could see out into the savanna that bordered them. The grass wasn't quite as tall as what we had operated in near the settlement, but it was still more than head high.

We were spread out in a surveillance line rather than a defensive formation, covering as wide a vantage as we could without becoming too separated to regroup in a hurry. My squad was strung out along nearly a hundred yards. The other squads were spread out the same way. There was no point to digging slit trenches. We expected orders to move as soon as it was clear what the enemy was going to do. But we did make what improvements we could to our positions—using loose branches and foliage from farther back to give us a little more concealment. Sometimes, it's the little things that make the difference.

By four o'clock, the last of our patrols had returned. There was no evidence of enemy activity in the woods or nearby on the savanna—no patrols sneaking up on us. Captain Fusik was satisfied with our positions. We lay quietly just inside the forest, most of us looking out onto the savanna, only a few squads stationed to cover our rear against the slim possibility that the enemy might come at us from that direction. We also had electronic snoops planted—but not nearly enough to make me comfortable with the coverage.

CIC tracked the activities of the IFer reinforcements as well as it could from the spy-eyes in the fleet. The new enemy force had taken a considerable time to organize on the ground. They did have artillery—self-propelled howitzers—about a dozen gun carriages. There was no sign of large rocket launchers, though, which was some comfort. The enemy started moving in two columns, a couple of hundred yards between columns.

By four o'clock, CIC had a decent estimate on their course. They were heading directly toward the patch of woods we were in.

"This is the only decent cover close to them," Tonio said, when I went to his position to see if he had heard the news. "They probably want to get their big guns out of sight, and this is the only rational choice for that. But there's not enough room for them to try to hide all their people as well."

"They can't get here before daylight," I said. "Maybe we'll get some artillery or air strikes in against them, slow them down, maybe force them to change course."

"I don't know about the artillery, but I don't expect any of our fighters to target them," Tonio replied. "The battle upstairs has heated up, and the fighters' first mission is to protect our ships and go after the enemy's ships. Besides, that keeps enemy fighters from giving *us* grief."

"In other words, we're on our own."

Tonio shrugged. "We'll do our bit and let the general figure out the rest of it. That's why he gets to wear all the fancy gold braid on his dress uniform. My guess is we'll be used to slow the IFers down and make them take more care about their own defenses while the general moves the rest of our people around for the main event."

I nodded and started back to my own position. I realized how edgy I sounded, and I wanted to get away from Tonio before he decided I was too nervous for my own good . . . which I might have been, even though I was calmer than I had been earlier. We weren't in a fight, and there was still a chance that we might not get into the kind of all-out mix-up that can get a lot of people killed. I don't know why I had been so nervous—worse than I've ever been, I think, except maybe for the first time I headed into a fight knowing it was coming—or why I was still on edge. It wasn't anything so clichéd as a feeling that this was going to be the time I bought it. Sure, that happens, but sometimes it can be a self-fulfilling prophecy. And I've known soldiers who had that "feeling" *every* time they went into combat.

If you say it often enough, there's a damned good chance you'll eventually be right.

What I felt was a more general malaise. The real fight for Unity hadn't started yet, but it was coming. It was close, and it might prove to be the worst fight I had ever been in. A lot of men were certain to die. There was a chance that I would be one of them, or some of my men might. I had to get my mind working straight before the fight started, to improve the odds.

I WATCHED THE DAY BRIGHTEN AS THE SUN CAME over the horizon in the east, giving brilliant green colors to the grass that dominated south of our location in the woods. The IFer regiments were still moving in our direction, but were at least an hour from reaching us. They were not observing strict electronic silence. With nine thousand men or more moving across open grassland, it wouldn't have done them much good. They were visible from space and knew it.

Their course had changed a little in the last half hour before sunrise. If they went straight on their current vector, only the eastern column would actually enter the woods where we were waiting. That was the column with most of the artillery. There were only a few places where those self-propelled guns could enter the woods without knocking trees out of their way, and the forest was thick enough that the mobility of the guns would be compromised in any case, but trees would still offer them more cover than tall grass.

Captain Fusik rearranged our positions to put the men with shoulder-fired rocket launchers where they could cover the most likely entry points for the enemy howitzers. I didn't read too much into that. There was a chance that the captain had received orders for us to try to knock out enemy guns, but it was more likely that he was simply taking a sound defensive measure. You put your weapons where the threat is greatest.

Apart from the slight realignment, we continued to wait. It wouldn't be long before the enemy vanguard would be so close that we would have difficulty slipping away unobserved, so every minute we stayed in place made it that much more likely that we were going to be thrown against the enemy reinforcements. In broad daylight.

"If we can draw them into these woods to chase us, we should have excellent opportunities to inflict great damage on them," Souvana said, when I slid next to him to see how he was doing.

"These woods don't go on forever," I reminded him. "The IFers have enough men to saturate them, which would mean we'd have to move out into that damned grass again." There was one other possibility, that they could simply surround the wooded area and move in until they had us boxed into the center. But I thought the enemy commander would most likely be too intelligent to waste time and manpower doing that—even if we had been more than a single company.

"By which time our own forces should have time to move into position to render some assistance," he said. No, there wasn't the faintest hint of nervousness in him. I hadn't expected that. Not only could I not hear any nervousness in him, I doubted that he felt any. Porracci view combat differently than most humans do. I think only the ghuroh approach the level of the porracci in their attitude toward war—on our side, at least; the tonatin have given every indication of similarly accepting the cost of battle.

Toniyi was whispering a prayer when I moved next to him. My translator buttons did not interpret the words, but I recognized the cadence from my first time on Dintsen, the divotect colony world where the war had started. The divotect use an old language for their religious rituals—it's a dead language used for nothing else, the way some on Earth still use Latin for religious observances—and I knew that language was not one our gear was programmed to interpret. Toniyi finished his prayer before he turned his head toward me.

"I was speaking to those who have already died," Toniyi said.

"I know. I've heard the prayer before." Too many times, during both of my visits to Dintsen, and after our other battles. "Let's do what we can to avoid joining those dead. I don't know exactly what we're going to be asked to do, but we'll handle the mission, whatever it may be."

"Yes, Sergeant," Toniyi said, nodding solemnly. Divotect heads look something like those of iguanas from Earth. They are rather larger in proportion to body size than those of any of the other sentient species in the alliance. With a battle helmet on, that imbalance seems exaggerated almost to comic proportions.

"Remember, even though we're out here by ourselves, the Alliance forces outnumber the IFers." The ratio might not be more than four to three, but we *did* have the better side of it.

Toniyi started to reply but stopped when we heard a whistle and looked toward the source. Tonio was on his feet, gesturing for me to go to him.

"Just keep your head and you'll do okay," I told my divotect before I got up and trotted over to Tonio.

"The IFers have changed direction again," Tonio said. "They're angling east, and it looks as if they might skirt this forest on the east side." He shrugged. "Either that or they're going to enter over there, instead of here where we've been waiting. Time for us to move. We've got to hit them before they get into the trees—if that's their intent."

"If it isn't, they might change their minds once we start hitting them," I said. "But at least we can slow them down, I guess. I assume that's what we're supposed to do." I nearly surprised myself with that. I sounded more confident, less worried—almost back to normal.

Tonio grinned. "If we can't wipe them out by ourselves."

WE DIDN'T HAVE ANY DIFFICULTY GETTING TO OUR new positions in time. We had a shorter distance to go and could move considerably faster than a couple of regiments. Since it was full daylight, we couldn't risk sending men out to plant land mines across the path the IFers seemed to be taking, but we would be ready to snipe at them from the flank, or ambush any patrols they might send out on our side.

Once we were up and moving, my nervousness faded even more. I had my men to look after, and you always have to keep an eye out for any surprises the enemy might put in your path—even when you think there's not much chance that they have. Maybe especially then, because that's when you're most likely to get careless. A busy mind has less time to worry about things it can't change.

CIC had gone tight-lipped again. I assumed that Captain Fusik, and perhaps the two lieutenants and lead sergeant, were getting updates that might affect us, but that news wasn't being shared on the march. When we got close to the southeastern corner of the forested area, we split into platoons, and there was considerable separation between them.

Tonio brought the three squad leaders in our platoon together after we got to our assigned position, at the north end of the company. We still only had three squads left, and one of those was at half strength; maybe that was why the captain sent us to the far end of the operation, the north, where we *should* be the last ones to encounter the enemy columns.

"We'll be operating by platoon," Tonio started. "The object is to harass any enemy patrols that come within range. It may fall to us to ambush the enemy's point detachment—two squads out in front of a full company, if the information I have is correct. This is all supposed to be hit-and-run. The captain said that we are to avoid getting pinned down at all costs. Stay mobile. Help is a long way off. We may have to stay on the move until after sunset." He paused. "That's only my guess—that General Chop will want to wait for dark to hit the enemy hard."

It was probably a pretty good guess. I would want to wait until dark, too, if I had my choice; but darkness was a lot of hours away, and we weren't going to be able to simply hide until it arrived. That's the way it goes, more often than not.

"Are we going to have anyone out in the grass to try to catch them from the far side?" I asked.

"No. We talked about that, but the captain decided against it. We'll stay in the trees as long as we can."

"Anyone watching to make sure they don't slip up on us from behind?" I asked.

"Just us," Tonio said. "Keep your eyes open."

"Yeah, you, too," I said. "And try to keep your butt out of the way of any speeding bits of metal."

I RELAYED EVERY BIT OF THE NEWS TO THE MEN in my squad. That's a safety measure, so the squad wouldn't lose time if something happened to me. No matter how many of us went down, the rest would still know what was expected, and the senior man would be in charge.

Tonio had second squad facing to cover our rear for the moment, but once we started moving—or once the shooting started—it would be up to all of us to keep track of everything around us.

"It should be another fifteen or twenty minutes before the enemy point comes within reach of the company," I said at the end of my little talk. "Unless the IFers have snuck people around through the woods, we should have *some* warning before we've got them in our laps."

"And if they get that close, remember to kick them in the balls," Souvana said. If anyone else had said that, I would have taken it as an attempt to lighten the mood. I was sure Souvana was serious though. He was not often moved to levity.

"Balls, teeth, or anything else you can reach," I said. "Just try not to get your foot stuck up somebody's butt." I enjoyed the laughs that earned, even though a couple of them sounded awfully nervous.

"Just remember not to get wasteful with ammunition.

Try to make every shot count." Lieutenant Spike came over then, and that more or less put an end to the pep talk.

Spike would stay with first platoon. Lieutenant Druvauna was with fourth platoon. The captain was with second, Tonio with third. That spread the company command structure out enough to minimize the chances for complete destruction. If we went to operating by platoon, or a decision had to be made immediately by the top man on the scene, there was someone higher up than a mere squad leader to handle it. It didn't bother me to have someone looking over my shoulder, as it were. If a really tough decision came up, I'd be glad to defer. Unlike many of the units I had been in during my ten-plus years in the army, I trusted everyone in the immediate chain of command above me.

A MOMENT OF SILENT MEDITATION—SIMPLY TRYING to clear my mind of every thought and breathing deeply and regularly to relax my body—helped me fine-tune my focus. My eyes remained open. Had anything moved within my field of vision, I would have seen it. I lay in a firing position with my rifle at my shoulder, ready to get into action instantly if I had to, but I felt safe taking the time. I had to push all the extraneous stuff far enough from my consciousness to make sure it wouldn't interfere at an inopportune moment. Our company might be, probably *would* be, called upon to take the first shots in what could be the climactic battle for Unity. Though I had no way to know, I suspected that neither side was likely to have any additional reinforcements arrive soon enough to affect the outcome. It might take a day or a week, but my guess was that the waiting and minor skirmishing were over. Once this fight was fully joined on the ground, it would continue until one side or the other was defeated . . . perhaps destroyed.

When I finished my meditation, I thought we should still have at least ten minutes before our first contact with the enemy reinforcements. But I was already listening for gunfire, and I started scanning the grassland for my first sight of the enemy. I had the magnification on my faceplate at its maximum 2X. After a scan, I looked over each shoulder as well, though there were other eyes to watch our backs. More rarely, I looked around at my men, assuring myself that everyone was paying attention—not that I had any real concerns that one of them might decide to take a nap. They would have had to be brain damaged for a stunt like that.

Ten minutes: there had been no gunfire, no new reports from CIC on the enemy movement. There was nothing of any immediate import to me and my squad. That was a little annoying. I felt that there should be *something* for us. Thinking *No news is good news* didn't help much either. It just shifted some of my annoyance from CIC to my own mind for not coming up with something a little less trite.

Fourteen minutes. I heard the sound of a relatively distant explosion—small, flat, almost certainly a grenade. That was followed quickly by a minor cacophony of automatic rifle fire, punctuated by occasional grenade explosions—tympani marking the rhythm of the first movement of this symphony. None of it was particularly close to our positions, but it was enough to give us a little extra edge—the kind of edge you need going into a firefight.

"Steady," I whispered, though I didn't have my radio transmitter on and none of my men were close enough to hear me directly. Still, I wasn't simply talking to myself. It was almost as if I were trying to get my message to the others by telepathy, by willpower.

That first firefight lasted less than two minutes, then ended abruptly, the coda a final few shots that sounded sharper for their isolation. There hadn't even been time for whoever was involved on our side to report over the company channel. Maybe someone called Captain Fusik directly. I wouldn't know about that. I couldn't monitor his direct channels to the lieutenants or other sergeants.

I didn't think it would be long before the next clash. As it worked out, I was right. Little more than three minutes passed before gunfire broke out again, not quite in the same place. The direction from where I lay was slightly different, and the sounds were louder, the action nearer. This time the noise didn't flare, then fade. It continued, and more weapons joined in, a crescendo—to continue the musical analogy I somehow got myself into.

Instinct made me check to make certain that my rifle's safety was off. I squinted a little as I continued to scan the terrain in front of me. I was watching more closely now, taking more time, more care. It was during that time that I started to hear calls on the company channel, just a few words here and there, not always complete reports. Sometimes it was just "Enemy movement on my left," or something similar. Twice it was reports of men hit and needing medical attention.

Fourth platoon reported that it was pulling back to escape an IFer attempt to encircle them. Third platoon moved to catch the enemy from the side. Then I heard a call from Sergeant Chouvana. He didn't identify himself. I recognized his voice. "IFer platoon coming to within one-fifty yards of us, slightly right of center." That would put the enemy between second squad and fourth squad, too far right for my squad to get involved immediately. But it did tell us how close the enemy was.

I shifted my position a little, and noticed the nearest of my men doing the same. We were all cheating a bit to the right, ready to give cover to the rest of the platoon if we needed to. That sort of thing is almost instinctive. But that particular IFer platoon withdrew as soon as they came under fire, back and to their left. That brought them more directly in front of us, but by that time they were out of easy range. I only saw one brief flash of movement, more than 250 yards out. I did not bother firing. The target was out of sight too quickly.

As soon as I was certain that this batch of the enemy was moving away from us, I glanced toward Lieutenant Spike, to see if he had noticed that enemy platoon—and to see if we might be getting up and moving. The ghuroh lieutenant turned toward me at almost the same instant. He shook his head and made a gesture with his hand, palm down. We were staying put. I didn't expect it to last too long, but everything was minute to minute. It can't be anything else in our brand of combat. Still, in spec ops, we go to both extremes. We might lie in ambush for hours, even days, then have to move hard and fast afterward.

I was certain we'd do more than our share of moving in the next hours—if not days or however long it lasted. For the time being, at least, if we got pinned down and *couldn't* move, we were going to be in BIG trouble.

"Heads up!" That was Captain Fusik's voice, on the all-hands channel.

I took my right hand away from the trigger of my rifle long enough to wipe sweat from my palm. I've always had that to worry about. I sucked in a deep breath and kept looking for the enemy. *Wait.* Time went into its stretch mode, where every second feels as if it takes several minutes to crawl past. I was acutely aware of every breath I took, without taking any of my attention from where it belonged. When I could spare half a second, I glanced toward the lieutenant, figuring that he might get the word before the rest of us did.

Gunfire erupted south of our platoon—no more than three hundred yards away. The volume was greater than in the earlier scuffles or the continuing low-level exchange that had been going on for the last ten minutes or so—farther away. The quick flutter in my chest was evidence that my body thought we were about to get into the mix, and then the captain was on the company channel again.

"Up and at 'em," he said. "Your course is one-six-eight degrees. Hit and back off quickly, on my command."

By the time Captain Fusik finished that, we were already up and moving, rifles at the ready, forming up by squad in a series of short skirmish lines. First platoon would hit the flank of the enemy. We *hoped* that they would be concentrating on the other platoons, that they wouldn't see us coming until we had done our damage and pulled back.

Then, when they *did* turn toward us, one of the other platoons could hit from a different angle. That had to be the nature of this game, given the disparity in strength. But if we played it right, we might do considerably more damage than we suffered in return. It would take skill and timing . . . and more than a little luck.

Luck was the part we couldn't calculate going in.

CHAPTER 19

WE GOT TO WITHIN 180 YARDS OF THE ENEMY, stalking, taking every care with moving from cover to cover, avoiding the sudden movements and jerky motions that draw the eye. The IFer patrol we were after was well in front of the left—western—column of the enemy force. From CIC, we heard that there was a gap of more than two hundred yards between that point detachment and the column behind them. That wouldn't give us much time to work.

We managed to spot the IFers before they spotted us, which was the point of the exercise. They were out in the open, wading through the deep grass instead of moving along the edge of the forest, where they would have had some cover.

What I saw were the backs of three tonatin helmets. They are distinctive enough that it's impossible to mistake them, even at extreme range. I assume that Captain Fusik was monitoring some of the helmet cameras in our platoon, because the order to open fire came five seconds after I caught my first glimpse of the enemy. We loosed a quick flurry of grenades, underscored by rifle fire from the rest of the platoon. The tonatin helmets I had spotted went down instantly, the men under them casualties. We chewed up a considerable patch of grassland even though the captain only gave us twenty seconds before he ordered us to start withdrawing on a compass heading of 115 degrees.

Before the tonatin patrol could return effective fire in our direction, they were being hit by our second platoon, and fourth platoon picked up after that. It was a quick cadence, with no gaps between the first few strikes. The captain ordered us back in from a different angle—two hundred yards from the point where we had hit the enemy the first time. That put us out in the open as well, fifty yards from the nearest trees. But we didn't get to take a second turn. Third platoon reported that the enemy's point unit had been neutralized—polite military-speak for destroyed. Maybe not all of them had been killed, but they were no longer a fighting unit.

We didn't have time to pat ourselves on the back, because there were a lot more IFers, and instead of a two-platoon point or flanking patrol, the next time it would be a full company, perhaps more, and they would be looking for ways to counter our attacks—or preempt them. They would be looking for us to try the same kind of sucker punch. If we did, we wouldn't get off as easily as we had this time. There hadn't been any casualties in first platoon, and I hadn't heard any reports of casualties in the other platoons—though no one would have broken electronic silence to report casualties unless there were serious wounds that needed medtechs immediately. Even then, concern for the safety of the rest of the unit might have kept anyone off the radio.

The captain relayed a new heading for us, and we moved again, back inside the wooded area—then south, just a few yards from the last rank of trees. The IFer main force was out on the savanna, three hundred yards from serious cover. To do much effective damage, we would have to leave the cover of the trees and get closer. We could put down rifle fire, but at three hundred yards, through that high grass, it would not be *efficient*. We had to be efficient or risk running out of ammunition far from any hope of resupply.

There was a clear demarcation line to the edge of the woods, almost as if the forest had been planted and tended by sentient beings rather than growing wild—I could see that the IFers now had three advance units, each two or three platoons in strength, spread out in an arc in front of the two columns. The main force seemed ready to bypass the woods altogether, but there was a flanking patrol—a full company—coming up under cover of the trees. Where we were, the flankers would pass to our west, while the main force passed to the east.

Tonio went from squad to squad to pass the orders. We were to take cover and lie low while the rest of our company hit at the flankers. Our job would be to slow down any reinforcement for that flanking patrol. If the flankers tried to retreat toward the main force, we would spring an ambush on them, slow them down to let the rest of the company get back into the act.

"This could get hairy for us," Tonio said before he left me, "so watch your head and your butt. Keep 'em down."

"You too," I said, but he was already running toward second squad.

WE HAD A BIT OF A WAIT, A CHANCE TO CATCH our breath. We had all fixed bayonets, a precaution in case the fighting got *too* close. I kept a nervous eye on the enemy main force, mostly by watching their positions on my map, worried that they might send a patrol-in-force our way—or even change course and put their whole army in our laps. If they did that, we wouldn't have many chances to escape with our skins intact. They could do to us what we were hoping to do to their flankers.

"When they get here, we keep our heads down until they're so close we can't miss. If we're careful, they won't see us, even if they're looking for trouble on this side. We hold off as long as possible, then hit them with everything we've got." I gave that message to both fire teams in my squad. Either Tonio or Lieutenant Spike would signal the start of our attack—by firing the first shots. Then it would be everyone laying down all the fire he could until we got a signal to stop, or until the enemy flanking patrol was out of range . . . or out of live, unwounded soldiers.

Ten minutes after Tonio left me, the other platoons of our company hit that enemy flanking patrol. Two platoons hit at once. The final platoon joined in after the IFer flankers responded to the initial attack. This time, it was not hit-and-run, the way we had smashed the point platoon in front of the one enemy column. Our people hit and kept hitting, trying to make the enemy flankers worry that we had a larger force than we did, perhaps strong enough to wipe them out.

The IFer flankers met the attack in place for nearly ten minutes before they started to withdraw slowly—heading east, directly toward first platoon—using steady fire-and-maneuver tactics, just as we would have in that spot. We got a "head-up" warning from Lead Sergeant Deelock. The retreating IFer patrol was within 250 yards of our positions. They had taken casualties, but not *heavy* losses. The company was still close to 90 percent in strength. It remained a coherent force, withdrawing under discipline. It was no mindless retreat.

I didn't expect that first platoon would be enough of a shock to the enemy patrol to change that last bit, but we could help whittle their numbers down to the point where they would be less of a threat, until they got help. The enemy main force was too close to assume that the flankers would be abandoned. It wouldn't take long for the IFers to reinforce that patrol or get my platoon in the middle. If we made things too hot, the enemy *did* have artillery on the ground, and they might use that, even though it would be like swatting mosquitoes with a sledgehammer.

A more likely response would be for the enemy commander to send more troops toward us, two or three companies at once—perhaps an entire battalion—to try to stop the attrition we were causing. He would *have* to try something major. We might only be nibbling at his side, but if we went unchecked, we could cause serious losses before the enemy could engage our main force. The holes we punched in the enemy organization would hurt them as much as the soldiers we killed or put out of action.

My rangefinder put the first tonatin I spotted this time 185 yards out. The forest was thicker near the edge, and the IFer patrol was being careful. For nearly a minute, I could see only that one enemy soldier, and *he* moved in and out of my line of sight, hidden by trees between us. I wasn't concerned by that. If I was having difficulty seeing enemy soldiers who were on their feet and moving, the enemy would find it almost impossible to see us lying motionless on the ground. We could let the enemy get almost within spitting range—close enough that we could take out a large portion of them before they were aware that they had an enemy behind them.

As a *practical* matter, I expected the order to open fire to come while the nearest enemy soldiers were between sixty and eighty yards away, perhaps a little farther, to let our men with grenade launchers operate effectively—dropping their little bombs out where the shrapnel would not endanger our own people.

You don't even *consider* fighting "fair" in combat. You take every unfair advantage you can find, and you keep looking for more. Screw the Marquis of Queensbury and his rules, and all the conventions for "civilized war" that people have come up with over the centuries. War is no game. If you don't play to win, you're asking to lose. To die.

As the enemy patrol moved closer—their attention focused on our three platoons that were pressing them—I spotted more targets, mostly the backs of heads, sometimes shoulders or half a torso. Still, it was here and gone again as trees came into the line between me and the targets. We were spread out enough that there shouldn't be much *dependable* cover for the enemy troops in the first few seconds after we opened fire. There was also a reasonable hope that those first few seconds would be massively lethal to the patrol.

By the time the nearest line of the enemy flankers reached a point 120 yards from us, I was getting nervous. I knew, intellectually, that we needed to let them get closer before we put them under fire. If we opened up at that range, too many tonatin might escape. We might have a real melee on our hands, one that would give the IFer commander time to move more soldiers into the fight.

One hundred yards. I heard a report from CIC that the enemy artillery—its remote-controlled gun carriages—was moving away from the columns, the self-propelled guns operating independently instead of rolling along as if on parade. That increased my nervousness. If they were beginning to maneuver—to avoid being targeted by our artillery—they might be ready to enter the fight, and at the current range, between seven hundred and a thousand yards from me, they could lay a shell within inches of the aiming point.

The flanking patrol we were waiting for closed to within ninety yards. There was some rifle fire going over our heads, coming from our platoons on the other side of the IFer patrol. I glanced up once and saw where a bullet had scored the trunk of the next tree to my left fifteen feet up. The angle seemed to indicate that it had come in from about seventy-five degrees to our line, a little from the right of dead ahead.

Come on, Lieutenant, I thought. *We've got to get working before our people get close enough that we might hit some of them by mistake.* I was beginning to get very antsy. The nearest IFers were close enough that I could make out the seams on their combat uniforms.

The lieutenant and Tonio opened up with their rifles. There wasn't enough of a gap between the two to tell who was first. The rest of us started pulling triggers as soon as the sound reached us.

"Mind your targets," I said on my squad channel. "Short,

aimed bursts or single shots. We've got our own people on the other side." And we didn't have unlimited ammunition.

It wasn't ten seconds after that when JL Spike ordered us to shift to the right. I guess he was also concerned about inflicting friendly casualties. We started crawling from tree to tree, stopping to fire anytime we saw anything that appeared to possibly be an enemy soldier. The grenadiers—one per fire team—kept up a heavier volume of fire, dropping their grenades around the area where we figured the bulk of that flanking patrol was. In heavy forest, grenades aren't as effective as out in the open. Tree trunks and limbs absorb too much shrapnel, and those trees can deflect grenades en route, unpredictably. That was another reason for not letting the enemy get *too* close. We didn't want any grenades bouncing back into our own laps.

It took the flankers nearly a minute to respond effectively. They chose what may have been the best of a series of poor options that were available to them. They charged us, the smaller of the units that had them targeted. They were going to try to roll right over us to get away from the larger force on the other side.

If they had started that maneuver immediately after we started firing, they might have had a damned good chance of succeeding, of getting at least half their men out of the trap. But those fifty-odd seconds they delayed cost them so many men that we weren't too badly outnumbered when they did rush us. In addition, we were flat on the ground, sheltered by tree trunks, and they had to expose themselves to close the distance between us quickly enough to give them any chance.

They got too close for us to use rocket-propelled grenades, so the grenadiers switched to their rifles. Forty yards. Thirty. By that time, our numbers were almost even, with the figures rapidly moving to our advantage. The enemy was too close for our prone positions to help any longer. I had started pulling a knee up to make the order I knew was coming a little easier to obey quickly.

"Up and at 'em," the lieutenant said—shouted—over the platoon channel.

We got to our feet firing—short bursts at targets we could see. I couldn't spare any attention to keep track of my men. Even when I saw someone go down at the edge of my peripheral vision I didn't dare take even a fraction of a second to see who it was. Or who the second man down in the squad was. I couldn't even be certain that only two went down. We closed with the enemy quickly once both sides were moving.

I scarcely had time to wonder how far behind these IFers the rest of our company was before we got right into face-to-face fighting with bayonets and rifle butts. A tonatin charged me. I could see his clawlike hand working the trigger of his rifle, but he was working with an empty magazine. My last couple of shots at him must have gone wide somehow. At least, I didn't stop him.

He thrust his bayonet at me, more or less on a line with my throat. I knocked the blade down and to the side with the bayonet end of my rifle, then came around with the butt, aiming for his head. He shifted his weapon along mine, far enough that he was able to push me back. That tonatin seemed to be nearly as strong as a porracci. I didn't quite lose my balance as I stepped back and turned, but he pressed, staying too close for me to get my rifle muzzle lined up to take him out with a bullet.

The tonatin was physically stronger than me, and he was at least my equal with the bayonet, moving his weapon with as much ease as I might twirl a drumstick. It was all I could do to parry his efforts, and he kept me totally on the defensive . . . for what seemed to be a year or two.

I slipped. My right foot went through something mushy and slippery, and I moved farther to that side than I intended—farther than the tonatin expected. He had started to swing his rifle butt for my head. If I hadn't slid through something a native animal left on the forest floor, he would have connected because my counter would have been too little, too late.

As it was, his rifle butt went over my head. My rifle was free for the instant I needed to line the muzzle up with his middle and blow off a burst of a dozen rounds that nearly cut him in two. I could see enough of his face through the tinted visor of his helmet to recognize a look of utter astonishment.

I turned to help the man from my squad nearest me. Souvana. His left arm was so bloody it looked as if he had dipped it in a barrel of red paint. He was wielding his rifle as if it were a saber, one-handed, and holding off a tonatin who had two good arms. I think Souvana might have taken the man out on his own if I had given him a little time. Instead, I drove my bayonet into the tonatin's back, slicing in from right of the spine. When he started to fall forward, Souvana's blade went into his throat.

Then, almost as if by magic, there were a lot more Alliance uniforms in the fight, giving us a two-to-one advantage. The other platoons had caught up with the enemy patrol. After that, the fight ended in seconds.

Not one tonatin from that patrol surrendered. Each fought as long as he could. The only prisoners we took were wounded too badly to resist. We left them for their people to collect. It was time for us to move, before the enemy got another crack at us. We had all we could do to move our own wounded.

WE PULLED STRAIGHT WEST, DEEPER INTO THE forest, to keep out of reach of the IFer main force. Our artillery helped, dropping just a few shells into the enemy columns. This wasn't an all-out barrage. Maybe we didn't have enough ammunition for the howitzers and self-propelled rocket launchers for that. If we had all that much ammunition for the heavy weapons, the general would have used them earlier, to flatten as much of the new enemy force as possible before they could get near the settlement. My guess was that we were trying to disrupt the enemy's movement and maybe give our company a little help getting out of the way.

We couldn't move at anything *near* full speed. Our wounded slowed us. The two men who had been hit in my squad were Souvana and Zhirie. Souvana had been the first I had seen fall, and he had gotten back up and kept fighting despite the loss of considerable blood. Porracci don't let wounds stop them for long. Once his arm had been bandaged, he was ready to go—and able to move under his own power. That was lucky. It probably would have taken three of us to carry him. Zhirie had been wounded more seriously. He had to be carried, but the medtech who treated him said he *thought* that the abarand would recover.

At least there were no IFers between us and the settlement.

CHAPTER 20

WE WERE MET BY SUPPORT PERSONNEL—
including medtechs with stretchers and portable medtanks
for the seriously wounded. With a full company of infantry
around us, we were able to relax a little. For the moment,
at least, we were on the sidelines. Once there were extra
hands to carry and care for the wounded, we made better
time. There were porracci and ghuroh to tote the stretchers,
so they could keep up with a fast pace on the march without difficulty. When we reached the northern edge of the
woods and had to cross that last long stretch of savanna,
there were more troops between us and any enemy force in
the area. I wasn't certain that I understood *why* we were
being afforded such deluxe treatment, but I didn't complain.

There were reports on the CIC channel about troop
movements, but I couldn't pay full attention. My brain was
seminumb, not uncommon after a fight. I had lost my
adrenaline rush. There is a kind of exhaustion that sets in
even when it might seem that it shouldn't. Our physical ex-
ertions certainly hadn't been enough to account for it, but
I was dragging, and a lot of the men around me also
were—with the usual exception of the porracci and
ghuroh.

The battle for Unity wasn't over. I knew that the worst

might be yet to come, but I could hardly have cared less. I had all the challenge I could handle to keep my eyes open and put one foot in front of the other. Our reinforcements were moving. The IFer reinforcements were moving. Everyone was playing for position, trying to get any possible edge over the other guy.

I did glean one fact from the broadcasts. The new IFer troops were sliding toward the eastern edge of our perimeter around the settlement—heading for the more wooded territory there. They wanted better cover for their soldiers and artillery, a chance for some concealment. I could hardly blame them for that. We tried for the same thing whenever possible. The last thing you want when someone is out to ventilate your body is to stand in the open and make it easy for them.

As usual, CIC was much less informative about our movements. Our company went back inside our original perimeter. We were holding that oval line, though with fewer troops than before. Captain Fusik was briefed after we got inside. He passed the word to his lieutenants and sergeants. I got the word from Tonio. One of our line battalions had moved out of the perimeter to link up with 2nd Combined Regiment. Two of the other three Ranger companies had moved out as well. They were concentrating on the IFers who had already been on Unity, doing what they could to keep them from linking up with their reinforcements.

Inside the perimeter, we were told to eat and get what rest we could, that we would have a few hours before any new action—*unless* the enemy attacked the perimeter. Otherwise, we would not be going out until sometime after sunset.

Souvana had to be ordered off with the medtechs for treatment. He kept insisting that he was still fit for duty, even after losing three or four quarts of blood. I had to get right in his face.

"What's it going to take to convince you?" I asked—shouted. "If I have to, I can take you down in eight seconds. That's how much blood you lost." For an instant, I thought he was going to take me up on that, and I wasn't *quite* certain that he was weak enough for me to take him. I guess Souvana wasn't certain I couldn't, and losing to me in hand-to-hand combat would be an unspeakable horror. He went with the medtechs.

Zhirie offered no objections. He was still nearly unconscious, though the medtech who treated him said he would be fit for duty within four hours.

I accepted that. As long as there were no limbs or major organs that had to be regenerated, or significant nerve damage, four hours would take care of most wounds. The problem in combat is keeping a man alive long enough for the medtechs to get him into a tank.

There was no hot food waiting for us when we reached our bivouac site, but there was hot coffee. Coffee is a vice most species have adopted since coming in contact with humans. They seem to like the effect of caffeine. Even divotect can get wired on coffee. There were also crates of battle rations, stacked by species. We got our coffee and food, then found places to sit. Robbie McGraw plopped on the ground next to me.

"We got off lucky," he said, while I took a drink of coffee. Under the circumstances, the drink tasted better than it was.

"So far," I replied. "This fight isn't over. The real battle hasn't even started."

Robbie shrugged. For the first time, I noticed that he had lost weight since joining the squad—more than seemed right; *everyone* lost weight on campaign. "Probably not, but we're in a lot better shape than we *might* be. The first damned batch of IFers who landed know how hard we can bite. It's got to make them pause. If they don't have any more troops coming in, we can take the ones on the ground."

I took the time to finish chewing the bit of meat in my mouth and swallowed before I answered. "I hope so, but it's not going to be an Alliance Day parade. We could be in for our hardest fight ever. These new IFers are all tonatin.

We're sure as hell not going to simply scare them to death."

"Yeah, I know." There was a long pause, while we both ate—though Robbie was only picking at his food—before he said anything else. "I keep wondering what it's going to take to *end* this damn war. Does it just go on forever, or until one side or the other doesn't have the soldiers or ships to send on another campaign? I get to thinking about the thousands of settled worlds, all the species, the colonies. I read someplace that the Ilion Federation might have the capacity to field a billion soldiers over four or five years."

"And the same for the Alliance," I said. "I saw that report, too. If you read it to the end, though, you saw that both sides would be bankrupt long before they could train that many men. That was the whole point of that committee's report, that neither side could afford this war in the first place."

"I guess the right people didn't read it."

"No shit." I stared at him, watching at the way he played with his food—absentmindedly. "You'd better start doing some real eating. The way you're losing weight, you won't be able to take either Oyo or Ala before long."

Robbie made a face at his ration pack. "No appetite."

"I don't give a damn. None of us have much appetite. That doesn't make any difference. Eat. I've got to know you're not going to faint from hunger. You can't pull your weight if you don't have any weight to pull. This is no place for a frigging anorexic prima donna."

I FORCED ROBBIE TO EAT THAT WHOLE RATION pack, then half of a second. I gave him a direct order to eat that much again at sunset, before we went out. And I told him I was going to keep an eye on him, and that he had best start putting some weight back on. He wasn't enthusiastic, but he did say that he would do what I told him to. Not that he had much choice—I threatened to have Kiervauna sit on his chest while I force-fed him if he didn't eat on his own.

Then it was time for sleep. I turned the volume down on my helmet radio—as low as I dared since I had to be able to hear any emergency call—and lay on my side. It wasn't much of a surprise that I fell asleep almost instantly. Nor was it any surprise that I didn't stay asleep. I kept waking, at sounds, maybe even at *dreamed* sounds. As muted as I had my radio volume, I woke at each call on one of the channels I was monitoring, even when the call was not for me. After the first stretch of sleep, I did not go very deep. It didn't take much to rouse me. And each time I woke, it was a bit harder to get back to sleep.

It was about thirty minutes before sunset when I quit trying. With trees over and around us, it was nearly dusky at the campsite, but not quite dark enough to need my helmet's night-vision help. Most of the squad was still sleeping—generally each man some feet from the next. There was one exception. Oyo and Ala were close together, back to back. Biraunta are similar to some species of Earth monkeys—not just in the way they look. They are intensely social, and feel more secure clustered together. They are happiest in a crowd of their own kind. One biraunta on his own, away from any others of his species, is a very nervous individual. That might contribute to their excellence as scouts. When you're alone doing a job like that, being nervous helps keep you sharp. You pick up clues a relaxed soldier might miss.

Souvana and Zhirie were back, certified ready for duty. They were both awake, sitting on the ground, apart from each other and from the sleeping members of the squad, looking in different directions. Souvana was eating—mechanically, methodically. Zhirie was just staring—at nothing in particular, so far as I could tell. I went and got down on one knee next to him, which put our eyes nearly on a level.

"How are you feeling?" I asked. He blinked several times as he focused on my face. Abarand eyelids move from both sides to the middle. Only abarand and divotect are built that way. The other species all have structures more similar to human eyes. It was still disconcerting, but I no longer flinched the way I had at first.

Zhirie let out a sigh, almost a musical passage the way abarand do it. "I dreamed I could really fly," he said, his voice wistful. I knew what he was referring to. Abarand derived from flying mammals. They still had rudimentary wings—like the flying squirrels of Earth—but like those squirrels, abarand could no longer truly fly, just glide. I hadn't seen Zhirie in the air, but Jaibie, the abarand who had been in the squad at the beginning, had been impressive. I saw him do a glide of thirty yards once—tree to tree. One of the abarands' beliefs is that when they die they will be able to *really* fly the way their primitive ancestors could. That belief is an important part of their religion and folklore.

"There is still work for you in this life," I told him. "You don't want to fly in a hurricane." That might not make much sense to a human, but it does to an abarand—or so I had been told when they gave us classes on the other species in the Alliance to help us understand each other.

Zhirie went through another routine of blinking before he nodded, using the human gesture rather than the abarand equivalent, which was a specific sort of flap of one wing, from the elbow out.

"Get something to eat," I said as I stood. "We'll probably be working tonight." He nodded again, and I walked over to Souvana. I remained on my feet there, standing in front of him.

Souvana looked up slowly. "Do you still wish to try to take me down in eight seconds?" he asked, his voice as soft as a porracci's could ever get, evidently not wanting to wake anyone who was still sleeping—a rare show of concern for his squad mates.

I grinned at him. "Not now that you're healthy again," I admitted. "Not unless I have to, and since we don't run this operation the way your people operate their armies, I don't."

Porracci determine rank purely by physical prowess. You square off against the soldier whose position you want and the winner takes the higher rank. Their entire society runs that way. I'm not sure it's any worse than the way we choose our political leaders; and in the case of the army, there might even be advantages to the porracci way.

He returned my grin, showing all thirty-six very large teeth. He could have fit a whole cantaloupe in his mouth. "Very wise," he said. Souvana still thought he was more qualified to be squad leader than I was, but he no longer reminded me of that every time I turned around or insisted that his way was superior to mine every time I made a decision. He was still quick with advice, but that's proper. Besides leading the squad's second fire team, he was my assistant squad leader. He was abrasive by nature, but, to give him his due, he was a damned good soldier to have at your side in a fight. I might not like him much, but I trusted him . . . and I respected him.

I GRABBED A RATION PACK AND WENT BACK TO SIT with my gear. Eat when you can. I had pushed that notion at subordinates so often that I did it myself almost without thinking. But I had hardly started eating before I had a call from Lead Sergeant Deelock.

"Get your men awake. Tell them to eat and get ready. Then you get over to the company CP. Captain Fusik will brief all the sergeants in ten minutes. We've got work to do."

CHAPTER 21

"THIS IS THE SITUATION," CAPTAIN FUSIK STARTED.
"It appears that the fight for Unity is approaching a climax.
There has been only scattered small-scale fighting since
we came back in earlier. The IFers are moving all their reinforcements toward the northeast sector of our perimeter,
and they've moved a third of the tonatin who were already
here to support that movement, with the rest apparently
poised to pressure the rest of the perimeter. We've done
what we could to harass the IFers, particularly the latest ar-
rivals, nibbling at their strength without doing any serious
damage.

"We're rearranging our dispositions. General Chop wants
to force a decisive battle before the IFers bring in more
troops. His staff and CIC estimate that there is a good
chance the Ilion Federation *will* try to vector additional reinforcements here. The pessimists say that those troops
might show up in-system virtually any second. The opti-
mists suggest that if they could bring more troops in that
quickly, they would have held the ones that have come in
back and brought everyone in at once, to overwhelm us in
one *coup de main.*

"I happen to agree with the latter opinion, but no one
asked me." He shrugged. "I've been wrong at least once or
twice, so don't take my optimism for gospel. Both HW

battalions will stage from inside the perimeter, targeting the main enemy force as practical—the intent being to keep the fight as far away from the colonists' settlement as possible. The line battalions will either stage from inside the perimeter or from where they are now—those units that are still outside. The local militia and a bare minimum of line soldiers will move to the inner line of defenses to provide a last line of defense for the civilians. All of the Ranger companies will sortie to get behind the enemy. We will operate as conditions permit—harass and distract the IFers by all possible means, attack their artillery units if we get a chance, and, in general, raise whatever hell we can.

"Our cup of tea—as some of those from Earth's tea-drinking regions might put it. B Company will exfiltrate by platoon. Initially, we will also operate that way. I will be with first platoon, Lead Sergeant Deelock with second, Senior Lieutenant Druvauna with third, and Junior Lieutenant Spike with fourth. If necessary, we will split into squads later on. That depends on the local tactical situation. The senior man with each platoon will make that determination if the need for electronic silence precludes confirmation from above. And if individual squads operate apart from the rest of their platoon, the squad leader will naturally assume tactical control." I could feel my forehead move into a quizzical expression. There was no need for the captain to get so didactic. This was all basic stuff. Routine. Maybe I'm not the only one who gets nervous before action.

"We will start moving to the perimeter in thirty minutes," Fusik continued. "Make sure everyone has all the ammunition they can carry, as well as food for three days. I don't know that this operation will take that long, but getting any resupply will be exceptionally difficult, if not impossible."

BY THE TIME WE LEFT OUR CAMP, EVERY MAN IN first platoon was carrying far more than his normal "basic

load" of ammunition—some double. I took the captain at
his word and made sure that my men did. In training, on
any "safe" world, we all would have griped at being forced
to carry that much extra weight, but no one said anything
now. A couple of men were bogged down with all the extra
ammunition they were toting, but they had taken it of their
own free will. I noticed that both porracci also carried
extra ammunition for the biraunta—the only ones in the
unit who didn't use the standard caliber ammunition. The
extra meal packs were almost an afterthought, and the
weight of rations for three days—*light* rations, since am-
munitions was more important than food—was almost in-
significant by comparison.

We ate as much as we could before we left. This time I
didn't have to prompt anyone to eat. Taste didn't count.
Hunger, or the lack of it, didn't count. We just put as much
food in our mouths as we could swallow and washed it
down with extra water. The easiest way to carry food is in
your stomach.

The CIC information channel was almost abnormally
quiet. There were only brief, well-spaced comments about
enemy movements, and nothing about our movements. We
were doing a lot of shuffling around, abandoning the outer
perimeter and falling back to the inner line—shorter, easier to defend. Add to that the Ranger companies, which
were all moving away from the perimeter and the movement of our reinforcing units that had stayed outside. It
was musical chairs on an enormous scale.

Between the two armies, there were twenty-five thousand soldiers moving toward what might be a pivotal battle in the war—on a world that no sentient being had ever
set foot on until the last few years, that few people except
those of us in the system had even *heard* of. Overhead, the
opposing fleets continued their own desultory battle, both
sides trying to keep their own ships safe while preventing
the enemy from taking part in the fight on the ground.

We had no problems getting through the outer perimeter. Although the line troops had started moving back,

there were electronic snoops and land mines planted beyond the perimeter, and we had safe paths clearly marked on our maps and helmet displays. Still, we went through the line one platoon at a time, with the rest of the company in position to provide support if an IFer patrol showed up at the wrong time.

It was unlikely that there would be more than a small enemy patrol in the area—if that. With the maximum effort the IFers seemed intent on making in the northeast quadrant, it looked to be fairly easy to slip out in the southeast. But we treated the situation as if we expected to find IFers waiting.

There was grassland to cross before we could get to the trees, and little of the grass near our initial perimeter was still standing. Major sections had been trampled flat. Others had been burned or chopped because of heavy rifle fire.

One thing I hadn't thought about was the strange fact that there were no rivers in the immediate vicinity of the settlement. The nearest was fifteen miles north of the extended village that the colonists had established. The few pieces of open water closer were generally very small creeks, the sort you can often step or hop across without getting wet. That seemed inconsistent—when it did occur to me—with the tall grass and the forests. It didn't seem to be the kind of verdant landscape that rain alone could account for. Maybe there were underground rivers, or springs.

Large rivers complicate operations for ground forces. They can either be barricades to your mission or a natural defensive bulwark. The fight for Olviat had featured a river that couldn't be waded and whose bridges had been destroyed. It doesn't matter how strong you are, a soldier carrying more than half his body weight in weapons and ammunition can't swim much farther than the average rock, and a self-propelled gun or rocket launcher makes that rock look positively buoyant.

THE IFER ASSAULT ON THE PERIMETER STARTED two hours before midnight. The point of the attack was where we had expected it, on the northeast part of the perimeter, coming from the forested area closest to our lines. There was no attempt at subterfuge. They just moved an entire regiment toward one point on the line. We had also concentrated forces there.

Although we were prepared for trouble, no one seemed to pay a platoon of Rangers any mind as we left the perimeter and moved at a rapid cross-country pace toward the trees. We reached that area, a mile from our now-abandoned front line, in under twenty minutes. Once we were safe from casual observation, the captain gave us five minutes to catch our breath.

"That's all we can spare," he told Tonio. The two of them had been moving with my squad, in the middle of the platoon. "We've got a lot of ground to cover."

After the break, the squads switched places. My squad moved to the point, with my biraunta in front as scouts. They got up in the trees—the first time they had really had a chance to operate in their natural element on Unity—and moved ahead to look for enemy patrols. Until we got near the rear of the enemy main force, we hoped to avoid contact with IFers. Skirmishes with patrols would slow us down even if we didn't suffer casualties, and any fighting would tell the enemy where we were.

Although spring was fairly advanced, the temperature had been moderate, and clouds had moved in before sunset. The wind was blowing at ten miles per hour. Even carrying all the extra weight and pushing the pace, I had only a light film of sweat on my face. My breathing remained easy.

We pushed on for another hour before the captain gave us a second break, and the squads shifted position again. That was fairly standard practice, to keep any man or squad from getting complacent doing "the same old thing." This shift left my squad with the tail end—rear guard. The captain used most of the break for a conference with Tonio and the squad leaders.

"We're going to have to slow down a little," Fusik explained. "Sometime in the next hour we'll cross into the IFer defensive zone. They'll have strong patrols on the flank and we're not far enough east to get behind them. If possible, I want to get past the IFer flankers so we can hit the nearest of their main columns. CIC says they have three columns moving in. The center one is concentrated at the apex of their advance, a wedge in depth, set up to let them keep up the pressure until they take one hell of a lot of casualties. The outside columns are stretched out more, ready to push forward or swivel to the side as needed. They hope to poke a hole in our perimeter, then roll up the line to one side or both."

"If we *are* detected by a flanking patrol, do we stop and fight or try to break contact immediately so we can get past them?" Tonio asked.

Fusik shook his head slowly. "I can't lay anything out solid in advance. We'll play this strictly by ear. Ideally, we'll get past the flanking patrols without being detected. If we are spotted, we hope to avoid a firefight, go inside the line of flankers. Just knowing we're operating that close to their main column ought to stir things up among the IFer commander. If we can't escape a firefight . . ." The captain shrugged. "As I said, we'll deal with that if the situation arises. Just keep an eye on me for orders."

"Any updates yet on how the main battle is shaping up, Captain?" I asked.

"Not really. The fighting has started." He gestured with a hand. "We can hear that." He waited for me to nod. "Don't worry, Dragon. We'll get our share. I don't think this fight is going to end in one night."

I tried to put a smile on my face, but I can't swear that I was successful. Some people take too much from my nickname. The last thing on my mind had been getting a share of the fight. I was more hoping that things would be going so well that we might not need to get up to our earlobes in the battle. If they wanted to finish it before I could join in, I'd lead the cheering.

"I just didn't bring my razor, Captain," I said, trying to

make the best of the moment. "Thought a couple extra bullets might do more good."

Captain Fusik damned near laughed out loud. Tonio shook his head, trying to hide a grin.

No, IT WASN'T ANY OF THAT "LAUGHING IN THE face of death" crap you see in bad adventure vids. We weren't *in* that kind of situation. It was just an attempt to lighten the mood, ease the tension—not just for me, but for Tonio and the captain as well. Bad jokes often work best . . . and if there's one thing I'm good at, it's bad jokes, the kind where the audience doesn't know whether to laugh or groan. Groans can be more satisfying, and the looks on their faces when I give out with a real stinker.

We got started again, with my squad in the back. I had Souvana's fire team last. He's good in that position—or any other—and he likes to be rear guard. As usual, he was Tail-End Charley himself, instead of in the middle of his team where the "Book" said the team leader belonged. With just about anyone else, I would have interfered, but I let the porracci corporal operate the way he wanted to—for the most part.

As we continued toward the flank of the enemy army, our pace continued to slow, in several discrete steps. The biraunta on point were in the trees, but not as far ahead of the platoon as earlier. The point fire team on the ground started moving almost in hesitation step, carefully searching the area in front of them for land mines, booby traps, or snoops—as well as looking for any indication of enemy soldiers in our vicinity.

After twenty-five minutes we were almost creeping. Like most of the men around me, I was hunched over to provide a minimal target. I held my rifle at the ready. There was a round in the chamber, and the safety was off. My finger was on the edge of the trigger guard—not on the trigger because it would be too easy to fire a burst by accident.

It doesn't take long to become almost paranoid, except

it isn't paranoia because there *is* someone out to get you. You know the enemy is in the area. You expect action almost any second, and as the seconds—and minutes—go by without action, your nerves start to knot around themselves. Up to a point, that's good, but you can't let it get too extreme, or you'll be too tight to react when trouble finally does come.

If you've managed yourself well—and that's where something like humor, even bad humor, can help—when the fight does start, that inner spring will unwind quickly, and you'll dive right into the shoot, relaxed enough to hit something smaller than the broad side of a barn. If you haven't managed your nerves well, the best possible result is that you won't be much use to your comrades at first. At worst, you might be dead, along with anyone close to you.

Time seemed to get stuck in molasses. I was right to the edge, my senses as alert as they could possibly be. Sometimes I think I could hear a worm burrowing along ten feet underground when I get like that.

I was too far away to see fourth squad's biraunta drop out of the trees and move back to report that he had spotted an enemy patrol, but it didn't take long for that news—passed along by hand signals—to reach me. The platoon stopped moving and went to ground, slowly, so undue movement wouldn't give us away. We alternated facing one side or the other while we waited for Tonio and the captain to confer and decide what to do. I divided my attention between the forest and looking up toward where the captain was—so I wouldn't miss the signal when it came.

After less than a minute, Tonio got up on his knees and passed the word. We were going to detour right to try to bypass the enemy patrol that had been spotted. They were moving obliquely across our front from northeast to southwest. I was to start my squad first. We were farthest from the IFer patrol and least likely to be spotted. Once we moved fifty yards or so, we would go to ground to cover the next squad.

I gestured to Souvana for his fire team to follow mine. Then I got my team moving. We stayed bent over, almost double, zigging slowly from cover to cover to keep as many trees as possible between us and the enemy. Trees and shadows. The two fire teams did not take turns moving. We had the platoon's other two remaining squads to cover us. They were between us and the IFer patrol—at least those IFers who had been spotted.

More than those IFers we knew about, I worried about running into another patrol—spotting us before we saw them. It might be unusual for the enemy to run two patrols so close together, but it wasn't impossible, and there was always a chance that our advance scout had only seen part of the enemy patrol. There was also a slight chance that the IFers who had been spotted were not a small flanking patrol but part of the left column of the main force. We might have passed the flankers without spotting them.

Fifty yards. I signaled my men down in an arc. We took cover behind trees. The next squad started moving, angling to pass behind us, heading farther east. It took them a long five minutes to get past us—Tonio and the captain with them. The captain dropped out of that line and plopped to the ground next to me, looking past the other side of the tree trunk that sheltered us.

We glanced at each other, but nothing was said. Then we both turned our eyes back toward the enemy patrol, though we couldn't see the IFers from where we were. Second squad went thirty yards past us. By the time they went to ground, fourth squad was moving, pulling south, directly away from the last known position of that IFer patrol, before they turned east. I guess they pretty much crawled the first ten or fifteen yards, doing everything they could to escape detection.

They almost made it.

CHAPTER 22

FOURTH SQUAD WAS HIT FROM TWO SIDES, NORTH-
west and southwest. A lot of weapons started firing at once.
My estimate was that there had to be an entire platoon of
IFers shooting, but it's hard to trust a guess made under
those conditions. I got my people turned around, looking
for any chance to assist fourth squad, but we couldn't see
much. The forest was thick, and we were too far away. A
lot of the trees had foliage almost down to ground level—
some of them shaped almost like Christmas trees, with
multitudes of long, thin leaves that were not quite needles.
You can't see through that kind of foliage, not at any distance.

We couldn't give all our attention to fourth squad's firefight. We had to watch out for ourselves, too. Now that the
IFers knew there were Alliance people in the neighborhood, they might send a lot more people in fast. The rest of
the company could come under attack at any second—literally.

Captain Fusik put a hand on my shoulder. "Hold your
fire." He was speaking on my squad channel and—I
guessed—second squad's channel at the same time.

I lifted my faceplate and leaned close to the captain.
"We can't just leave them out there without help."

The captain also lifted his faceplate—about halfway,

just enough to let him talk without using his radio. "We won't. But fourth is in as good cover as they can find. The IFers are either going to have to move closer or come at them from more angles. We're just holding to get a better shot at the IFers."

He really didn't owe me an explanation, and he didn't wait for me to acknowledge it. He slapped his faceplate back down. So did I.

Fourth squad wasn't doing any shooting. I couldn't have said if they had done any at all since being attacked. If it hadn't been for what the captain said, I would have assumed that the men of fourth squad were all dead or too badly wounded to fight. But the captain wouldn't risk live men for dead. That can be a hard decision to make, emotionally, but it's almost always right. If fourth squad was a total loss, we would have tried to slip away from these IFers—save the payback for a later time, when we could do it right. Payback, not revenge.

I shifted position to get a wider view, trying to see around the copse of low trees. The IFers had quit shooting, apparently on command because they all stopped at once. Discipline. I did not lift my head to look around. I want to keep my head right where it is, firmly attached to my shoulders, and those IFers might be waiting within a hundred yards just looking for some turkey to get curious. It's been years since I gobbled.

How many are closing in? I wondered. I had a nervous itch running up and down my back. That's not just a cliché. I felt that itch, moving as if there were a tiny animal scrambling back and forth, using my spine as a highway. Somewhere, closer than I liked, there were a couple of regiments of enemy soldiers—maybe ten thousand men. One hell of a lot of them might get close enough to hit us before we could pull fourth squad out of the grinder and get away.

I didn't bother looking to see what my men were doing. They would be doing what I was doing—looking for the enemy and waiting for the captain to decide what we were going to do.

The silence seemed impossibly complete. Before the shooting started, there had been occasional sounds from birds or small animals. Now, even they were silent, probably doing what we were, sitting and waiting, alert for danger and trying to avoid it. My breathing had gone shallow and slow. Good sound pickups can hear a deep breath at forty yards or more. You can't hold your breath, not for more than a few seconds, without risking an involuntary gasp for air.

It couldn't have been more than two minutes that this tableau continued. My guess is that Captain Fusik was on the radio with whoever was left in charge in fourth squad—listening to reports on casualties and what fourth's survivors could see of the enemy. The captain was not simply going to meditate and come up with a brilliant plan out of his imagination. He was too damned good a soldier to try. A brief interruption of electronic silence was a safer risk, especially for fourth squad, since the enemy knew where they were.

The captain tapped my shoulder. I turned my head. He lifted his faceplate and leaned closer to whisper, "Fourth squad has six men alive. Two are hurt too badly to move on their own. We're going to cover fourth. They'll pull their wounded with them. We need to move first and second squads to give us a better angle to cover the withdrawal. Fourth can't see any enemy soldiers, but they have to be close to where they were at the start of the action. Hang here for two minutes with your squad. I've got to get over to second. I don't want to use the radio." Tonio was with second squad. "Two minutes, then start your squad toward the right side of fourth. Get out about sixty yards and wait. Once we're all in position, I'll signal fourth to start pulling back."

"Yes, sir. Wait two minutes. Take my men sixty yards out toward the right of fourth squad. Then wait."

Fusik clapped me on the shoulder, then started crab-crawling on elbows and knees. It looks awkward and feels worse, but it's fairly efficient. I had marked the time at the instant the captain told me to wait two minutes. I didn't want to wait too long. The enemy might have a different schedule.

I USED HAND SIGNALS TO PREPARE MY MEN AND to make sure they would be watching me for the order to start. I also kept an eye on the time. The captain had said two minutes, even though he would need that long to get to second squad and give his orders. Second squad would need at least three minutes to move into position. Five or six minutes can feel like eternity, and there was no way to be sure the IFers would give us that much time.

Maybe I shaved a second or two off the two minutes, but since we were going to have to wait again once we got to our new position, I figured it didn't matter much—and if it did, moving early would be better than trying to move late.

I had Souvana lead with his fire team. We would leapfrog each other, with half the squad down and ready to provide covering fire while the other half moved. We stayed low and moved slowly, five or six yards at a time, more concerned with stealth than speed. Each time I crawled forward, I expected to hear incoming gunfire. That dancing itch on my back was going faster and faster.

After I had moved with my fire team for the second time, I started to pick up vague infrared warm spots beyond fourth squad. I assumed those spots were enemy soldiers, but I couldn't be sure. I couldn't get any definition of shape or a precise distance. There was too much obstruction between us, and the spots did not seem to be moving.

I gestured with my hand flat, palm down, to warn my men about staying low. They shouldn't have needed a reminder, but I would have been remiss in my duties if I had not given it. If I was picking up possible enemy targets, the IFers might be picking up vague indications of us; and if their gear was even a little better than ours, they might have targetable images before we did. We slowed our movement.

Motion might be the kicker that gave the enemy better information than I was getting about them. Crawling on your stomach is a lot slower than crawling on hands and knees, but it's safer. You present a smaller target, harder to pick out from the background. The next time my fire team stopped, I took a second to glance in the direction of Captain Fusik and second squad. I couldn't see anyone. I didn't expect to, but I had to look.

By that time, second squad should have been on the move, angling across to cover the other flank of fourth squad.

Maybe another three minutes before anything happens, I thought. *Or a little more.* That was, of course, assuming that the IFers didn't preempt the captain's plan by starting something on their own. I was more than a little surprised that they hadn't done something already, that they hadn't pressed in on fourth squad right from the start. It wouldn't have taken much to overrun one squad that had already lost several men. Six men, two of them wounded too badly to move on their own and maybe even unconscious, couldn't do a hell of a lot against fifty or more attackers. The only excuse I could think of for the IFers not continuing their attack was that they must not be certain how many more of us were in position to join in.

That must mean that we're not *dealing with a large unit,* I thought. *It must have been a flanking patrol, not one of the main columns.* A patrol, maybe a platoon or two, certainly no more than a short company. That gave me a small measure of relief, but I did not make the mistake of taking that estimate for gospel. I had to allow for the possibility that I might be wrong. There might be a lot more IFers lying in wait, using the remnants of fourth squad as a lure to bag more of us at one time. That could be a very smart tactical move.

I kept scanning the forest, past where fourth squad was, looking for confirmation that those warm spots were actually enemy soldiers, and trying to get a count on those areas. While that would probably not give me an accurate

number—since many of the IFers might be totally con-
cealed by tree trunks—it could give me a working minimum: *they have at least so many troops waiting.* After that,
it would be a matter of trying to estimate what percentage
of the total I was seeing.

Souvana's fire team got to their next position. I got my
team moving again, slithering through the leaves and other
detritus on the forest floor. The move would take us to
where the captain wanted us to wait. When we stopped and
moved into firing positions, we were spread out in a line
with two yards or so between men. Then Souvana brought
his team up on the left, and we were in place. Now all we
had to do was wait for the captain and second squad to get
where they were going. Or wait for the IFers to open up.

The next five minutes were among the longest in my
life. One small bird issued a tentative chirp almost directly
over my head, maybe thirty feet up, and it startled me so
badly I almost jumped out of my pants. It started my heart
racing so loudly I thought it might be audible by the men
on either side of me. I needed half a minute or more just to
calm the beat down again. Then I swallowed hard. My
mouth was dry, but I didn't dare take a drink of water. The
movement, and the time, were simply more than I could
risk.

From maybe seven or eight hundred yards away, I heard
shooting—a brief firefight, much like the one that had
caught our fourth squad. My guess was that one of our
other platoons had encountered enemy soldiers. This time,
it sounded as if the gunfire was two-way, not a one-sided
ambush. The sudden outbreak of shooting had less effect
on me than that one chirp had a minute or so before. And
the next burst of fire—on the other side, even farther
away—had even less effect.

Lay it on, boys, I thought. These distractions I welcomed.
If there were other minor firefights going on, the IFers would
be less able to concentrate on us. It should make extracting
the survivors of fourth squad somewhat easier. I looked over
my shoulder again, wondering how far the captain and sec-

ond squad were from where Fusik wanted them to be. *They should be in position by now,* I told myself, but since I didn't know exactly how far they had needed to travel, I couldn't be certain of that. *Any second now.*

Fifty of those seconds went by. I was starting to hear a distant fight going on, the explosion of a couple of artillery shells, most likely. The rumble was not much different than distant thunder, the kind where you just barely see the glow above the horizon. It was too far away to have any impact on what we were going to do—try to do. Still, I was aware of it, background noise, a pulse to accentuate the waiting time. I knew the main battle had been going on—for several hours, by that time—but with our own needs, I had nearly lost track of the occasional distant echoes of that fight. In the silence now, maybe I was simply aware of those sounds again. I'm certain they hadn't stopped the main battle just so I could concentrate on what was happening closer. Your brain can get weirdly focused under stress, picking and choosing what it will take notice of.

Another thirty seconds passed. When the captain finally spoke on the platoon channel, it startled me badly even though I had been waiting for it. "We're in position. Fourth, start pulling back with your wounded. We'll cover you."

I was already in a solid prone firing position, safety off, my finger on the trigger. All I needed was a target. I knew where fourth squad was. I had their recognition blips on my head-up display. They didn't waste any time moving once the captain gave them the word. Unless the wounded were biraunta or abarand, it would take two men to move each of them. I figured that neither of the wounded could be porracci because the squad wouldn't be able to move even one porracci and another man. The squad leader, Chouvana, was porracci. There was, or had been, one other porracci in the squad.

It was one of the porracci I saw first. I thought it was Chouvana, but I couldn't be certain at the distance. Whoever he was, he was carrying a smaller individual, a biraunta, on his back. The porracci was crawling on knees and one hand, holding his rifle in the other. That put the bi-raunta on his back awfully high, certain to be visible to any IFers within eighty to one hundred yards. If nothing else, the wounded biraunta would be a tempting target.

I saw the flash of gunfire from a muzzle that was aimed almost exactly in my direction, but not precisely at *me*. I spread a short burst right around those flashes, mostly below, since I didn't want to waste ammunition shooting over his head. *One down,* I thought, certain that I could not have missed. I rolled to my right, to make certain that no IFer could return the favor that easily, and ended up in another good firing position.

There was more gunfire now, in both directions. Fourth squad was not being targeted expressly. The IFers were more concerned with the rest of us. We were less than a hundred yards apart—in some cases significantly less. That meant that we had to be careful with our rifle fire and *extremely* cautious about using grenades, either RPGs or hand. Because fourth squad was in the middle, we had to be most cautious about grenades. Fourth squad might suffer from any errant explosion.

For five or six minutes, the gunfire was general, on both sides. With the noise close by, I wasn't certain about any more distant fighting. I *thought* that maybe one or two of our other platoons might be involved in firefights as well, but I couldn't be sure. The only sound I heard from the main battle was an occasional artillery round exploding, and even that did not always register.

Fourth squad was moving away from the worst of the gunfire, and still escaping notice, for the most part. They were not suffering additional casualties, at least, and that was the important thing. Captain Fusik started moving second squad again, as if they were going to try to flank the IFers and roll them up from the side. Maybe that's what the IFer patrol thought as well. They started withdrawing north, back toward their main force.

"Keep up the pressure as long as you have targets," Fusik said on my squad's channel; there is a bank of indicator lights that I can see on my helmet display to tell me which channel is in use. We were in contact with the enemy so there was no need to observe any degree of electronic silence. "We'll get fourth squad out of the way, then set up to cover you. Second platoon is also moving to help cover our withdrawal."

I clicked my transmitter to acknowledge, then shifted my fire team a little to the right, and a couple of yards closer to the enemy, moving to new trees, keeping up the fire. I was only looking for a little better angle, a way to avoid wasting so many bullets on tree trunks, not a way to close with the enemy, but if they thought that was what we were doing, it was okay with me. The IFers quit returning fire at about that time. That meant they were either trying to end the skirmish or wanted to change position without showing us where they were going. Even odds, I thought, and you have to prepare for the worst, not assume the best.

Second platoon was moving to assist us, so they must have been able to break off from whatever fighting they had been in. Lead Sergeant Deelock was with second platoon, or had been at the start of the mission. I had no way to know if second platoon had lost anyone in the skirmishing I had heard earlier. Second must have been the nearest of our other platoons, but I wasn't certain how close they were, how long it would take them to get into position. At least they would narrow down the angles that the IFers could come at *us* from.

That wasn't exactly what we had hoped to do. By this time it was pretty clear that we had run into a flanking patrol and had not gotten through to harass the enemy's main force. Still, if we could withdraw from this little fracas—and the others at least a couple of the other platoons seemed to have found—we would still have a chance to accomplish our mission. The IFers might not expect us to try to penetrate the flanking screen again. Or maybe we'd simply catch a little better luck and slip through that screen unseen.

Once it was clear that the IFers were intent on breaking contact, Sergeant Chouvana and his men got to their feet and ran, zigzagging from cover to cover, trying to make it difficult for anyone to hit them. Just because the IFers weren't shooting just then did not mean that they might not want to try a tempting, easy target. The other porracci in fourth squad was obviously unhurt. He was carrying a ghuroh over his shoulders and not moving much slower than anyone else in the squad. They passed us on the left. I gave them a twenty-yard lead, then got my people up, and we started pulling back in the same direction. We moved more slowly though, keeping our faces toward where the enemy had been and shifting from cover to cover.

We were not firing now, since the enemy wasn't shooting at us. The captain hadn't said anything specifically about the situation, but—as a general rule of thumb—I figured that we were also going to be content to break contact. We didn't want the IFers to know where we were either. We were on our feet and moving back in order. I could see our second squad also pulling back the same way. Their attention was focused more to the left, in case the IFers were trying to come around us on that flank.

ONCE THE PLATOON HAD REUNITED, WE TOOK long enough to treat the two wounded from fourth squad before we started moving again—northeast, almost back on our original heading. Captain Fusik had stopped second platoon from coming any closer. We didn't need their assistance, and we weren't going to mass more people together simply because of the skirmish. All four platoons from the company would continue to operate independently.

It was after two in the morning when we started north again. Captain Fusik left our platoon's fourth squad with its wounded. In another half hour or so the wounded ghuroh would be able to walk. Fourth squad would make its way south, then east, back toward the perimeter around the settlement. That might be fine for them, but it left my platoon at half strength, since we had been operating without a third squad almost since the beginning of the campaign.

CHAPTER 23

CAPTAIN FUSIK DECIDED THAT IT WAS TIME FOR us to start moving as separate squads—to give us a better chance to get past whatever other flanking patrols the IFers might have out. The captain stayed with my squad. Tonio went with second. Since the captain did not use the radio to give similar orders to the other platoons, it would be up to the senior man in each to decide how to try to get closer to the main enemy force. Since our training is geared toward operations at the lowest level, the squad, it seemed more than likely that we would all be moving that way before long.

We saw signs of troop passage—tracks in wet spots, moss that had been scraped, leaves that had been dragged or turned on the ground, freshly broken twigs, and so forth—to show where enemy patrols had passed, but we crossed what we thought would be the zone the flankers would be covering without spotting enemy troops. The left column of the IFer main force might be within a hundred yards of us to the north, but by this time the tail end of the formation might be several hundred yards west of us. The word from CIC was that the IFers were still pushing forward, and beginning to enlarge their front against the perimeter around the settlement, spreading out to left and right.

Captain Fusik turned my squad more to the west when we started to spot signs that a force considerably larger than a platoon or two had passed. This had to be the track of the enemy's left column—at least a full battalion, eight hundred men or more. After we had gone nearly two hundred yards, just to the side of that track, the captain had me stop the squad. "I've got to risk using the radio," he told me, face-to-face, whispering. "I've got to make sure everyone knows the enemy has moved past here, get everyone turned so we can come up on their rear. Once I get off, we'll move as quickly as we can."

I nodded. Most of our company was farther east, farther from the enemy. The captain pulled his faceplate back down and used the company command channel to spread the word. That connected all of the officers and sergeants in the company, so I heard what he said. He was only on the air fifteen seconds, just long enough to give very terse orders, the ones he had laid out for me before.

"Now, let's move," he told me when he had finished.

We moved. I sent my two biraunta out as scouts, but even once they got up in the trees they had difficulty putting any distance between themselves and the rest of us. We were jogging on the ground, moving not quite on a straight line but not zigzagging as much as we might have in other circumstances. Still, we ran quietly, without disturbing much of the ground we passed over. You can't avoid leaving *some* sign of your passage, but after a few hours, those signs would no longer be so obvious.

After two hundred yards, we slowed a little. Captain Fusik turned my squad a little more to the right, going behind the concentration of the enemy force. We weren't close enough to *see* the enemy yet, and the sounds of battle were still a considerable distance in front of us—little louder than they had been before the skirmish that caught fourth squad. But there was artillery fire going in both directions, and some of it was exploding not too far from us—maybe less than a mile away. We might be getting that close to the enemy's artillery, since the IFer heavy weapons were what our big guns would be after.

When we stopped to catch our breath, I went to the captain and asked him about that.

"Your squad doesn't have any rocket launchers, so we'll leave the enemy artillery to the squads that do," he said. "They know to be on the lookout for them."

"They'll have troops guarding the people controlling the artillery, sir," I reminded him. "The operators can't be *too* far from the guns." There's no need for remote artillery operators to be in line of sight with their guns, or even particularly close, but it's a lot easier to control them if you're not too far from the area where the self-propelled gun carriages are maneuvering.

"We see those troops, we'll do what we can. Right now, let's concentrate on getting close enough to the enemy's main force to do some good."

I thought about mentioning the fact that some of the other squads in the company might trip over the enemy howitzers or their operators, but he would know that. And those other squads were going to be moving even faster than we were, knowing that they had a lot more ground to cover. There was every chance that some of our people might run into real trouble, but there wasn't much that the captain or I could do about that.

NOT TEN MINUTES LATER AN ARTILLERY SHELL EX-ploded within two hundred yards of us—close enough for us to feel the concussive wave of air and heat pushed aside by the blast and the slight shaking of the ground. A tree trunk cracked after the explosion and started a chain reaction as it fell through the interlinked branches of trees around it. We dived for the ground and stayed down until the bits of debris quit falling around us. Nothing large got as far as we were, but there was dirt and small rocks and who-knows what else.

I hadn't heard the rumble of the treads and engines of

any SP guns, but they couldn't be too far away, unless our artillery's target acquisition system had gone all to hell. There had to be enemy gun carriages operating fairly close. I guess the captain figured the same thing. When we were getting back to our feet he came over to me and lifted his faceplate just a little.

"Looks like your guess was right," he said. "Just figures that the squad that stumbled on the enemy guns first would be one without a rocket launcher."

"I'm no prophet, Cap," I said. "I was just being myself, the eternal pessimist. I'd rather have been wrong. But if we're this close to the guns, we can't be far from the operators either, or the troops guarding them."

"So keep your eyes open. It might be nice to off a few artillery operators, but I don't think we'd like the odds getting to them." He shook his head a little. "That would sure as hell get the IFers' attention. We'll detour a little to the left, farther from where that round went off." He gestured. I whistled to get the attention of the others in the squad and gave the same gesture. But I called the biraunta back and told them that we wanted to avoid contact. If they saw anything, one of them should come back to warn us, and the other should look for a way around.

We spread out a little more on the march, putting more distance between men to minimize casualties if the enemy spotted us and got in the first shots. I was near the front, and the captain was closer to the rear. We had three people between us. That's fairly standard as well, putting as much distance as practical between the commander and the second-ranking man. The more rungs on the chain of command that go out at once, the greater the confusion that can result, even in a spec ops squad, where we try to make sure that every man knows precisely what the mission is.

Although we wanted to put distance between us and where the enemy big guns might be—*must* be—we also did not want to draw attention to ourselves, so we kept the pace relatively slow now, trying to blend in, avoiding jerky motions that could draw a distant eye. I felt hypersensitive to my surroundings. That's normal for a dicey situation, for me, at least, and for a lot of guys I've talked with about it. Everything starts to work at extreme speed, as if the brain fires up afterburners. In several respects, it's like the way shuttle pilots accelerate toward the ground on a combat landing. Sight, hearing, even smell seem to become abnormally acute. The brain processes everything more rapidly. But simultaneously, time seems to go more slowly—some sort of balance, I guess. Every breath, every heartbeat seems to come as a discrete event, noted in passing, with clear gaps between one and the next.

Another artillery round exploded, maybe at about the same distance from us as the first had, but more to the west as well as north of our line of march. This was a more massive explosion than the first, almost certainly an artillery rocket rather than a howitzer round. The rocket warheads pack several times the explosive force. It shook the ground noticeably, and caused a lot more damage, toppling every tree in an area of forest at least sixty yards in diameter and starting a number of small fires. The glare of the blast temporarily overwhelmed the night-vision systems in our helmets, momentarily blinding those of us who were looking that way when it went off.

Once more we went to ground and waited for the concussive wave and the subsequent fall of debris to pass. There was a lot more stuff raining down on us than after the previous blast, another indication that it had been a rocket and not a shell that went off. *Maybe it hit a gun,* I thought, though I had not heard any secondary explosions—the kind that could come from shells being cooked off by the primary blast. *That might account for all the extra crap.* We got up and started moving again. Captain Fusik signaled another slight change in our course—trying to get us farther from the wrong end of the artillery.

"We can't go much more than another hundred yards in this direction," he said when we stopped for a moment. "We need to start angling back north, get between the IFer artillery and their infantry. If they've moved their guns that much closer to the front line, it may get dicey, but we're not going to do any good if we're too far out on the flank. We might slip past the edge of the battle and run into our own perimeter." If nothing else, that would be an embarrassing mistake. It might be a deadly error as well, if a nervous soldier on the line wasn't looking for friendly forces in front of his gunsight.

"Just point the way, Cap," I said. "If I'm going to get zapped, I'd just as soon it was trying to do something useful than get it by accident."

FIVE MINUTES LATER WE TOOK A SHARP RIGHT turn, heading just a little west of north—about 280 degrees by the compass. I hoped that the enemy artillery was all east of us by that point, but there was no way to be certain—or to be certain that they would *stay* farther east and not move directly toward us while they were trying to avoid our counterbattery fire. Those big guns stay on the move constantly when they're in use, because that's the only way they can hope to survive the battlefield environment. That's also why the big guns are remote-controlled, to cut down on the personnel losses.

Three minutes after we made the turn, Oyo dropped out of a tree about halfway between the captain and me and moved toward Fusik. I headed over to hear what he had to say. The rest of the squad stopped with us, and everyone got down on the ground, sinking slowly into position.

"An enemy force, Captain, at least one full company, more likely two—perhaps a full battalion. About three hundred yards from here. They're moving west, but slowly, in two columns. Ala thinks there are more troops farther west, ahead of what I saw, and others beyond to the north, but he wasn't positive."

Captain Fusik unfolded his electronic map and scrolled to get it centered on the position Oyo had mentioned. "Ala is probably right," Fusik said. "We're getting close enough that we have to be near the left column, and pretty damned close to the main battle. Damned near within spitting distance. We're only a mile and a half from the nearest point of our perimeter. Most of the IFer force should be concentrated just west and north of us." He looked at me then. I kept my mouth shut, waiting for him to decide what we were going to do. The situation was well beyond the range of a buck sergeant. I wasn't going to suggest how the captain should deploy a single squad against maybe six or seven thousand hostile troops. It seemed to take forever for the captain to speak again, but it was probably not more than twenty seconds.

"We'll attack. As soon as we engage, I'll broadcast and tell the rest of the company to move in as quickly as they can and get a piece of the action. Have them latch on wherever they can. We need to give the IFers something to worry about on this side." He was still staring at me, so I nodded, just to acknowledge that I had heard him. "I'll make sure CIC and the general know what we're doing and where we are as well." I don't know if he was trying to reassure me or himself. We were going to turn the stove on ourselves, then jump on the burners.

"We'll move in, strike from grenade-launcher range, then shift farther west before we hit again," Captain Fusik continued. "The second time, we'll look for the best defensive position we can find. I doubt that we'll get much chance to move after that. They're going to come after us fast."

"Most likely, Cap," I said, nodding again. I was relieved to find that the prospect didn't have me pissing in my boots. I had been in rough spots before, but maybe none that I knew were going to be horrible before we got there. "They'll put any troops that aren't close to engaging on the perimeter to squash us. We still look for an avenue out after the second hit?"

"We look, and we'll take it if we can, but we've got to put enough pressure on to make them come after us. We just nibble and run, they might not bother. We need to draw off as many IFers as we can to lessen the pressure on the perimeter.

That's getting weak, from the last report I had from CIC. We need to sow some confusion and give the enemy general a few extra headaches." The captain got more detailed updates than what were available on the general information feed. He might also be getting instructions directly from regimental headquarters. I didn't know how closely General Chop might be managing the operation.

I KNEW IT WAS GOING TO BE HAIRY AS HELL. THE phrase *Dragon's Last Stand* ran through my head—as if I were reading the headline from my obituary. Special Operations Squad. That's what the description reads, not Suicidal Operations Squad. Our platoon's third squad had already been effectively destroyed on Unity. The company had lost other squads during the war.

But it's something we try to avoid—fervently, religiously. Last stands leave no room for a sequel, and they kill the "They lived happily ever after" ending all to hell.

My deepest hope at the moment was that there would be other squads close enough to hit the enemy very quickly after we started the action. If the enemy was able to concentrate on us for any length of time, they would be able to wipe us out without breaking a sweat, even if there was only a single IFer company close. That would give them a tactical advantage of about twenty to one, and they probably had a lot more than one company within reach. And I hoped our main force, the line battalions facing the enemy force directly, would be able to push out of the perimeter and crush in from the far side quickly enough to give the IFers too much trouble for them to worry about us. If everything worked exactly as we hoped, we might still get through this in fairly good order.

But nothing ever goes *exactly* as you hope in combat.

WE WERE EXTREMELY CAREFUL ABOUT MOVING into position for the attack. Yes, we wanted to draw their attention, and once we started firing, they were going to know exactly where we were, but we wanted the advantage of firing the first shots—a *lot* of first shots, and first grenades. Getting in the first blow can make all the difference in the Galaxy, especially when you've got grenades or the like, and we absolutely *needed* that advantage to have any hope of surviving the fight.

On the move, I arranged my people the way I wanted them. Both biraunta were on the ground now. They would be too vulnerable in the trees once the shooting started, and getting down safely at the point of contact was too iffy. Captain Fusik was near the middle of our skirmish line and a couple of steps behind the rest of us, where he would be able to have a better view—*not* far enough back that he would be any less a target for enemy gunners. If anything, that kind of position is a little more dangerous because the enemy can assume that the man back by himself is commanding the unit. I was near the right end of the line, Souvana near the left end. The spacing was between two and three yards from one man to the next, not uniform, allowing for everyone to drop to some sort of cover.

In skilled hands, RPGs are accurate at two hundred yards, or a little more, in the open or in lightly wooded areas. In thick forest, they're not going to be entirely accurate even at half the range. There's too much wood that can deflect an arcing projectile along the way, or cause a premature detonation. The closer we could get, the better, but we didn't want to trade the advantage of more accuracy with the rocket-propelled grenades for giving the enemy the first shot. It was going to be a balancing act, and a test of nerves. Captain Fusik would give the order unless I saw something that wouldn't leave time for me to ask for permission—something like the faceplate of an enemy helmet looking in my direction and a rifle being raised.

We were 160 yards from the enemy—I had just spotted a helmet moving across my field of vision, but not looking at me—when the captain gave the order. *"Now!"*

CHAPTER 24

THE TWO MEN WITH GRENADE LAUNCHERS, KIER-
vauna and Razor, were the first to fire. The launchers hold
a clip of four grenades, and it takes approximately three
seconds for a well-trained grenadier to get four aimed
shots off. Before the first grenades had traveled half the
distance to the enemy, starting to rip through the leaves
and small branches of the forest canopy, the rest of us
opened up with automatic rifle fire, spraying the area
around where we had seen the enemy. The bullets leave the
rifle at supersonic speed. They reach their target before the
sound does. And they overcame the maybe one-second
lead of the first grenades.

That meant that a few enemy soldiers died before they
could even know that they had come under fire. I could
imagine men looking up when they heard the approach of
the grenades, but not being able to react before the bullets
arrived. The rest were just diving for the ground when the
grenades started to explode around them. By that time,
Kiervauna and Razor had reloaded and were firing second
clips of grenades, moving their point of aim with each
shot, spreading bloody mayhem around an area maybe
sixty yards wide and thirty deep. We had made a solid
mark on the enemy before anyone managed to get a shot
off anywhere near our direction.

The first time I saw a special operations squad put that much firepower into a concentrated target zone, I couldn't believe that anyone could survive such an onslaught. There were hundreds of bullets and tens of thousands of bits of shrapnel flying, including both the primary shrapnel and the secondary shrapnel thrown off by the solid objects broken apart by the blasts. You could grind hamburger that way if you were inclined to the spectacularly macabre.

People can, and do, survive attacks like that though. Whether by chance or divine intervention, some men come through that kind of assault without a scratch even. Body armor can't account for all of that. No species completely armors itself, and not even the best military body armor is 100 percent protection even over the areas it covers. The armor material can have defects that only the stress of use reveals. It may have worn too much through age, a seam might not be tight, or a bullet or piece of shrapnel can hit with enough force and just the right angle to penetrate armor that meets or exceeds specifications. Occasionally, the force of a bullet strike—or a series of strikes—can do enough damage to a body even though the flak jacket itself is not penetrated.

We laid down all the metal hell we could for twenty seconds, then started moving, taking turns by fire team, one covering the other, wanting only to get somewhere else before the enemy could return the favor. Only the team that was still in our old position fired; the team moving did not, to avoid giving the enemy any pointers about where we were going. When my people started moving, we went silent, to give the enemy a chance to lose track of all of us. By the time we started shuffling rapidly along the ground, there was considerable rifle fire coming back toward us, but the opposition had not brought any grenade launchers to bear yet. And, for a time, the hostile fire was going behind us instead of right at us.

Souvana led the way, taking us more north than west, definitely closer to the enemy, but obliquely. That was probably the best choice under the circumstances. He had been given no instructions, but neither the captain nor I was inclined to suggest anything different.

Rationally, it would seem that we should be heading away from the enemy. If we had been intent on the sort of hit-and-run tactics that spec ops squads normally practice, that is what we would have been doing. As long as the IFers thought we would behave rationally, we could get away with the maneuver. Going closer to an enemy that outnumbered us might seem too suicidal for them to react to immediately. For a couple of minutes, they were shooting in the wrong direction and aiming at the wrong distance.

Still, we could not go too far in that direction without risking crawling right into the laps of the people we were shooting at. Bayonet range, hand-to-hand combat range: *that* would be suicidal for us. It was still dark, but the enemy was equipped with night-vision systems as sophisticated as those we wore.

If we could get right in the *middle,* in the gap between a couple of enemy platoons, we might have a chance to get where they couldn't shoot at us without shooting more of their own people. But reaching a point like that is the snag. Going in, they can fire on you from both sides and do shark's-tooth stitchery on you. We were trying to confuse the daylights out of the IFers, but we needed help with that, and I still had no idea how long it would be before some of the other squads in our company could get into position to stir the mix a bit.

Fifty or sixty yards from where we had first attacked, we stopped to launch more grenades and more rifle fire against the IFer unit we had engaged. This time we didn't have as much of a safe lead time. The IFers were watching and listening more closely. They might have heard the passage of grenades through the trees and started spraying their own fire almost as soon as we did. Since we were all on the ground, most of the bullets passed harmlessly overhead, and the IFers still hadn't brought RPGs down on us. Had they concentrated all their grenadiers nearer the front?

That seemed to be stretching possibility, but it still seemed to be the most likely explanation. The troops we were firing at hadn't seen much, if any, combat yet, so they couldn't have run out of RPGs.

I did not consciously think through all of that at the time, of course. It was just something noted subconsciously, something to consider when decisions have to be made. You try not to question a stroke of luck until you're certain you don't need it any longer. Okay, call that superstition. I won't argue the point. It works for me, or seems to. That's all I ask.

It did give us a chance to move again, despite our earlier concern that we would get pinned down before we could change positions a second time. Once more we aimed across our front, at a shallow angle to the assumed line of the enemy column. My fire team was in front this time. We stopped firing before we started crawling. Souvana held his team back longer than he should have, perhaps, and they kept firing while we moved. Finally, though, Souvana got his people on their way—after an order from Captain Fusik, who was with my team at the moment.

Second fire team crawled toward us, just as fast as they could scuttle along without getting their bellies more than an inch off the ground. I had my team hold their fire, hoping that the IFers would lose track of where any of us were. Souvana's team was also not firing. The IFers finally found the triggers on their grenade launchers, apparently. At least three RPGs dropped in and around where second fire team had been shooting from . . . fifteen seconds after they had quit shooting and left that location.

Still, there was some scatter to the pattern, and the kill zone for one of those grenades is theoretically forty yards. One came close enough to pepper Zhirie with shrapnel from behind—or below. That meant it was the least armored part of him that absorbed the shrapnel. It pushed him forward a little, and his helmet plowed a bit into the ground before he came to a halt. I looked for vital signs from him on my monitoring system, but there was nothing.

He was dead—another abarand finally free to really fly, if their belief in what the afterlife meant was correct.

We kept moving. There was no possibility of checking to make certain that Zhirie was dead, no time to waste on the faint possibility that it was only an electronic failure. I had seen the way his body had jerked when he was hit. We couldn't even risk going back to him to salvage his ammunition, though I would have loved to do that. We might need all the ammo we could find before this was over.

FOR THE MOMENT, THE IFERS SEEMED TO HAVE lost track of just where we were—while we moved as silently as we could. That couldn't last long. As close as we were, they would be able to read the heat signatures of our bodies—and of our rifle barrels, all of which had warmed up considerably in use. The body heat might be mistaken for that of their own people, but the rifles probably would not. Someone would get an angle on us that wasn't blocked by a tree or underbrush, and a rifle barrel would stand out in infrared like a thousand-watt light tube. But while the moment lasted, the enemy was spraying bullets—and the occasional grenade—over a lot of territory where we weren't. That was what made it so obvious that they didn't know our exact positions.

Fusik made a gesture, urging us to start moving again. We went, staying as nearly flat as we could. Silence wasn't quite so important with all the gunfire, but we needed to stay on our bellies, both to avoid making targets of ourselves and to keep our hot weapons and bodies as low as possible so that they wouldn't give us away. I spotted one narrow stretch that didn't seem to have any rifle fire coming out of it and aimed for that point. Maybe it would put us between companies, or platoons. That was what I was hoping for—barring a miracle that would suddenly make all the IFers around us turn the other way to fight somebody else.

I scooted along for some thirty yards—now somehow

out in front of the squad—and the gap ahead was even more noticeable. After stopping for maybe thirty seconds to survey both sides, I decided to keep going, to press the possible opening for all it might be worth. At one point, maybe another twenty yards along that route, I think I came within ten yards of an enemy soldier on my left, but he was looking back toward where we had been earlier. I don't think he heard or saw a thing. Of course, I might have been holding my breath part of the time, or trying to. Somehow, I got far enough past him before the involuntary gasp came when my body decided it wanted air whether I was willing to let it have it or not.

Ten yards north of that man, I shifted around on my side, hidden almost completely by a tree trunk, and brought my rifle to bear on him. I wasn't going to fire unless he spotted one of the men behind me and tried to score a quick kill. I'm all for getting rid of as many enemy troops as possible, but I hoped to be able to let this one—a tonatin, at that—live at least a little longer if it meant that my people would get through the line and maybe to someplace marginally safer beyond.

I really didn't think it was going to work. All that tonatin grunt had to do was glance to his left a little. Some hint of movement might catch his eye, some slight sound. For all I knew, he might have his sound pick-ups cranked to maximum the way I often did in similar situations. Or another IFer, one I hadn't seen, might be as close on the other side, or might slide down the line to pass along an order. Almost any little thing could do it. Then the shooting would start, become general, and our luck would run out for the last time.

Ala made it through the gap safely. Biraunta are small enough to get away with more than the larger species. I gestured for Ala to keep going past me, then find a place a little farther on where he could turn and help me cover the rest of our people. Claw was next, then Kiervauna and Captain Fusik. Toniyi was the last of my fire team. Everyone went past me. Then they fanned out a little, off the path, getting into position to take out the enemy soldiers near us.

That lone tonatin I could see hadn't moved his head the entire time I had been watching. He was staring south, looking out at whatever he might be seeing in the forest. As long as he wasn't seeing any of us, I didn't care what he did. That tactical mistake kept him alive. There might have been just a thin line of IFers left to try to deal with us. Once we all got past that line, we *might* be in the clear. For a few minutes.

It wouldn't be for long. Even if we did get free of the little mess, we would soon be looking for another chance to raise some hell in the enemy's ranks. That was what we were doing there to begin with. All we were doing was buying ourselves a little more time.

Robbie was the first man through the gap from second fire team. Oyo and Razor came next, too close together, and Souvana was the last man past the line. Naturally. Souvana wouldn't have had it any other way. Also naturally, when he came even with me he made a very small gesture, telling me to go on ahead, that he would bring up the rear. Arguing the point would have been foolish. I let him have his way. If he got a bullet up the ass for it, that was his worry.

No MATTER HOW DILIGENTLY I TRIED TO PAY AT-tention to what we had to do next, there was a repeated, *We did it!* banging around in my head. It was incredible, a textbook infiltration that had gone perfectly—and then some. That we were still up to our armpits in deep doo-doo couldn't detract from that. If anything, we were probably in a much worse position than we had been before. More than likely, we had the IFer army totally surrounding us, with little chance that we would be able to sneak back out as successfully as we had snuck in.

We moved a little farther away from the enemy we had spotted, then simply lay motionless for a moment, gather-

ing our wits and taking a bit of a breather. We weren't
arranged in a perimeter, just spread out next to trees and in
what minimal underbrush there was, blending in, trusting
our camouflage and thermal insulation, keeping our eyes
open and our weapons ready. I guess I wasn't the only one
amazed that we had made it, or drained by the exercise.
After a moment, I looked toward Captain Fusik. Our next
moves were up to him.

With silence close by again—the IFers had apparently
quit firing at where we had been earlier—it was easier to
hear the more distant sounds of battle. The loudest noise,
and the closest, was to the west. That was where the main
battle was being contested, the fight that would decide who
won Unity. We could hear artillery rounds going overhead
on their trajectory from gun to target. Since both sides had
artillery, they had to concentrate on each other's heavy
weapons rather than on the frontline troops. Off to the east,
there was sporadic gunfire, seemingly in half a dozen different directions, scattered around nearly half the compass,
from north-northeast to south-southeast. That would be
where the other Ranger units were skirmishing with the
IFers.

I tried not to think about what kind of casualties the rest
of the company might be taking. That might have made it
too difficult for me to move along and get back into the
fighting myself. I was scared, but I didn't want to give my
fear a chance to take over and start making decisions for
me. That might turn me into a coward, make me do things
that I would regret the rest of my life . . . no matter how
long or short that life might be. When you're in the middle
of the total chaos of war, you have to hold on to yourself,
no matter what.

Captain Fusik started the squad moving north again. There
were several men on that side of me, all of my fire team and
Oyo from Souvana's team. I saw the captain's gesture and
nodded, then tried to swallow. I couldn't. My mouth and
throat were too dry. My tongue might have been coated with
sand. And there was no way I could pull my canteen out to

take a drink. We were too close to the enemy—to at least one of them. If I had taken a drink it would have been my last, and maybe the last that any of us would have.

When it was my turn, I started crawling again, trying to work my tongue in my mouth to maybe generate a little moisture. I couldn't try clearing my throat. Silent, gaping yawns did not help, the way they sometimes did. It was becoming a dangerous distraction, but I had crawled ten yards or more before I was able to make myself stop.

Ten yards . . . ten miles . . . ten light-years. It took an eternity. I had a twitching in the back of my neck, knowing there was that one tonatin soldier we had snuck past. We might have tried to sneak up on him from behind—slit his throat with a knife. Anyone in the squad, except possibly the biraunta, should have been able to do that efficiently, without giving him a chance to cry out; but it might not have been totally silent, and any noise might have given us away to the other IFers who had to be close. You don't leave one man all alone. There might be five, even ten, yards between men, but there would be *someone* close enough to see—and react.

We covered five more yards—another eternity. Some yards apart, the captain and I each raised our heads a little to look all the way around, trying to spot where the next batch of enemy soldiers might be. We took a considerable amount of time, moving in increments of under an inch, both lifting up and turning, scanning slowly, both for what we could see and for what heat signatures our sensors might pick up.

The nearest sign I saw was due west of us, a lot of moderate heat, bodies, beginning perhaps 250 yards away. I glanced toward the captain, caught his attention, then looked back toward the heat signatures, knowing he would look where I was looking. After a few seconds, I turned my head toward him again, and he nodded, then made a series of cautious hand signals, his hand low, no more than ten inches off the ground.

We had found our next point of attack.

━━━━ **CHAPTER 25**

WE DIDN'T RUSH INTO IT. THE CAPTAIN, SOUVANA,
and I crawled into a clump of bushes together for a conference, but even then we used more hand signals than words to communicate, and those few words were in the softest possible whispers, almost subvocal, trusting our sound pickups to make them audible inside our helmets. We didn't know what sort of sound equipment the enemy might have in operation looking for interlopers, so we didn't take unnecessary chances.

I did take time for several short sips of water, careful not to let my canteen make any sloshing noises. The captain and Souvana both took my cue and had drinks themselves. *I wish it was whiskey, or at least beer,* I thought, but that water tasted pretty damned special just then.

The enemy soldiers we were going to attack might be 250 yards away, but there were probably other IFers a lot closer, and not just a few. We tried to spot those others, and did note several hot patches in the forest. One IFer—too small to be a tonatin—trotted east from the main concentration, following a trail that wouldn't come closer to us than forty yards. From the man's size and the way he moved, I guessed that he was human. The IFer army was not exclusively tonatin—it just seemed that way sometimes.

We stayed down and watched where the runner was going. He had to be a courier, a messenger, carrying orders. There had to be more IFers on the far end of his run, and that was a matter of some importance to us. With a fix on his course, we were able to track him even after we lost visual contact, and we knew how far off he was when he stopped—a little more than three hundred yards east of us and maybe thirty yards north. There was a concentration of warm targets there, and beyond. My rough guess was that it was most likely a reserve battalion.

That defined the maximum "safe" space we had to operate in. Captain Fusik unfolded his electronic map—the slight glow of the screen made that a touchy decision even though we figured we had at least fifty yards from *any* enemy soldier. I hoped that the cover of the bushes would be enough to keep the glow from giving us away. We got the overlay of enemy positions, mostly given away by electronic emissions that had been plotted by CIC. We also had our own position marked on the map, and the locations of some of the other spec ops squads.

The map offered us nothing reassuring about our position, showed us no easy route out once we started raising a ruckus again. There was one other spec ops squad—I thought it was probably Tonio with our platoon's second squad—about four hundred yards away, but half of that enemy reserve battalion was between us. None of our company's other segments were within twelve hundred yards. Of those whose positions we could see on the map. There was a chance that a squad or two might be closer, without displaying recognition codes that our watching ships could see.

We could see a lot of enemy units. Directly west of us, with the nearest elements 250 yards away, were more than ten thousand IFers pushing against the defensive line between them and the colonists. East of us was that battalion-sized unit, maybe eight hundred men. There were fewer known enemy positions directly north or south of us— mostly picket lines, like the one we had infiltrated, but there were enough locations highlighted to show us just how difficult it was going to be to break through again once the enemy knew which side of their lines we were on—the inside.

Captain Fusik did not rush his decision. I was kind of glad he didn't. I wanted him to take all the time he needed. Maybe he could come up with a truly brilliant plan that would give us an even chance to escape with our hides still holding full complements of working organs. It was more than five minutes before the captain started laying out what we were going to do. We couldn't do much fancy zipping around. All we were going to do was find the densest piece of forest within two hundred yards of the enemy rear and start laying hell in on top of them. We were going to settle in and make the enemy come to us, so we wanted the densest part of the forest, with thick tree trunks and heavy main branches—the type of stuff that would deflect some incoming RPGs and absorb as much rifle fire as possible—around us. The terrain was basically flat, so we weren't going to get any benefit from rolling ground or rock outcroppings.

It felt a little weird, as if we were picking the place where we were going to die.

PRAYERS HAVE NEVER COME EASILY TO ME, though I've tried often enough—and *not* just when I was going into something that looked like it might be lethal. It's just that I've never known who to address them to, or if anyone was even listening. "Hey, You, whoever You are, if You're even there," just doesn't seem like the proper start.

I guess most folks have got their own ideas about that, and few of them agree on much when it comes to religion. When all those believers say, "I'm right and anyone who disagrees with me is wrong," they don't allow room for differences of opinion. And it's not something you can trust to logic or even a polygraph machine.

Humans seem to be the champion species for coming up

with different versions of a god or gods, and ways to worship, placate, or cajole. But religion is not expressly a human institution. Every species we've met has something we would recognize as religion. They just don't have the proliferation of gods, religions, and rites. They wonder where they came from, where they're going, and whether there's any purpose to what comes between. Just like us. But they don't fight wars over whose interpretation is right. They don't parse and speculate endlessly. None of them have the bewildering confusion of gods and rites that humans have managed throughout their history.

The captain pointed to a spot, first on the map, then straight out from where we were sitting. "You see anything better?" he whispered, looking back and forth between Souvana and me. I looked at the real spot, not the one on the map. I looked a little to either side of it as well. Then I shook my head. It wouldn't have taken much to be "better," but the choices weren't there.

Souvana shrugged, then whispered, "One spot is as good as another for this," he said, with bravado and resignation seeming to tangle in his tone. The trace of resignation surprised me in a porracci, especially Souvana. He was always the ultimate in positive thinking. Maybe I wasn't the only one with intimations of mortality.

Fusik nodded and we moved out of the bushes and back to the rest of the squad. Now that the decision had been made, there was no point in wasting time. The captain started the squad moving immediately. Souvana took the lead. That saved the bother of explaining to anyone where we were going, and the what was implicit. There was no use beating that into the ground either. Captain Fusik got between the two fire teams. I was back near the end of the crawling parade, with only Ala behind me.

The place the captain had chosen was about 160 yards behind the nearest enemy troops we knew about to our west. There were four fairly large, tall trees, clustered so close together that their branches were extremely interlocked, beginning no more than twenty feet up. It was almost a little house, except that it only had corner posts, not walls. The space in the middle was nearly rectangular, with the east and west sides about 50 percent longer than the north and south sides. There was no ground cover in the area except for a little moss. The canopy was too thick to allow sunlight through for anything else. There were thick roots around the bases of the trunks, almost buttresses. Those would give us some cover ... though not as much as I would have liked. Near the trunks, some of those flaring roots stood more than a foot above the ground. The soil was too hard to give us any chance to scoop out slit trenches or pile up dirt in front of us. It was almost like metal. Even Kiervauna could barely scratch through the moss and dirt, not enough to do any good.

This is it, I thought once we were all in position. Resignation brought calm, not despair—not even fear; the time for fear was past. My mind seemed unnaturally clear, my thinking to the point, not distracted by ... irrelevancies. I knew what we had to do, and I was under no illusions about the probable outcome. Between now and then, though, I would do the best job I knew how.

I had pulled a couple of full magazines for my rifle out of my belt pouch and laid them at my side where I could get to them very quickly. The two hand grenades I was carrying came out, too. I left my pistol in its holster, but I had the holster unsnapped. Most of the others were doing the same thing. Souvana had already finished laying out all his stuff. He had also fixed his bayonet on the end of his rifle. When I did the same thing, the rest of the squad copied us. Kiervauna and Razor had their grenade launchers at their shoulders and their remaining clips of RPGs at hand. They were looking at me for a signal.

I took a deep breath and looked toward Captain Fusik for the order. When he turned his head in my direction, I nodded. We were as ready as we were ever going to be.

The captain returned my nod, then spoke one word on the squad channel. "Now."

• • •

AGAIN, WE GAVE THE GRENADIERS JUST A BIT OF a lead—little more than a single second. Then we all opened up. Even Captain Fusik was using his rifle as readily as if he were the lowliest private in the squad. At the same time, he was talking on the radio, reporting to Colonel Hansen, the battalion commander, and probably carrying on conversations with the leaders of the other segments of our company.

Kiervauna and Razor weren't pumping out grenades as quickly as they could this time. They were being more sparing, and spreading their payloads over a wider area, all the way out to the extent of their range. Their stock of grenades was getting low, and they might be more useful after the fight had been going on for a few minutes. Initially, they were more interested in getting the most efficient use from the grenades they expended—wanting visible targets, concentrations of enemy soldiers.

We knew there were thousands of IFers out there, past the muzzles of our weapons, even though we could only see a few score helmets when we started shooting. The front line—the line where the two armies were fighting—was little more than a thousand yards away, and the IFers were heavily concentrated in the area between us and the front line. Any bullet we put out there had a fair chance of hitting a good target . . . if it didn't end up in a tree trunk. Our rifles had enough muzzle velocity that the trajectory was extremely flat over the first seven hundred yards. We weren't likely to hit anything at that range in the forest, though—there was too much wood in the way, even after several hours of the main battle raging.

It was only in the first few seconds that we had clear targets. Once the IFers in front of us knew we were there, they went for cover. It only took a few more seconds before some of them got turned around and started returning fire. And it wasn't long before some of them figured out exactly where we were. Bullets started to come right at us—still a little high. But, then, once the IFers were on the ground, a lot of our stuff was high as well.

The advantage we had was that there were more IFers behind those who were firing at us. Behind us there were only more IFers. They were going to have to be careful to keep from shooting into their own troops, especially once the fight got closer. If the IFers tried to come at us from both sides, the chance of hitting their own people was going to slow down any effort to get to us.

Back when I was a raw recruit suffering through boot camp, one of my drill instructors with a flair for the dramatic hit us with the line, "Your status in Hell depends on how large an honor guard you take with you." It impressed some of us trainees. It wasn't until years later that I learned that the DI had not made up that statement. It was a quote dating back to a time before humans had ever left Earth, before we met any of the other sentient species. But it was an impressive quote to hit tired, scared recruits with. It stuck in our minds. I know that I used it a few times myself when I was assigned to training duties.

THE IFERS DIDN'T SEEM TO BE IN ANY HURRY TO close with us and stomp us flat. There was movement out there, a long way off, but they were playing it smart, moving men to both sides to get several angles into our little nest—angles that gave them clear lines of fire that didn't endanger their own people. But they weren't moving closer. Yet. They were staying out beyond two hundred yards, putting enough rifle fire in our direction to make sure we couldn't go anywhere. I suspected that they would be moving in from the other direction too—men from that battalion or so we had spotted farther to the east—but that would complicate matters for them. It wasn't going to make much difference to us though, not that I could see. It might postpone death for us for five or ten minutes, but they already had more than enough people around to do the job. It was just a matter of how much of a hurry they were in to finish us.

Bits of bark, small branches, spikes of wood splintered from trees. There was a considerable amount of debris zipping or falling around us. Out in front, a lot of foliage was being shredded. Up where our grenades had been going off, there were two small fires showing a little flame and a lot of smoke. That's not really common with fragmentation grenades, but it does happen.

I felt completely at peace. There was no time for fear, or for anything but being as efficient with my rifle as I could be. If I didn't have clear targets—soldiers—I always had the muzzle flashes of their rifles to guide my aim. Short bursts, preferably three or four rounds at a time—draw a line just below the last muzzle flash. It might almost have been a training exercise back at Fort Campbell, without men on the other side trying to kill me while I tried to kill them. There was no frantic feeling. I took my time about targets, being as careful with my ammunition as I could be . . . given the circumstances.

We had a longer period of grace than we had any right to expect. We had decent positions and the IFers didn't try to rush us. The firefight had been going on for nearly ten minutes before we suffered our first casualty. A long, tight burst of rifle fire hit Toniyi's helmet—first shattering the helmet, then shattering the top of the divotect's head. I didn't have to look for vitals. There was no way he could have survived. He probably had no time to even realize that he had been hit.

Two minutes later, an RPG exploded overhead, against the trunk of one of the trees that sheltered us, and much of the blast came into us. Captain Fusik took several pieces of shrapnel in his right arm, then had a chunk of wood conk him on the head. He apparently lost consciousness, but only briefly. I didn't notice at the time, but I guess I caught a chunk of that shrapnel in my hip. Ala and Kiervauna had minor wounds as well.

I guess we've about had it, I thought. I accepted that, too calmly, maybe. By this time all any of us could do was try to take as many of the enemy with us as we could—that infamous honor guard for Hell. When I heard gunfire coming from a new direction, off to the southeast, I assumed that it was more IFers coming to help finish us off and shifted my position a little so I could work against the new threat. I was a little longer realizing that some of the fire that had been coming our way had stopped. I could still hear the guns firing, but there was less crap coming toward us.

"You trying to hog all the fun?" I recognized the voice as Tonio's, but I had difficulty believing that I was hearing it. "We're about ninety yards from you. I think we're going to have to stay where we are for a bit though. The IFers have spotted us, and they're not being very polite."

"I hope that 'us' you're talking about is the whole damned army," I replied, knowing that Tonio probably only had second squad with him—minus any casualties they had suffered getting to us. My voice still worked, but it didn't sound all that steady. "I'm no pig. You're welcome to all the fun you can bite out of this shit."

"The whole damned army is a little busy right now," Tonio said. "They're trying to get to you from the other side. They should be about five hundred yards from your position. You'll have to settle for a smaller 'us' for now." His voice was not as bantering as his words. I guess he was under no illusions either.

That's okay. If you've got to die, you might as well die among friends. The front line was five hundred yards away? It might as well have been five hundred miles. There were still a lot of IFers between us and salvation. Even if the IFers retreated, they would have to run right over us to get away from our main force.

IT GAVE US ANOTHER RESPITE, MORE TIME TO think about what was coming. Tonio was bringing another squad in to help us. The IFers had started moving that reserve battalion in our direction as well. Maybe their commander had decided that they couldn't spare any of the troops west of us. We were worth bringing in the reserves. I guess a soldier could take some pride in that. We were doing our job. In the meantime, the IFers had enough people keeping us busy to hold us in place. Of course, that was all guesswork on my part, but I'd say it was a pretty good guess.

Captain Fusik regained consciousness. I crawled over and told him that Tonio and second squad were close. That gave me a chance to check the captain's condition as well. He was still a little fuzzy, slow to respond. He said that his vision was blurred, that he probably had a concussion. "You take over here until Sergeant Xeres arrives," he told me. "I may not be thinking straight." He seemed to fade out then, but only for a few seconds.

I took a minute to check on the rest of my squad. Kiervauna hadn't taken time to slap patches over his shrapnel wounds. They were still bleeding, but not profusely, just matting down his fur. The wounds didn't seem to be affecting him at all. Oyo had tended Ala's wounds, and had taken a bullet in the shoulder while he was at it. Ala stopped the bleeding, packing bandaging against both the entrance and exit wounds, but Oyo was in no condition to contribute to the fight. Biraunta are slight. It doesn't take much of a hit from a bullet to incapacitate them. Or kill them.

The fighting came closer on the side where second squad was, more intense. We had only a brief warning from Tonio: "We're coming in." The gunfire in his direction escalated again. Thirty seconds later, I saw Tonio, Sergeant Chouvana, and another soldier—a human—running toward us. I had my people do what they could to cover them, just laying as much fire as we could manage in the direction of the IFers who were trying to stop Tonio and the others. The human fell, and slid to a stop. Tonio dived over my head into the minor cover of our position, doing a somersault before he came to a stop. Chouvana skidded past me on his stomach. Chouvana, second squad's

leader, was bleeding from several wounds. The way he
came in, I wondered if he was dead. But after just a few
seconds he showed signs of life and lifted up an inch or
two to scuttle the rest of the way in. Then he turned around
so he was facing out again, ready to start fighting again.

"Anyone else coming?" I asked on my link to Tonio. We
were looking at each other, and not more than four feet
apart, but I used the radio. That was faster. Tonio shook his
head. He didn't need to draw pictures for me. The rest of
second squad was either dead or left behind, wounded too
badly to continue.

Gradually, we spread around a little more, so we could
cover all four sides better. If the enemy was bringing in
people from the east to dig us out, or to bury us where we
were, we had to get ready for them. As best we could. We
were four humans, one with a concussion and not seeing
too well; three porracci, two of them wounded; two
ghuroh; and one biraunta still able to fight. Oyo was unconscious now—better off for it, I thought. It wasn't just
that being out would spare him some pain. That way, he
might miss the grisly finale.

There was a massive explosion little more than a hundred yards due west of our position—an artillery rocket. It
opened a gaping hole in the forest and a crater in the
ground. A flash of orange flame, a moving wave of smoke,
deafening sound. Wood and shrapnel came our way, thud-
ding into the trunks of the four trees that sheltered us and
ripping through the foliage above our heads. In the relative
quiet after the shock wave went past, I heard another rocket
whistling far overhead, diving toward its terminus.

"Down!" I screamed on my squad channel, and I flattened myself on the ground, worried that the new rocket
would land almost in our laps. I wasn't too far wrong. It hit
about seventy yards west of us, maybe twenty yards south
of where the previous one had come down. We could feel
the heat of the blast, and the concussive force blew hard
against us, a physical slap. Hot. Stinging. It took the breath
away from us for an instant before the air pressure equal-

ized again. Branches broke in the trees overhead. They came down on us. One hit Sergeant Chouvana across the back. I could hear his grunt of pain.

"That's our own people!" I still had my transmitter open, though I wasn't aware of that at the time. "They trying to save the IFers the trouble of burying us?" I took a deep breath. It hurt. I became aware of a pain on my left side—cracked or broken ribs. I closed my eyes long enough to take another breath—measuring how far I could inhale before the pain became . . . difficult.

"They're trying to keep that IFer battalion east of here from getting to us," Tonio said. "Somebody's watching out for us."

I knew that. The words had escaped before my mind could censor my thoughts. Right then, the best thing we could hope for was a lot of artillery rounds coming in that close—maybe even closer—to chew up the IFers before they could come in and kill the rest of us.

I noticed silence then—nearby, at least. The sounds of the main battle, off to our west, were still there, still very noticeable, but there was nothing right close, within a hundred yards or more. There was no incoming rifle fire at the moment, and none of us were shooting as we tried to assess the damage we had taken from that last rocket, get the debris off our weapons, and so forth. Chouvana got the heavy branch off his back, slid out from under it, rather. I did not assume that the pause meant that our troubles were over, but I was grateful for even a brief respite. I took my canteen out and poured a little water into my mouth—sloshing it around before I swallowed.

Swallowing was painful, too. I hadn't taken in much water, but I had trouble getting that down. I reached for my pocket and pulled out a pain patch, then slid it up under my body armor and tunic. If I got it right over the affected ribs the analgesic would take effect that much sooner. Sore ribs were a distraction, but I couldn't just take the rest of the fight off. I had to be able to continue fighting. In the situation we were in, there is no "excused duty."

I scarcely got my hand back out after putting on the pain patch before the IFers started shooting at us again. This time, it was all coming from the east. The enemy reserves were on the scene.

WE FOUGHT. WE LAY BEHIND THE SHELTERING roots and trunks and gave these IFers everything we had. Literally. The enemy appeared to be sending a full company against us. A couple of platoons would advance while the others put down covering fire. A few grenades got launched in our direction as well, but that was one thing we were moderately protected against. Most of those projectiles hit and exploded before they got to us, or were deflected to one side or the other.

Most, not all. One came in at my side of the squad. I saw it hit the ground, before it exploded. Chouvana threw himself over the grenade, trying to cover it with his legs. He also pinned my legs in the effort.

The grenade exploded. I felt searing pain that seemed to run up both legs. I would have sworn that my legs were on fire. Chouvana hadn't quite judged his jump correctly. The explosion was below his pelvic region, and he caught a lot of the shrapnel between my legs. The blast also tossed him clear of me.

At the time, I wished it hadn't. I could see the damage that the grenade had done to my legs. The right one had been severed just above the knee. The left . . . well, the leg bone was still connected to the thighbone, but it looked as if someone had packed hamburger around the knee. Somehow, the blast had flipped me over as well. I was lying on my back instead of my stomach, and my head was propped up, leaning against a protruding root.

Although I was losing blood by the bucket, my mind still seemed clear. I knew what I had to do, so I started pulling web straps from my pack to use as tourniquets. But my fingers weren't working too well. There was an instant when I realized that I wasn't going to make it, followed by surprise when Robbie McGraw got to me and took over. Then I guess I blacked out, but I didn't stay out. There was pain, too much pain, but it was receding.

"I stopped the bleeding and put a couple of pain patches on you," Robbie said. I tried to respond but couldn't. My mouth and vocal cords had mutinied. I was just barely conscious—eyes open, awake, but unable to do anything but watch. Robbie left me, crawling over to Captain Fusik. The captain had also been wounded. I assumed that he was still alive, but without basis.

I have no idea how long the fighting continued. I may have faded out a couple of times, but never for long. The pain was still there, but bearable, somehow more distant than my legs. During one of my lucid periods, I noticed that I was holding my rifle again—sort of. The weapon was across my body, and my hands were on it.

The sky seemed a little less dark. Dawn had to be fairly close. One of the trees that marked the corners of our doubtful redoubt cracked. The trunk leaned inward, kept from falling by its neighbors. There was a rain of bits of bark, twigs, and leaves.

Something hit my side, hard, then landed on top of me. The impact had jarred me past the edge of consciousness, at least briefly. When I opened my eyes again—or whatever—I saw Razor lying on top of me, across my abdomen. But it wasn't all of Razor, just his head and part of his torso, along with one arm. His helmet had been blown off. His face was bloody, shredded almost as badly as my legs had been. But his eyes were open.

Staring at me.

I managed to shrug his remains off, but the effort strained me. I faded out of consciousness again. When I was aware next, I could see Tonio, Souvana, Kiervauna, and Robbie—close together, facing west. They were on their feet, bayonets extended. *Here it comes,* I thought, wishing I would pass out again and *sleep* through the miserable end to the debacle. But it didn't look as if Fate was going to do me that favor. I *felt* more alert than I had since before that grenade mangled my legs. I was going to have to watch the end, see the last of my comrades—and friends—die before I joined them.

Tonatin heads, helmets, started to appear between my comrades. I saw two of them go down. Then Kiervauna fell, a bayonet in his side. I realized that I was still holding my rifle, and I tried to get it aimed toward the gap. I sucked in breath until my ribs felt as if they were stabbing through my lungs. My finger closed on the trigger. The recoil almost yanked the rifle from my grip. More tonatin fell, including the one who had stabbed Kiervauna, but I can't say that I had anything to do with it. I just didn't know. Tonio took a rifle butt across the side of his head and went to one knee. Tonio. I got my rifle aimed and shot the tonatin before he could finish off my best friend.

Souvana fell backward, tripped over something or someone, and nearly fell on top of me. He got back up quickly though, and moved back to his position between Tonio and Robbie. Tonio had managed to get back to his feet as well. There were more tonatin coming into view. I fired my rifle until the magazine was empty, much of that time barely able to cling to the rifle . . . and consciousness.

Three men to stand off a battalion, I thought, and then—for the longest time—I had no thoughts at all. I could have slipped into death without being aware of it.

POSTSCRIPT

WAKING UP ALIVE WAS A SURPRISE. THERE WERE
still a lot of painkillers coursing their way through my system, so my first thoughts were rather muddled. But I did
realize that I was still alive without any corny wondering
things like, *Is this what death is like?* I faded out and in
several times before I was able to stay conscious for any
length of time—long enough to get past the wonder that I
had somehow survived what had looked like a totally unsurvivable situation.

Usually there was someone next to me when I woke—a
surgeon or medtech. Maybe it was whatever they were
doing that brought me out of the abyss. It had happened
several times before my mind even figured out that I should
ask what was going on, and I had a couple of failures to
communicate. My mind might have started thinking again,
but my body wasn't ready to cooperate.

Strong daylight, the sun almost overhead. Fading daylight, with the sun dropping toward the horizon. Okay, I
was outside, somewhere, and on my back. Memory was
slow to return. It was late afternoon before I was able to
stay conscious long enough to think back and start to put
answers to the sudden questions. We had been close to
being overrun. There had only been three men still on their
feet . . . and I hadn't been one of them.

That was when I recalled the grenade that had done such damage to my legs—amputated one and left the other in such bad shape that it probably . . . I struggled to lift my head and look toward where my feet should be. I finally managed to get my head up an inch or two, but that wasn't enough to let me see anything other than the fact that my body was in a medtank, apparently from the neck down to wherever my body now ended.

A tank. The IFers probably would not have wasted a med-tank on a prisoner. That seemed to indicate that our own people had got to us. *Us?* I wondered if any of the men with me had survived. Had I been the only one to luck out? How long had that last fight lasted? I passed out, or fell asleep, before my mind could struggle too long over those questions.

DARKNESS. MY EYES WERE OPEN, SO I GUESSED that it was night. There were a few points of light close, though I could not see the lights themselves. This time, my mind did not feel so foggy. I thought I might be able to stay awake longer. Maybe I'd even be able to ask questions when someone came to check on me.

I listened with my full concentration, but all I heard were small noises close by. If the battle was still going on it had to be at a considerable distance from wherever I was. My range of movement was very limited. I could raise my head that inch or so. I could turn my head a little to either side—not much more than that same inch. Nothing below my neck seemed inclined to obey mental commands. Well, I knew I was in a medtank, so *that* wasn't any great surprise. It would have me immobilized.

Slowly, I got around to realizing just how long I must have been in the tank—certainly a dozen hours, maybe eighteen or more. A tank can repair most injuries in four hours or less. *They've got to regenerate your leg, maybe both legs,* I told myself. *Remember when Kiervauna lost a leg. He was in a full tank more than two days, then in a partial tank over the leg for a couple of weeks.*

Kiervauna. Tonio. Souvana. Captain Fusik. Oyo. Ala. Robbie. Claw. I didn't know what had happened to any of them. Razor had died. I remembered his head staring at me. Chouvana must have died in the explosion that got my legs. Toniyi was dead. *Who else?* I could feel the tears burning my cheeks and welling up on my eyes until I could scarcely see at all. Blinking didn't do enough, so I kept my eyes closed for a time. But I was still awake.

Remembering. Wishing I could forget, but afraid I would.

IT WAS NEAR DAWN WHEN THE SURGEON CAME around to talk to me again. He looked as if he hadn't slept in days. He sat on the ground next to me, which put our heads at about the same level.

"You look terrible, Doc," I said. My voice was weak and squeaky, but I guess it was understandable. The surgeon actually managed a small laugh.

"I must be if my patients start saying that," he said. "I've been afraid to look in the mirror."

"Unless this is Halloween, don't." I was fully alert by that time, and feeling no pain. I couldn't feel much of anything except on my face. There was a bit of a breeze, cool, wonderful. "Tell me straight, Doc. Did I lose both legs?"

"Above the knee on both of them. The left one, I had to finish the job the explosion started. There was just no way to save it. Better to start over. The right one, I had to tidy up the end. You were pretty damned lucky, Sergeant."

"Tell me something I don't know, like what happened."

"If you mean what happened to you and the men you were with, I can't say. I don't know. If you mean the overall battle, that's just about over. All but the cleaning up."

"We won?"

There was a rumbling noise from his throat before he spoke. "They're calling it a victory. Myself"—he looked around, at what, I couldn't tell—"I call it a bloody butchery. There weren't enough medtanks to get everyone in when they needed it. That meant some men had to wait. A few didn't make it."

IT WAS A COUPLE OF HOURS LATER WHEN **I** HAD visitors—*welcome* visitors—Tonio, Captain Fusik, and Souvana. By that time, I was feeling a little stronger. I still couldn't move anything but my head, but I could move that as far as my bed and the medtank would allow.

"I hope you're not the only ones who made it," I said.

"Kiervauna and McGraw are both in medtanks, just down the row a little," Tonio said. "Claw was evacuated to one of the ships. He's out of the medtank now, but it was . . . close."

"If it hadn't been for you and McGraw, none of us would have made it," Captain Fusik said. "You *must* be part Dragon, still fighting with both your legs gone and hardly any blood left in your body. I wouldn't have believed it possible if I hadn't seen it, and the way my head was ringing, I wasn't sure I could believe when I *did* see it."

"I guess I'm just too dumb to know when I'm supposed to lie down quietly and die."

"At the end, there, you, Souvana, and McGraw were the only ones still able to do anything," Tonio said. "You held the IFers off long enough for our people to break through and reach us."

"You have the spirit of a porracci," Souvana said, softly.

I stared at him, suspecting that he had just paid me the highest compliment he could think of. Quite a change from our early relationship. "Thank you," I said. "That means a lot to me."

I LEARNED MORE DETAILS LATER. **A**LL OF THE SUR-vivors from my squad, as well as Tonio and the captain, had been wounded. Kiervauna's spine had been severed.

Robbie had lost his left hand and forearm—and kept fighting one-handed until he passed out, just after the last IFers decided to head in the other direction. Both Kiervauana and Robbie would be out for the weeks that regeneration would take, as I would. Claw had been in desperate condition when elements of the porracci 3rd Firestorm Battalion got to us. No vital organs had been hit, but he had lost as much blood as a ghuroh could and still survive. Tonio and the captain both had head injuries and bullet or bayonet wounds to the body, but they had needed no more than four hours in tanks.

The last IFer troops on Unity were neutralized three days later. More Alliance ships came in to drive the IFer fleet out of the system.

It was ten days after I lost my legs when Ranger Battalion of 1st Combined Regiment was returned to Earth. There was an awards ceremony held in the hospital at Fort Campbell. Souvana, McGraw, and I were all awarded the Order of the Golden Galaxy, the highest medal given by the Alliance of Light. And we were all promoted—me to platoon sergeant, Souvana and Robbie both to sergeant. They skipped Robbie right past corporal.

That was the good news. The bad news, as far as I was concerned, at least, was that the three of us were being transferred out of 1st Combined Regiment. The political council that governs the Alliance had sent out a directive that said that OGG winners were not to be risked in combat. We were transferred to training cadre at the Ranger School at Fort Campbell.

THAT WAS EIGHT MONTHS AGO. I STARTED WRIT-ing about my time in the 1st Combined Regiment while I was growing my new legs and learning to use them, and once the habit was started, I kept writing after I returned to active duty—training men from all the species in the Alliance for duty with the Combined Regiments. There are seven of them now.

The war continues. My old regiment has been in combat twice without me. They just got back from the second of those campaigns, on a world whose name I can't pronounce—or *spell* without help—two days ago. Claw didn't make it home this time. Kiervauna is the only original member still in the squad that was mine. Tonio is lead sergeant for B Company, Ranger Battalion now. *Major* Fusik is the battalion's executive officer.

Just this morning I put in a request for transfer back to 1st Combined—the way I did the last time they came home after a campaign. My current boss told me that the policy of not sending Order of the Golden Galaxy winners to combat assignments is still in effect. But he's sending the request through anyhow. One of these days, if the war goes on long enough, I might get lucky.